Con...
fro...

Coming S...

*To Colton Parayko: Hardworking defenseman.
Precious cinnamon roll. Inspiration for Tristan
and this entire story.*

*And to Jonathan Toews, who will never read this
dedication but is entirely responsible for Piper falling
into the world of hockey and never once looking back.*

OFF THE ICE

———

Avon Gale & Piper Vaughn

Piper Vaughn

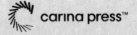

carina press™

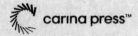

carina press™

ISBN-13: 978-1-335-21576-5

Recycling programs for this product may not exist in your area.

Off the Ice

Copyright © 2019 by Avon Gale & Piper Vaughn

This is the revised text of the work first published by Riptide Publishing, 2017

This edition published by Carina Press, 2019

This edition published by arrangement with Harlequin Books S.A.

www.CarinaPress.com

Printed in U.S.A.

Authors' Note

We're so thrilled the Hat Trick series has found a new home with Carina Press! Aside from minor edits, this book remains mostly unchanged from the first edition. We wanted to keep the story as close to what it was originally, both for the readers who are already fans of Tristan, Sebastian and all the other Hat Trick boys, and for the new readers we hope will join us along the way.

OFF THE ICE

Chapter One

Tristan slumped farther into his seat, struggling to rearrange his limbs in a way that didn't make him feel like a bundle of hockey equipment shoved into an undersized duffel bag. Between the small chair, the tablet arm, and the narrow aisle—apparently none of which had been designed with people of Tristan's size in mind—it took a lot more work than he'd anticipated to find a comfortable position. Luckily, the lecture hall was still nearly empty, and the few students who'd trickled inside completely ignored his fidgety attempts to situate himself as they went about preparing for class.

No one spared him more than half a glance, and no one appeared to recognize him, either. Atlanta wasn't much of a hockey town, no matter how much the NHL tried to make it one, and Tristan wasn't an all-star, besides. He'd never graced the front of a Wheaties box, and he hadn't once been stopped in the street by a fan in the years he'd been playing defense for the Venom. It seemed even less likely in the off-season, though up to now, he hadn't been around to test the theory.

For the first time since his signing, Tristan wouldn't be spending the summer at his family's farm in Wisconsin. Instead he'd be taking a couple of classes toward completing his unfinished business degree at Georgia State. But after spending three seasons immersed in the world of professional ice hockey, it felt strange to be back in school, like starting over again.

Tristan tried to shake the awkward-new-kid feeling and adjusted the bill of his Milwaukee Brewers cap, pulling it lower over his eyes. If there was one small comfort, it was that sitting at a desk with a book bag at his feet felt familiar to him in the same way all arenas did after a lifetime of playing hockey. The lingering funk of sweaty athletes that no amount of disinfectant ever quite vanquished, the gleam of freshly resurfaced ice, the narrow benches and green-and-orange water bottles—those things remained unchanged. Just as, regardless of the state or the university, one classroom was much the same as any other.

More students shuffled into the room. To Tristan's surprise, one of them—a stylishly dressed hipster wearing a cobalt button-down, skinny-fit khakis, thick-framed glasses, and a bright-red cardigan straight out of *Mister Rogers' Neighborhood*—bypassed several rows of empty seats and paused at the desk next to Tristan's.

"Mind if I sit here?" he asked, jerking his chin at the desk. "I hate being so spread out in these big lecture halls. I'd rather not have to yell across the aisle to talk to someone." He laughed lightly. "Besides, I like to have a note buddy in case I miss a class. So, do you mind?"

Tristan shook his head. "Go ahead."

"Thanks." Hipster Boy set down his messenger bag and settled primly into his seat. With his pomaded sidepart and—hopefully ironic—handlebar mustache, he reminded Tristan of the black-and-white picture of his great-grandfather that sat above the mantel in his parents' den. And to think, like most of the other students in the classroom, this guy was probably a few years Tristan's junior.

Hipster Boy turned to Tristan, extending a hand. "I'm Steven. And you are?"

Tristan engulfed fine-boned fingers in his much bigger paw and tried not to squeeze too hard. "Tris."

"A pleasure," Steven said before flipping open his messenger bag. He withdrew what looked like a Moleskine leather notebook and uncapped an honest-to-God fountain-tipped pen.

Was this guy for real? If he pulled out a little pot of ink, Tristan was going to lose his shit and start laughing.

Steven didn't. Thankfully. But as he sat there, spine straight as a ruler, not a hair out of place or wrinkle to be seen, Tristan felt like a scrub in comparison.

Tristan usually didn't give much thought to fashion. His postworkout outfit consisted of a threadbare Grateful Dead T-shirt and a pair of old gray sweatpants that had seen better days. He wasn't exactly red-carpet ready. Tristan had chosen the items for comfort, not style, as always when he wasn't attending an event for which his contract required him to look presentable.

But Steven... Tristan would bet he never stepped foot out of the house looking anything less than pristine. Sitting next to him made Tristan feel weirdly self-conscious. He ignored the feeling and people-watched from beneath the brim of his hat until, at precisely ten o'clock, a tall, dark-haired man swept into the lecture hall, slamming the door shut behind him. The girl a couple of rows in front of Tristan startled and dropped her pen.

"Welcome to Sociology 3201: Wealth, Power, and Inequality," the man said as he set a messenger bag much like Steven's on the desk at the front of the room. "If you're not registered for this class, this would be the time to leave."

No one moved.

"If you bothered to read your syllabus, you'll know my name is Sebastian Cruz. If you've taken any of my classes or spoken to my former students, you'll also know I expect assignments to be turned in on time and I don't tolerate excuses. I'm not here to be your friend or mentor. This isn't *Dead Poets Society*, so don't expect me to be your buddy. I'm here to teach, and you're here to learn. As long as you keep that in mind, we'll get along fine."

He glanced around the room, his dark eyes narrowed in his sharp-featured face. He got to Tristan and stopped. "Classroom rule number one: no hats. You're not at a baseball game. Show some respect."

Tristan pulled the cap off as heat gathered in his face. He tossed it atop his book bag and combed his fingers through his hair. No doubt it looked a mess after being damp and crushed under his hat for the past hour. "Sorry, sir."

Professor Cruz ignored him and kept talking. Or rather, ranting. Tristan groaned inwardly. Great. Another hard-ass who ran his classroom like some kind of drill sergeant. Tristan hated the type, but whatever. He'd survived coaches who would make Sebastian Cruz resemble a cuddly little lamb. Tristan couldn't be intimidated easily, even if, yeah, it embarrassed him to be scolded like a high schooler in front of his peers.

Eh, you win some, you lose some in the professor roulette. If there was one thing hockey had taught Tristan, it was self-discipline. He enjoyed sociology and thought the classes would be beneficial to him as a potential businessman. Tristan could cope with Mr. Don't-Expect-Me-to-Be-Your-Buddy for seven weeks.

"So power and inequality," Professor Cruz was saying, "let's talk about how that relates to blue-blooded Manhattanites and me, growing up as a Puerto Rican welfare kid in the Bronx."

Well, he didn't waste any time, did he?

Tristan flipped open his MacBook and started taking notes as Professor Cruz lectured. Warm and fuzzy the guy was not, but he certainly didn't lack in passion for the subject matter. Soon, Tristan was fascinated. Professor Cruz absolutely came alive as he spoke. True, he suffered from a bad case of Resting Asshole Face, and Tristan wouldn't go so far as to call him handsome, not exactly. Still, there was something compelling. Professor Cruz—tall and whipcord lean with warm golden-brown skin and wavy raven-black hair—definitely qualified as eye candy.

"In the New York social stratosphere, some of these people are akin to royalty," Professor Cruz said. "Anyone ever watched *Gossip Girl*? I'd love to tell you that show was unrealistic in its portrayal of rich, entitled teenagers, but it wasn't far from what I experienced growing up alongside some of them. Of course, the difference between us was, my mother was the hired help, and for that reason, we existed in entirely different realities.

"See, when you're a child of such absolute privilege, you grow up with an entirely skewed worldview. These people have no concept of what it's like to subsist on food stamps or to struggle from paycheck to paycheck. They're on the far right of the social spectrum, the very top of a modern-day caste system, and the blue-collar workers, such as my parents, are the laboring class. The

privilege of wealth is going to be a major theme over
the next several weeks. Get used to hearing that word,
folks: *privilege*. You're going to be sick of it by the time
I'm done. And that brings us to your first assignment…"

Tristan fought back a smile as Steven muttered something unpleasant under his breath. *Should've read the
syllabus, bud.*

Tristan had. He'd already started the homework due
before they met again on Thursday. Sure, he would've
rather been playing hockey still, but in a way, Tristan
was almost relieved the Venom's season had ended in
the first round of the playoffs. He didn't think Professor
I-Don't-Tolerate-Excuses would give him a free pass on
an assignment—even for a Stanley Cup Final.

*The problem with wealth is that it makes some people
have money and some people poor.*

Sebastian read the opening line of the assignment he
was grading out loud and groaned. "No shit, Sherlock,"
he muttered, his voice echoing in the quiet of his apartment. He'd tried grading with some music in the background, but it seemed somehow sacrilegious to mix Pink
Floyd and his students' idiocy. As if it were somehow
tainting what was good and pure with drivel.

The assignment wasn't terribly taxing, especially for
students enrolled in an upper-level sociology course, but
so far he wasn't impressed. He hadn't wanted to teach the
summer course, even if the material was near and dear
to his heart and definitely something for which he had
an academic passion. Summer courses were intensive
and time consuming, and the only thing that made it all
worth it was that he generally loved the subject matter.
Even when it resulted in grading papers with sentences

like *The problem with wealth is that it makes some people have money and some people poor.*

Rubbing his temples, he kept reading through the end
of the paper, which had arrived via the course's PAWS
site. He made a few notes about consulting the reading—*and by that, I mean, actually do it*—and gave it a
cursory mark in the C-minus category, which was the
norm so far for all the papers he'd read. The worst had
been a paper in which the student had opined over the
unfairness of not having access to a trust fund before a
certain age, since his parents had worked hard for their
millions and wasn't the point of having money to share
it with their children?

That paper had nearly driven him to drink, but he'd
written *Perhaps you might benefit from further reading
on the concept of poverty* and assigned a barely passing
grade. He had a feeling he knew exactly whose paper that
was too—the blond hottie in the gray sweatpants. The
boy with the full mouth and the gorgeous body, who'd
immediately irritated Sebastian by slouching and wearing a hat. Sebastian remembered with a certain amount
of pleasure how the kid's fair skin had turned noticeably
red after Sebastian had corrected him. He looked exactly
like the kind of person who'd write a whiny paper about
not having access to a trust fund to blow on…whatever
rich kids spent money on. Sebastian had no idea. Chuck
Bass with the Nice Ass did, Sebastian was sure of it.

The final paper he graded was much better, talking
about the idea of class and wealth and what it meant to
have a sudden and rather jarring transition from one to
the other. The paper was well written and referenced the
reading, which was enough to earn it a solid B right there.
There were a few clunky transitions and some of the stu-

dent's thoughts were a bit muddled, but overall it was a fairly erudite examination of the sudden gain or loss of privilege that came with the movement from one social class to another. Sebastian gave the paper a B-plus, made a few suggestions for how the student could improve the presentation of his ideas and, because it really had been the best one in the whole bunch, added *You clearly did the reading and thought about the assignment from an interesting angle—well done.*

From Sebastian, that was high praise indeed—especially on a first assignment. It at least gave him hope that there would be the potential for some interesting and productive dialogue, which had seemed a dim prospect while grading the other students' assignments. Chuck Bass might be hot, but Sebastian had a feeling he'd spend most of the class asleep—if he even bothered to show up.

When Sebastian was finished grading, he finally checked his texts and found a few from his friend R.J. Marcus, a professor in the Math Department at Georgia State. He'd been the one to encourage Sebastian to take on the summer class, with the argument that if Sebastian wanted to be tenured before he turned thirty-five—which, of course he did—it would go a long way in improving his chances if he showed he was a team player.

Sebastian didn't point out that team players were a myth in academia, because R.J. was one of the good ones and was fast becoming a close friend. After exchanging a few texts, he changed clothes and went to meet R.J. at a nearby bar for a drink. After those papers, he needed about seven.

"That bad?" R.J. asked, when Sebastian slid into the booth next to him and proceeded to down half his Scotch in one swig.

Sebastian fixed him with a sharp look, the one that most of his students had a hard time meeting for too long. "One of my students wrote a very sad treatise on the inequality of trust fund distributions based on age. He referred to it as, quote, *ageablism*. That's really the word he used."

R.J. snorted and leaned back in the booth. He shook his head. "Wow. Hey, look, it's only for seven weeks." R.J.'s smile flashed against his dark-brown skin. "My first year, I had to teach a math class in which one of my students answered all the proofs with long, involved puns."

"At least those are funny," Sebastian groused, fingers tracing the rim of his glass.

"They were *bad* puns," said R.J. "And I don't know. *Ageablism* is pretty funny. I mean, you'd laugh if you did that kind of thing."

Sebastian, well aware of his reputation, smiled slightly. "There's one good thing about the class, though I'm afraid he won't be around that long." Sebastian told R.J. about Chuck Bass, he of the gray sweatpants. "I'm almost sure that punk was my trust fund brat, but goddamn."

"Well, there you go." R.J. toasted him with his beer. "Does he have one of those awful trust fund names like, uh…" R.J. squinted up at the ceiling. "Whatever those are?"

Sebastian snorted. "I've been calling him 'Chuck Bass' in my head. The kid from *Gossip Girl*?" R.J.'s look suggested he didn't know what the hell Sebastian was talking about. Sebastian shrugged. "Like I bother to learn their names, R.J. Come on. They'll be gone by the time I do, and I won't see any of them again anyway."

R.J.'s eyebrows rose, but all he said was, "Hot Guy is a better nickname than, uh… Ageablism Guy. Right?"

"Well, I'm probably a lot older than he is," Sebastian pointed out, letting the Scotch and the music—and R.J.'s cheerful, upbeat company—mellow him out. Also, it was the weekend and he had a few days off before he had to address his class and explain how to capture and wrangle that mythical, elusive beast known as a thesis sentence into submission. "And I'm sure I won't be seeing much of him when he gets his paper back. But, until then, I'll enjoy how he fills out that pair of sweatpants." He grinned evilly.

It wasn't a laugh, but it was close enough.

Chapter Two

Tristan swung his club and watched as the ball veered wildly off course and landed a few lanes away. He winced and sent the guy down the row an apologetic wave. *Damn.* Why did he bother going to the driving range? He sucked at golf. It just seemed like something he should do because so many of his teammates played during the summer, but he never actually seemed to get any better.

"Were your eyes closed during that shot, Holtzy?" A beefy hand shoved his shoulder, and he turned to face Morley, his defense partner on the Venom. Trevor Morley was handsome, if somewhat rough around the edges, with spiky golden-brown hair, blue eyes, and a brick-wall physique. He exceeded Tristan's six foot four by a few inches and outweighed him by probably twenty pounds of solid muscle. During games, Morley played with a mean-as-hell scowl. He had a reputation in the league as someone not to be fucked with, but off the ice, his teddy-bear personality shone through, and he delighted in being the biggest prankster on the team. They'd become close friends in the years since Tristan had joined the Venom as a wet-behind-the-ears rookie.

Tristan leaned on his club. "Maybe we should call it a day and go to lunch."

"Not until I finish this bucket. Practice, bro, practice. You'll never improve your swing otherwise."

Tristan grumbled good-naturedly and grabbed another ball.

"When Ryu gets back from training, we'll have to get him out here too. You both need to up your games. It's no fun slaughtering you two every time. You know I thrive on competition."

Tristan laughed. It was true. Ryu, his best friend and the Venom's backup goalie, also sucked at golf. Unlike Tristan, who took it in stride, it pissed Ryu off not to be good at something. Ryu was currently in Sweden participating in a camp run by Kris Karlsson, a legendary goalie from the nineties. Until he returned in a couple of weeks, their improbable trio was down to a duo.

"Are you coming out tonight?" Morley asked as he adjusted his stance, eyes focused on the field. "You should've seen these chicks we met last weekend. They're supposed to be at the Empty Bottle again tonight." Morley swung with such perfect form he could've been posing for the cover of *Golf Digest*. The ball flew straight and landed near the farthest yardage marker. "They were strippers, man," he added, grinning. "I'm sure one of them would be more than happy to take a ride on your pole."

Tristan sighed. "Seriously? We've talked about this. Dial back the sexism—we've both got sisters."

"Yeah, yeah. Allow me to rephrase. We met some lovely ladies, dancers, who I feel would be honored to meet a studly gentleman hockey player such as yourself." Morley rolled his eyes. "So? Are you in?"

Instead of answering immediately, Tristan pounded a ball out onto the field while he tried to come up with an excuse to bail.

It wasn't that he didn't enjoy partying with his team-mates. They were fun guys. Family, really, after three seasons. But with Tristan being one of the few singles on the Venom's roster, they expected him to be constantly chasing skirt. Little did they realize he had no interest in women. Not sexually anyway. He'd known he was gay since he turned thirteen—and he'd known it was some-thing he'd have to hide if he wanted a future in hockey for just as long. Things were slowly getting better, but as Michael Sam's short-lived NFL career could attest, there were reasons for the lack of openly gay athletes in professional sports.

Tristan wasn't the only gay man playing hockey. Hell, he'd been fucked by enough players to know, and the teammate he'd dated in college had also gone on to the NHL. They still hooked up whenever their current teams crossed paths. However, the existence of other queer players didn't mean Tristan could admit the rea-son he had no interest in partying with the guys was because they weren't going to the right clubs. Tristan might not mind a bit of harmless flirting, but he *hated* pretending. He'd rather stay home alone than be forced to put on an act.

Someday he might be ready to be honest with his friends. *Someday.* Not now.

Of course, hiding such an intrinsic part of himself wasn't exactly ideal. Whenever Tristan hooked up with someone, he dealt with paranoia about being outed for days afterward. The loneliness, the sense of being dis-connected, untethered from everyone and everything sometimes left him with an unbearable ache in the pit of his stomach. But nothing in life was perfect. Tristan was living his dream and getting paid well—*very* well—

to play the sport he loved. How many people could say the same?

"I don't think I can make it," Tristan finally replied. "I have a paper due on Tuesday, and I still have to do some research." It wasn't a lie. He was only taking a couple of courses to ease himself back into student life, but Professor Cruz—dark-haired, scowly Professor Cruz, whose wiry body made Tristan think things he shouldn't—had already assigned two papers in the week and a half since the summer session started.

Morley's eyebrows spoke volumes, being nearly at the level of his hairline. "'Research'? Bro, I don't even understand why you're taking those classes. This is our only time to relax without Clancy riding our asses. Why do you need a business degree anyway? You're making bank with your new contract extension."

Tristan lifted a shoulder. The contract extension was actually the reason he'd decided to go back to school. It meant he'd be in Atlanta for the next three years, barring an unexpected trade. Plenty of time to finish his degree. "I was about to start my junior year when I got drafted. I'm halfway done. I don't want those credit hours to go to waste, you know? I want a plan for after hockey."

"But, dude, you're what, twenty-four?"

"Twenty-three."

"Even better. You won't be retiring for ages. If you play your cards right, you can live off your earnings for the rest of your life. You won't need to get some boring-ass nine-to-five."

Tristan set a fresh ball on the tee. "Yeah, maybe. But there aren't any guarantees. You know that. I could get hurt the next time I step on the ice, and bam! No more contracts. No performance bonuses or endorsement deals. No day with The Cup. It'd be over."

Morley blanched. "Bite your fucking tongue, bro. You shouldn't even be thinking about that, let alone saying it out loud."

"I can't *not* think about it," Tristan said mildly. He whacked the ball and watched it soar nearly straight upward before plopping onto the grass a few yards in front of him. He sighed, turning back to his friend. "It's the realist in me. Besides, my parents have been on me to go back for years. I don't fantasize about some white-collar job in international relations, but it feels smart to do this now. That way, if I'm ever forced to quit hockey, I'll be qualified to do something other than play-by-play announcing for some dinky local TV network. And that'd be if I got lucky."

Morley gave an exaggerated shudder and quickly crossed himself. "You should find some wood to knock on." His expression was dead serious. "You're freaking me out with all this talk of injuries and quitting."

Tristan laughed and knocked on his head. "There. Satisfied?" Tristan was as superstitious as the next hockey player, but Morley had him beat. He even prayed before every game "in case Jesus is listening," though Tristan knew for a fact Morley only stepped foot in a church once a year for Christmas Mass.

"Close enough." Morley peered down into his bucket. "Five left. Let's finish this up and grab some lunch."

"Yep." Tristan lined up another shot and gave Morley a questioning glance. "Last one finished buys?"

Morley nodded without looking up. "You're on."

Tristan grinned. No need to tell Morley he was on his final ball.

* * *

Sebastian stood in front of his class, eyes sweeping over the students who had bothered to show up. It was a couple of weeks into the summer term, and as expected, the class size had shrunk considerably since the first day.

What wasn't expected, however, was the presence of Chuck Bass, who hadn't missed a single class. Not only that, but he hadn't worn a ball cap since the first day—although he was still showing up in those sweatpants, which Sebastian was doing his level best to ignore.

Today he was wearing a Pink Floyd shirt. Sebastian wondered if blondie was even old enough to know who they were, and resisted the urge to go full-out classic-rock hipster and ask him. He had a class to teach.

"Today we're going to talk about perception," Sebastian said, leaning back against his desk. "The way we perceive others has to do with a variety of factors, and the assumptions we make because of them. Humans have a tendency to place people into a hierarchy, and we design that hierarchy in several ways."

He wondered if he was losing them, but Gray Sweatpants was typing away at his computer—a newer model MacBook, Sebastian noticed—so either he was taking notes or blatantly ignoring Sebastian in favor of updating his Facebook. Sebastian noticed the painfully trendy young man with the notebook, the one who always sat next to Gray Sweatpants and probably took notes in calligraphy given that fancy pen, was absent today.

"One way in which we organize individuals into a hierarchy is based on the things we've been talking about in this class so far this semester—perceptions of wealth, class, that sort of thing. But we also make designations in this power hierarchy based on other factors, and I wanted to take a bit of time to talk about those. Race and gender, for example…and sexuality."

Sebastian waited a moment to see if mentioning that got anyone's attention, but besides Gray Sweatpants glancing briefly upward, the rest of the class were staring at their computer screens. One young woman was on her phone and one guy was slouched in his seat against the wall, half-asleep.

And these were the students who'd bothered to show up.

"You put me in a position of power in this classroom because I'm the professor," Sebastian continued. "But there are other, more subtle factors that you might not even be aware of—the position of where I'm standing in the room, for example. It's very similar to what happens in your mind when you go and watch a rock concert." Sebastian waved a hand. "Or whatever music you kids are into, nowadays."

That got a slight smile from Gray Sweatpants. Interesting.

"Musicians are literally raised to a position above you on a stage, so your mind fills in the hierarchy clues and places these people above you. You do it with me because I'm standing while you're sitting, I'm speaking while you're quiet, and I'm awake while you're sleeping." He stared hard at the dozing kid in the back, who didn't realize Sebastian was addressing him at all. Several of the others did, though, and it wasn't only Gray Sweatpants who smiled this time.

"Now, what about me changes your perception of my place in the power hierarchy?" Sebastian's mouth quirked. "Before you awkwardly avoid my eyes and figure out how to answer this, I'll do it for you. I'm Puerto

Rican. Does that make any of you question if I'm really in charge of this classroom?"

There were a few gazes exchanged among the engaged students in the room, and a few mumbles and awkward smiles.

"And how about if I tell you that I'm gay?"

That got their attention, most noticeably Gray Sweatpants, who looked up sharply from his computer. Sebastian met his big, wide blue eyes and stared at him, waiting to see if Mr. Trust Fund had anything to say about that.

"Now, I'm telling you this for a few reasons. One, my primary interest and area of study—which you'd know if you bothered doing any research about your professor—is LGBT issues in Latinx urban communities, and how traditional ideas of gender and class are challenged by openly queer individuals.

"Two, I want to spend some time discussing perceptions and how we, as individuals, challenge those perceptions in our day-to-day life…as well as the images we present to others. I want you, in your next assignment, to talk about a role you play in a community that you have a particularly strong tie to—familial, cultural, I don't particularly care which—and where you think you fit in the so-called 'power hierarchy.' Then, tell me something about you that might challenge that perception and why."

He paused. "This is a very personal assignment, so I hope you will take the time to really think about what I've said and deconstruct your own place in one of the social spaces you inhabit."

Gray Sweatpants was still watching him, and Sebastian found himself meeting the kid's big blue eyes for the second or third time. Maybe it was because none of the other students were bothering to interact with him in any way, or maybe it was just the kid was hot and those wide eyes and that full mouth were giving Sebastian ideas he shouldn't have in class.

Or maybe there was something else. Maybe Gray Sweatpants was looking so intently at him because he—

Stop it, what are you doing? You're in class. Save your pervy fantasies for later.

Sebastian glanced at his watch and realized it was time to end class. "That's all for today. I'll expect your papers turned in to me via the class site by the end of the week."

He watched as they all stood up and assembled their things, heading toward the exit singly or in small groups. He thought he heard one of the girls murmur, "...really gay?" on her way out of the door, and he had to stop himself from snorting.

Gray Sweatpants was the last one out the door, and the girl probably would have had her answer if she'd noticed how Sebastian unabashedly eyed the guy's ass in those pants on his way out. But she was already gone, and the only other person left was the kid asleep in the back...and he was snoring, so Sebastian doubted he noticed anything much at all.

Chapter Three

Over the next couple of days, Tristan gave serious consideration to the topic Professor Cruz had assigned. What "social space" did he inhabit? Hockey, of course. The dressing rooms, the arenas, the charter planes and busses. Tristan spent most of his time with other athletes. Where did he fit into the hockey power hierarchy? What role did he play—aside from the obvious answer of "defenseman"? Did he ever do anything to challenge that role?

Tristan typed a first draft, which was more of a stream-of-consciousness-style brain dump than anything. It ended up a seven-page ramble that had no real purpose or sense of direction, but luckily, there were a few diamonds amid all that rough. Those ideas Tristan cut and polished into a more cohesive second draft. One he thought Professor Cruz would appreciate.

Sexy, dark-eyed, *gay* Professor Cruz, who put his sexuality out there like it was nothing. Who lifted his chin and practically dared anyone in the class to say something negative.

What would it be like to be able to do that in front of a group of strangers? To be totally candid and honest about who he was? Tristan wouldn't know. He couldn't quite imagine saying the words to his family or his teammates, let alone a lecture hall full of people whose respect he wanted to keep.

Professor Cruz had certainly earned Tristan's respect
with his frankness. And his bravery. Even if the guy was
out flying rainbow flags every weekend, it couldn't be
easy to share that aspect of his personal life, potentially
opening himself to criticism or bigotry. Tristan admired
the courage that took as he sat there ruminating on his
place in the world of hockey and the homophobia that
still pervaded the sport, particularly in the junior levels.

No one had stood up in front of the league and proudly
declared their queerness to the masses. But that wasn't
something Tristan planned to address in this paper. Or
anywhere else, for that matter.

He refocused on the task at hand—deconstructing his
place within the hockey community, and what about him,
aside from his sexuality, challenged the perceptions of
outsiders. The answer came in a flash that left Tristan
feeling foolish in the aftermath. Obviously, the fact that
he was back in school pursuing a degree made him different from many of his teammates. He still considered
it worthwhile to complete his education, though he had
a salary most people would envy and friends like Morley who questioned why he would bother.

His topic decided, Tristan tackled the paper with renewed energy. He was in the middle of reworking his
closing paragraph when a *ping* from his MacBook alerted
him to a new message.

Tristan's Gmail inbox was open, and a little green box
flashed in the corner—a chat invite from Steven. They'd
been emailing consistently since the first day of class.
He'd already begged Tristan to send him notes a couple
of times, but he'd never initiated a chat before.

Curious, Tristan accepted the invite to see the message.

Steven: Hey, how's the paper going? Did you figure out your subject yet?

Tristan: Yeah. Almost done, actually.

Steven: Oh man, seriously? I've got nothing so far.

Tristan considered for a moment. Are you part of any clubs? Play any sports? Or are you involved in a church or anything?

Steven: No I'm not really into any of that. IDK. I'm stumped.

There was a pause. Then Steven sent another message: Would you mind letting me read your paper? Just so I can see what you did. I can proofread for you!
Tristan hesitated. But, really, what harm could there be? Besides, he could do with a second set of eyes.

Tristan: Yeah, sure. Will send in a bit.

Steven: Thanks, man, you're a lifesaver! Hey gotta go but I'll read it later and get back to you.

Steven signed off before Tristan could reply.
Another hour passed before he felt ready to let someone else see his work, but eventually, Tristan completed his revisions and sent the paper off to Steven. Not too shabby, if he said so himself. It might even earn him an elusive A from Professor Cruz.

After a quick shower and a protein shake, Tristan checked his phone to find a stream of texts from Morley.

Morley: Bro remember that movie I wanted to see? Its @ the cheap theater now.

Morley: Shootouts car chases hot chicks EXPLOSIONS!! Fuck yeah lets go!!!

Morley: Dont ignore me ill show up @ ur house and drag u out the door in a headlock.

Morley: Cmon bro im bored af.

Tristan snorted. What the hell. He could use a couple of hours of mindless entertainment. What better way to decompress than with over-the-top special effects and excessive amounts of gunfire?

Tristan could think of one thing, but it had been a while since he'd gotten laid and he wasn't in the mood to deal with Grindr or trying to go out to pick someone up. For now, his hand and Vin Diesel fantasies would have to do.

Tristan: Sorry, was working. Yeah, let's go. Come pick me up.

Morley replied almost immediately—with a row of five thumbs-up emojis, an eggplant, a peach, and three bombs.
Translation: I'm on my way.
Tristan laughed and shook his head.

The papers came in by the end of the week, and to be fair, most of the students appeared to have at least tried

to apply to their papers what Sebastian had been talking
about. One student talked candidly about being raised
Mormon and estranged from the church, one talked about
their family, and a few others talked about activities they
belonged to—an a capella group, a dance team, and a
LARP group (though Sebastian wasn't exactly sure what
that meant).

Most interesting so far was, oddly enough, about a
student who was apparently heavily involved in playing
lacrosse—a sport that Sebastian knew absolutely nothing about and had no idea if GSU even had a team. But
he wasn't that big into sports, so it was entirely likely
that the college had a team and that this student, Steven
Wheeling, was a lacrosse player and had chosen to write
his paper on his experiences. It was a good paper, and
while Sebastian couldn't relate entirely to the athletic aspect, he did know what it was like to challenge miscon-
ceptions people had based on one aspect of his identity.
He left a few notes and resisted adding any sort of personal message—it would be inappropriate.

Sebastian recorded the student's grade in the PAWS
system, clicked back to his desktop and opened the next
Word document. For a moment, he thought he'd clicked
the same document and reopened the lacrosse paper,
because the opening paragraph was exactly the same.

Well. It was the same, but instead of the word *lacrosse*
it said *hockey*. Frowning, Sebastian glanced quickly at
the pages and realized he was reading an almost word-
for-word version of the earlier paper. The only difference was the sport, and Sebastian might not know much
about college athletics or the lacrosse team, but he knew
for sure GSU did not have an ice hockey team. He copied a few paragraphs and ran it through a plagiarism

checker that the school gave professors access to, but nothing came up.

This wasn't a paper in a fraternity file that had been used over and over again. This was one person's paper that had been stolen. Sebastian thought about Gray Sweatpants and the trendy kid with his notebook, and how he'd heard them exchanging emails the first week of class. If he had to pick which one of them was a student athlete lacrosse player and which one was a frat boy who thought their gay professor would buy the idea of a hockey team at a Southern school…

Seething, Sebastian stared hard at the screen and drummed his fingers on his desk. He couldn't say why he was so disappointed, because honestly, he shouldn't have been surprised. He'd been warned about the possibility of plagiarism, of course, and had figured that it would crop up sooner or later in one of his classes. He considered contacting the dean and reporting it, and he'd have to do that eventually. But first, he was going to confront the plagiarist—Tristan Holt, according to the document—and give him an appropriate lecture. It might not do any good, because people like that never learned. Likely it would go in one ear and out the other, but Sebastian was going to make sure it at least burned on its way through the kid's empty skull.

Tristan Holt and his sweatpants were one piece of eye candy Sebastian wouldn't be enjoying the rest of the semester, because Sebastian was going to make sure he never set foot in his classroom again.

Chapter Four

Tristan was in the middle of making his morning protein shake and rocking an air guitar solo when his smartphone abruptly stopped streaming Led Zeppelin's "Black Dog" and started playing the familiar chorus of Fleetwood Mac's "Go Your Own Way." The song was one of his mother's favorites, and he'd assigned it as her personal ringtone ages ago. It always reminded him of the mornings he'd woken to find her dancing around the kitchen while she cooked.

Grinning, Tristan switched off the blender and accepted the call. He propped the phone between his ear and shoulder. "Hey, Mom."

"Hi, sweetie. What are you up to?"

"Making some breakfast. I have class in an hour." Tristan popped the lid off the blender pitcher and poured the pinkish-brown mixture into the tall glass waiting on the counter. Strawberry-banana-spinach didn't make for a pretty shake, but it tasted good, and the vanilla protein powder wasn't as offensive as others he'd tried. "How are you?"

"I'm fine. Washing up." That explained all the banging in the background. "Hannah and I have been canning all morning. We picked blackberries yesterday! I'll send you some jam next week."

"Yes, please. You know I love that stuff." If he didn't watch himself, he'd eat his mother's blackberry-honey jam straight from the jar.

"How are your classes going?" she asked as he slugged about a third of his shake in one go.

Tristan swallowed, swiping the back of his hand across his mouth. "Good. My sociology professor is keeping me busy, but my corporate finance course is more laid-back. It's mostly discussion, but I think I'll stick with two classes when the season starts again."

"That's smart. You'll have to find the right balance," his mom said. "You know, Dad and I are very happy you decided to go back. We're so proud of you, and we hope you'll be playing hockey for a long time to come, but it never hurts to be prepared."

"You're right." Tristan smiled so his mother would hear it in his voice. They'd had this discussion many times before. "How are things on the farm?" He hadn't quite overcome the guilt of not being there to help, as he'd done for at least a portion of every other summer since he learned how to walk. "Do you need me to come up?"

"No. Thank you, sweetie, but we're fine. Hannah and Brian are here. We've got it covered."

"Okay. Well, I'm done with class at the end of July. I might visit for a week or two in August. Otherwise, I won't see you guys for months." Tristan set down his shake and went to the fridge to take out a carton of eggs.

"We'd love to see you, of course. But don't worry about the work, okay? Focus on your studies. Your brother says hello, by the way."

"Tell him we're still disappointed about that game seven," Brian's muffled voice yelled. "He should've never let Gibb get past him. That guy is slower than Grandma skating backward in a snowstorm."

Tristan snorted a laugh. Gibb played for the Venom's biggest rivals, the Memphis Marauders, who they'd lost to in the first round of the playoffs. Gibb wasn't the quickest or most adept of skaters, but he *was* one of the league's top-scoring defensemen and had a ferocious slapshot that had topped 105 miles per hour during skills competitions. Not many players were willing to dive into the path of a puck moving at that velocity.

"Tell Brian I'll let Gibb know my brother insulted his skating abilities and wants to challenge him to a race the next time I see him."

"Oh, I put you on speaker. He heard you just fine." His mother laughed while Brian sputtered.

Brian took the phone from their mother, and they talked about Brian's last fishing trip while Tristan scrambled egg whites, microwaved some turkey bacon, and threw a couple of slices of whole-wheat bread into the toaster. By the time he'd finished eating, he only had twenty minutes to get to the GSU campus.

Tristan said good-bye to his brother and dumped his dishes in the sink. He rushed out of the apartment, not wanting to risk Professor Cruz's ire by being late, even if, after the last few weeks, some twisted part of Tristan had started finding the man's dark-eyed death glare sort of stupidly hot—especially when those sable eyes caught and held his own, as they had when Professor Cruz talked about his sexuality during their last class. Tristan thought he'd spotted interest there, but probably he was only imagining things.

He made it to his seat seconds before Professor Cruz sailed into the lecture hall and slammed his messenger bag onto the desk with unnecessary force. His gaze swept the room, lingering on Tristan for a long, tense moment that made Tristan squirm, though probably not in the way the good professor intended.

His movements were tightly controlled as he unpacked his laptop and connected it to the projector screen. Tristan couldn't stop himself from eyeing the lean lines of Professor Cruz's back, the breadth of his shoulders beneath the crisp white material of his dress shirt, the taper of his waist down to his round, fine-looking ass. Distracted, Tristan tongued his lower lip while wondering what Professor Cruz did for exercise. He had the body of a runner, wiry and strong instead of bulky from weight lifting. Tristan had several inches on him, but then, when he wasn't among athletes, Tristan was often the tallest person in the room. It wouldn't be enough of a height difference to make kissing difficult, though…

Jesus. What are you even thinking? Focus.

Steven leaned closer to whisper, "Is it me or does he seem even more pissed off than usual?"

Tristan hid a chuckle behind a cough and earned himself a hard glare from Professor Cruz. Out of the corner of his eye, he could see Steven's mustache quivering as he fought back his own laughter.

Tristan's amusement withered at the expression on Professor Cruz's face. Steven was right. Not that Professor Cruz could be described as cheerful on the best of days, but right then, he looked about ready to commit murder. *Damn.* What had crawled up his butt and died? And what the hell was wrong with Tristan that the ferocious glare being aimed his way made him hot instead of putting him off?

Professor Cruz released Tristan from his stare and

started lecturing, his voice a deep, familiar rumble. Tristan could easily envision that stern, no-nonsense tone ordering him around in bed, and it made his dick stir with interest.

Tristan bit back a groan. *Fuck.* The very last thing he needed was to be caught fantasizing about Professor Cruz during class. For one, it was inappropriate as hell. Two, the jockstrap and sweatpants Tristan wore hid absolutely nothing. If he chubbed up any further, his hard-on would be unmistakable. What if Steven looked over and noticed?

Tristan had a sudden, uncomfortable flashback to high school algebra, back when his horny teenaged body popped a boner at the mere whiff of another hot, sweaty boy. He remembered sitting in his seat, mortified and silently praying Mr. Martin wouldn't call on him to solve a problem in front of the class. The residual humiliation from having to shuffle up to the board with a book covering his crotch was enough to wilt his erection even now.

Ugh. Tristan cringed at the memory.

But how could he help himself? Tristan couldn't be the only student looking at Professor Cruz differently after his revelation last week. Perceptions always changed the more you learned about a person, whether it be their sexuality, political views, or the way they treated homeless people on the street.

In this particular situation, Tristan imagined most of his classmates probably weren't picturing a naked Professor Cruz forcing them onto their knees, but hey, he'd already been having that fantasy. Professor Cruz's admission simply took his lusty daydreams from purely hypothetical jerk-off material to an entirely possible, if not very likely, reality.

Tristan tuned back in to the lecture. Professor Cruz was talking about nepotism and how it related to crime and punishment and the privilege of wealth. Tristan pushed aside his smutty, wayward thoughts and forced himself to concentrate so he could open a new document on his MacBook to start taking notes. He'd done well on the last two papers, and he wanted to keep that momentum going.

He wanted—no, *needed*—to flip the big, dumb jock stereotype on its head. People rarely acknowledged the sheer amount of discipline and dedication it took to be involved in professional sports. Tristan worked his ass off to keep his body honed and develop his skills during the regular season, and he continued those routines throughout the summer. He couldn't slack because they weren't actively playing, and many of his peers worked just as hard. But so often athletes were ridiculed as stupid, overpaid brutes undeserving of their contracts or accolades and incapable of any thought beyond hitting pucks with sticks or scoring touchdowns.

There was more to Tristan than his ability to block a shot. Professor Cruz had asked for them to get personal, and Tristan's experiences had given him plenty of source material for his last paper. He was proud of what he'd written, and he hoped his grade reflected the effort he'd put into it. Tristan might not be the strongest of writers, but he knew he'd been improving with every assignment. His competitive nature ensured he constantly strove to be better, even when his only competition was himself.

When the class ended, Tristan gathered his belongings and followed Steven down the aisle on his way out of the lecture hall. Tristan had a break before his next class, which he usually spent in the library, but as he passed Professor Cruz's desk, he heard, "I need to see you in my office, Mr. Holt. Right now."

Tristan almost kept walking, assuming Professor Cruz was speaking to someone behind him, until he registered the "Mr. Holt" and looked up to find himself the sole focus of that dark-eyed stare.

"Okay," Tristan said. It sounded more like a question. He waved for Steven to go ahead without him.

Professor Cruz nodded sharply. "Follow me. My office is on the first floor."

Brow furrowed, Tristan trailed Professor Cruz down a couple of flights of stairs to a door wedged between a men's restroom and a storage closet. Tristan waited for him to unlock it and followed him inside the small office.

"Have a seat," Professor Cruz said.

As Tristan sank onto the chair in front of the desk, he looked curiously around the room. There was a distinct lack of pictures or personal items, save for a large framed print of the album cover for Pink Floyd's *The Dark Side of the Moon* mounted on the wall next to the bookshelf. Tristan smiled a bit at that—they were one of his all-time favorite bands—but before he could comment, Professor Cruz set aside his messenger bag and settled into his seat.

He didn't speak until he'd withdrawn a sheaf of papers from one of the drawers. He separated them into two piles and slid both across the desk to Tristan. "Do you have anything to say about this?" Professor Cruz hiked an imperious eyebrow.

Tristan leaned forward. One pile of paper appeared to be his latest assignment. The other had something about lacrosse in the title and had the name Steven Wheeling in the top, left-hand corner.

Tristan chewed his lower lip, knowing he probably appeared as confused as he felt. "No?" he finally said.

Professor Cruz's face darkened. "No? Do you think this is some kind of joke? You clearly copied your classmate's paper, and it's beyond insulting that you actually thought I wouldn't notice. You do realize once I report this, there *will* be disciplinary action, up to and including your immediate removal from my class and a failing grade for the course. Allow me to assure you, I am very seriously considering making that my recommendation to the committee."

Tristan jerked back in his seat and raised his hands. "Whoa, whoa, whoa. I think there's been a misunderstanding. I didn't copy anyone's paper."

Professor Cruz huffed and shot him an unimpressed glare. "The evidence sits right before you, Mr. Holt. I spoke to Mr. Wheeling this morning. He told me he'd sent you his paper to proofread. You might have changed the sport to hockey, but otherwise, it's clearly identical."

Horror hit Tristan like an unexpected punch to the stomach. Queasiness welled in the wake of the shock, tightening his throat. For a few seconds, Tristan didn't even dare to speak. If he opened his mouth, he might puke from the violent rage churning in his guts. He yanked the papers closer and quickly scanned the one with Steven's name in the corner. It was, almost word for word, an exact copy of the paper Tristan himself had written.

"That asshole!" he burst out.

"Please restrain yourself, Mr. Holt. Don't blame Mr. Wheeling for the fact that you got caught."

Tristan shook his head. "You don't understand. This is *my* paper. He asked me if he could see it because he couldn't decide on a subject. *He* offered to proofread for *me*. He told me he doesn't even play sports! I can show you the chat history if you want proof."

Professor Cruz stared at him. For the first time, Tristan got to see him nonplussed.

After a long pause, Professor Cruz cleared his throat. "Show me."

His hands trembling with barely contained fury, Tristan dug his phone from his backpack and pulled up the Google Hangouts app. He opened the conversation with Steven and scrolled to the top before handing the phone to Professor Cruz.

The silence stretched. Then, wordlessly, Professor Cruz returned the phone. "My apologies. Mr. Wheeling was very convincing when we spoke this morning."

"What proof did he show you?" Tristan asked.

Professor Cruz hesitated.

Tristan laughed without humor. "None, then. You assumed I was the one who copied because, what?"

Professor Cruz lifted his chin. "It appeared that—"

"It *appeared*," Tristan broke in. "So, because I look like an empty-headed jock and he's some hipster nerd, he had more credibility than me? You didn't ask him to prove his work? I can show you my first draft of the paper too, if the chat history isn't enough."

Professor Cruz held up a slender hand. "It's enough. I believe you."

"And?" Tristan arched his brows, wishing his shaky voice hadn't so clearly projected his annoyance.

"And Mr. Wheeling will be disciplined appropriately, I assure you."

"Good." Tristan grabbed his bag and got to his feet, staring down into dark, unreadable eyes. "Are we done here, Professor?" He needed to get out of this office before the tenuous grip on his temper snapped.

"We're done."

Tristan stalked to the door, his heart racing. He paused on the threshold and looked over his shoulder. "You know, for all your preaching about privilege and tolerance in class, you seem pretty biased yourself. Maybe it's time for a bit of introspection, Professor."

He walked away without waiting for a response. Fury blazed bright in his chest. Tristan wanted to go back in there and really rip Professor Cruz a new one. Instead of doing something rash, he slammed out of the closest exit into the hot summer afternoon.

Tristan wasn't sure what made him angrier—the plagiarism accusation or that fucker Steven cozying up to him in class and then stealing his paper. Steven must've known what Professor Cruz wanted to talk to Tristan about today, and he hadn't even looked guilty when Professor Cruz asked to see Tristan in his office. That little *shit*.

No, Tristan *did* know what pissed him off more—the assumption that he, *Tristan*, would be the one to steal someone else's work, based solely on appearances. Professor Cruz, a college-educated man who taught *sociology* and should theoretically be above stereotyping, had clearly slotted Tristan into the "dumb, blond jock" category without giving him the benefit of the doubt. It was unfair, and more than that, it was infuriating.

"Son of a bitch!" Tristan snarled, startling a short guy who'd been walking unnoticed beside him.

The guy squeaked, wide-eyed, and scrambled away.

Tristan raised his hands, palms out. "Oh, no, sorry, man. Sorry. Not you."

The guy took off without answering, and Tristan cringed as guilt cramped his stomach. Breathing harshly, he detoured from the walking path and stopped under the shade of a tree.

"Get a grip, Holtzy," he muttered, shaking out his limbs. He hadn't been this enraged or disappointed since his disallowed goal lost the Venom game six of the first round of the playoffs, forcing the game seven that ended their run at the Stanley Cup Final. If he saw Steven right now, Tristan didn't know what he'd do. Choke the little fucker, probably.

Breathe. Breathe.

Good thing Tristan was fairly certain Professor Cruz would ensure the thieving douchebag never stepped foot in his class again. That was the only upside in this situation. The rest of it was a disaster. Tristan's ill-advised crush on his professor had thrown him off-kilter, causing him to invent a connection between them that didn't actually exist. Why should it matter what Professor Cruz thought or assumed? The dude was a judgmental, sanctimonious prick. His opinions meant less than nothing. And if there was a bigger boner-killer than being threatened with disciplinary action—and not the fun kind—by the guy he'd been thirsting for, Tristan couldn't imagine it.

God, he felt like such an asshole for even entertaining any of those sex fantasies in the first place. Professor Cruz had ripped Tristan's rose-tinted glasses right off. Maybe it was for the best. Tristan didn't need to be lusting after one of his teachers anyway. In another four weeks, he wouldn't have to see Professor Cruz or hear his name ever again.

One thing was certain: Mr. Sociology needed to take a

long, hard look at his own personal prejudices. If Tristan wanted, he could report Professor Cruz to the school board or the chair or whoever the hell was in charge of these kinds of things. He'd have to check the handbook to find out for sure, but Tristan couldn't imagine they'd appreciate hearing one of their staff members had made such a gigantic screwup. Lucky for Professor Cruz, Tristan wasn't inclined to be petty. But that definitely wouldn't stop him from being pissed off.

Chapter Five

After Tristan left his office, Sebastian sat in his chair and stared moodily at his computer screen while he cursed himself for being such an asshole.

He'd completely misjudged the situation and made assumptions based on Tristan's appearance, which was *totally* unprofessional—not to mention went against everything Sebastian taught as a sociologist. What the hell was wrong with him that he'd been so quick to assume Tristan was the plagiarist frat boy?

He couldn't deny that he was glad Tristan wasn't a plagiarist, but it didn't change the fact that *he* was disappointed in himself for his own behavior.

"So, because I look like an empty-headed jock and he's some hipster nerd, he had more credibility than me?"

Groaning quietly, Sebastian stood up and shoved his things back in his messenger bag. He knew he was going to have to apologize to Tristan. Some sociology professor he was. They should revoke his PhD and send him back to undergrad.

Maybe it was the lingering effects of the Catholic upbringing, but Sebastian had a strong desire to confess his stupidity to someone so he could feel better about what he'd done.

Preferably over alcohol, but it was way too early in the day for that.

As he made his way to the Math Department, he kept a wary eye out for Tristan, and wasn't sure if he was relieved or disappointed not to run into him. Remembering that flash of hurt in Tristan's bright-blue eyes made him wince, and he was in a bad mood when he knocked on R.J.'s office and waited for his friend's gruff, "Come in," before shoving the door open.

"Hey, Seb," R.J. said, but his friendly smile dimmed somewhat as he took in Seb's stormy expression. "You need help hiding a body or what? You look pissed as hell."

"I'm an idiot," Sebastian said bluntly. "I did something exceedingly stupid, and I can't believe myself."

"Um." R.J. gestured to the chair in front of his desk. "Have a seat and tell me about it."

Sebastian gave him the short version, telling him about the plagiarized paper and how he'd immediately assumed Tristan was the plagiarist instead of the original author. He'd just mentioned Tristan's name when R.J. held up a hand to stop him.

"Wait—wait. You said Tristan Holt…you don't mean the hockey player, do you?"

"His paper was about hockey, yeah," said Sebastian, momentarily confused. "Does he play for GSU? I didn't know the school even *had* a hockey team." Sebastian scowled. "Then again, apparently I don't know much of anything, today."

"Dude." R.J.'s eyes went wide. He was apparently ignoring Sebastian's momentary lapse into dramatics.

"Tristan Holt doesn't play hockey for the college. He plays hockey for the Venom."

"The...what?"

R.J. snorted, typed something on his computer and then gestured for Sebastian to come around his desk. "Look."

Sebastian walked around and peered over R.J.'s shoulder. There, on the screen, were images of Tristan in green-and-gold hockey gear. He took in Tristan's broad shoulders, looking even more so in the pads, and then glanced at R.J. before finding his eyes drawn once more to the screen.

"The Atlanta Venom is an NHL team," R.J. explained. "Your student is a professional athlete."

That would explain Tristan's papers—the very insightful paper about hockey, and, Sebastian realized, the first assignment about finding oneself suddenly jumping from one economic class to another. A glance at the Wikipedia page R.J. pulled up showed that Tristan's entry-level contract had been nearly two million dollars. Even spread out over a couple of years, that was a hell of a lot of money—especially for a twenty-three-year-old. And that was *before* a recent contract extension.

R.J. was still extolling Tristan's virtues as a defenseman—apparently he was a hockey fan—which was not helping Sebastian feel better about his fuckup. Nor did it help when R.J. said, "That's impressive he's got this great career and he's getting his degree at the same time. Takes a lot of dedication."

Sebastian crossed his arms and shot R.J. the same sharp stare he gave his students. "You're not helping."

R.J. shrugged. "I don't think there's really anything

I can say that will. You fucked up and you know it. Did you apologize?"

"Of course," Sebastian snapped, perhaps a little too hastily. At R.J.'s disbelieving look, he scowled harder and raked a hand through his hair. "I— All right, no, not really. But I was going to. He left before I had the chance."

R.J. tilted his head to look up at Sebastian, who moved away when he realized he was looming over his friend and practically crowding him. "Well, you should probably do that."

"Yes," Sebastian said, testily. "I know." He went back and grabbed his bag from the chair, shouldering it. "Meanwhile, I have to do something about the student who actually plagiarized."

R.J. gave him a sympathetic look that was completely and utterly contrived. "You're sure you got the right one this time, Cruz? You need me to google any more student athletes for you?"

"Oh, shut up," Sebastian muttered, but despite his surly tone, he knew that R.J. wouldn't take it personally. It was obvious that Sebastian was only upset with himself. "You want to meet later for a drink?"

"I promised to run a study group tonight," R.J. said, clearly regretful. "Rain check?"

"Sure," said Sebastian, and promised that yes, he would apologize to Tristan and no, he wasn't going to ask him for hockey tickets.

After leaving R.J.'s office, Sebastian headed home and changed his clothes to go for a run. He was training for a half marathon, and technically he should do a seven-mile run today. Lucky for him, that wasn't a problem—he was in the mood to run at least ten. Of course, the heat and humidity of the Georgia summer day was enough to make him reconsider the longer distance. But every time he thought about what had happened with Tristan, he forced himself to keep going until he was covered in sweat and his muscles burned from exertion.

Once home, he showered, fixed himself a light supper and drank practically a half gallon of water. He felt better than he would have if he'd gone out for a drink, and he was glad that R.J. had that study group after all.

Once he was finished with the dishes, he sat down and pulled out his notes for the next class meeting. He'd already made it clear that he never deviated from the syllabus, but this time, he was going to make an exception. As he jotted down a few reminders and reviewed the class roster, mind cleared from the exercise and determined to make up for his mistake, Sebastian started putting together a plan.

"I know the syllabus says we're supposed to discuss the systems of power that are put in place to keep people stagnant in their circumstances, but there's something else I want to address." Sebastian faced his class, his eyes touching briefly on Tristan's.

"Our last assignment was about perceptions, and how those perceptions can affect our behaviors—both positively and negatively." Sebastian leaned back against the desk, his posture far more casual than normal. "In my case, it was the latter. I made an egregious assumption based on appearance, and it was both unprofessional and shortsighted of me." He gave a slight nod to Tristan. "Even those of us who study these sorts of things for a living aren't immune. That's how powerful these biases are."

Sebastian then asked the students if they wanted to talk about the experiences they'd written about in their last assignments. At first it was a bit like pulling teeth, but after a while, they had some actual dialogue about the ideas and concepts they'd been discussing. It wasn't precisely lively, but it was more interactive—and more engaging—than classes had been thus far.

After class, Sebastian waited for Tristan to walk past his desk and stopped him with a quiet, "If you wouldn't mind staying behind for a few minutes, Mr. Holt, I'd appreciate it."

Tristan was wearing those sweatpants that were so distracting, and his hair—which had been damp when he'd shown up for class today—had dried into soft spikes. He shifted his backpack and nodded, waiting quietly while the other students filed out of the room.

A few of them actually told him to have a nice weekend, which was a change. Sebastian acknowledged them with a nod, trying not to focus entirely on the young man waiting next to him. Tristan smelled like soap and faintly like fabric softener, as if those distracting sweatpants had been taken directly from the laundry that morning and pulled on over freshly showered skin—

"Professor Cruz?"

Sebastian cleared his throat, realizing with a slight twinge of embarrassment that they were alone. "Yes, Mr. Holt. I owe you an apology for my assumption that you'd plagiarized your paper. You're right, it was entirely my fault for assuming that you were the plagiarist because of the way you looked."

Tristan smiled a bit. "Yeah, well. I'm used to people making assumptions about me."

Sebastian nodded. "I'm sure you are, but it doesn't excuse my behavior. Your assignments have all been very insightful, and I meant all of the comments that I've left for you. I'm not sure what you're planning on doing for your final paper, but I'm looking forward to reading it."

"I'm...thinking about a couple of things." Tristan raked a hand through his hair. "I haven't narrowed it down yet, though."

"Well, if there's anything you'd like to discuss with me, please feel free to do so. Also, just to reassure you, Steven Wheeling has been removed from this class and assigned a failing grade for the summer term. He was made to understand that stealing a classmate's paper is entirely unacceptable." Sebastian wanted to add something else, but he didn't know what.

"Okay, good," said Tristan. "Thanks, Professor Cruz."

He liked the way that sounded, Sebastian realized, in a way that was as inappropriate as his erroneous assumption of plagiarism had been...only in a completely different way. "You're welcome. I appreciate the opportunity to apologize, and thank you for accepting it." He paused. "I also think it's wonderful what you're doing, pursuing your education in addition to playing a professional sport. That must take an incredible amount of dedication."

If anything, Tristan looked embarrassed by Sebastian's entirely genuine praise. His fair skin pinkened slightly, and it gave Sebastian even *more* inappropriate thoughts about what else he could do to make Tristan flush like that.

"Some days it's more work than others." Tristan gave

Sebastian a nice smile, teeth slightly crooked in a way that was somehow just as attractive as the rest of him. "Have a good weekend, Professor."

"You too, Mr. Holt," said Sebastian, and didn't even pretend not to stare at Tristan's ass on his way out.

Chapter Six

Tristan wished he hated Sebastian Cruz. No one who knew the circumstances would blame him if he did. After the plagiarism accusation, Tristan's hatred would've been entirely justified. And being threatened with academic consequences for an act he hadn't committed *should* have been enough to snuff out any lingering lust Tristan might've felt for someone so completely, incredibly off-limits.

Except it hadn't. Tristan didn't hate Professor Cruz. At all. In fact, Tristan wanted him more than ever. The sexual fantasies had only gotten more graphic, more arousing, in the days since that damned class last week, and the apology afterward.

Tristan knew how much it had cost Professor Cruz to admit to his fault and confess to his personal biases. The man didn't exactly lack in pride, and it seemed to Tristan he was probably used to being on the defensive—as a gay man, as a person of color. None of that excused Professor Cruz's behavior—and maybe forgiving him made Tristan a soft touch—but it wasn't in his nature to hold a grudge. Tristan respected someone who owned up to their mistakes. It took courage and a level of self-awareness that a lot of people lacked.

Also…there was the small matter of Professor Cruz's thorough, and unsubtle, appraisal of Tristan's body.

He'd caught the quick once-over Professor Cruz had given him at the end of class, and he'd felt that same stare burning into his ass as he walked out of the lecture hall.

It wasn't a stretch to assume Professor Cruz might be as attracted to Tristan as Tristan was to him. Imagining how the man's intensity would carry over into sex made Tristan want to pant. It didn't take much more than that—and Professor Cruz's apology—to reignite the burgeoning flare of lust Tristan had been trying so hard to stifle.

Sebastian Cruz wasn't a classically handsome man. He was too sharp-featured, too forbidding. Yet somehow that severity fascinated Tristan. He appreciated the bold, striking lines of Professor Cruz's face. They made him interesting. And the way Professor Cruz scowled and generally seemed annoyed by the universe at large made Tristan's balls feel heavy and his stomach warm with want. What that said about Tristan's psyche, he didn't know. He'd always been attracted to authoritative men. He liked bossy tops, and judging by what he'd seen of Professor Cruz, Tristan couldn't picture him being anything but demanding in bed. Of course, it didn't hurt that Professor Cruz had the sort of body Tristan's wet dreams were made of.

So if Tristan left class on Tuesday and jerked off to the fantasy of being fucked hard over the desk in Professor Cruz's office, well, no one else had to know. And if he did it again on Wednesday morning before going to meet Ryu, that was between him and his right hand.

Ryu had returned from Sweden over the weekend and seemed more than ready to get back to their usual routine. They followed a similar exercise regimen and often worked out with the same trainer, so it made sense to do it together. Tristan knew they made an unlikely pair. Him, the son of simple Midwestern farmers; Ryu, raised in Los Angeles and born to a world-renowned surgeon and a former gold-medal-winning Olympian. But Tristan was closer to Ryu than anyone else on the team.

Ryu stood at about five foot ten, small for a goalie, and his dark, silky hair was cut into a feathery, face-framing style—layered up top, long enough to brush his collar in the back—that made him resemble a Japanese rock star more than a professional hockey player. He also possessed the same eerie intensity nearly every goaltender seemed to share, and compared to most of their rowdy teammates, Ryu might be considered downright taciturn. He wasn't, though. His sense of humor was quietly snarky. He made Tristan laugh, and his self-possession appealed to the part of Tristan that missed spending time with his easygoing family.

He'd only known Ryu for a little over a year. They'd bonded last season after Ryu had gotten called up from the Rattlers, the Venom's AHL affiliate, as the backup's backup when Elliott, their starting goalie, broke his leg in two places. Elliott had retired shortly afterward, and Ryu had stayed on the team instead of being sent back down to the Rattlers.

During Ryu's first game in net, Tristan had thrown off his gloves and punched out the winger who kept crowding Ryu and spitting ethnic slurs. No one messed with Tristan's goalies. Ever. Especially not like that.

Thus, their friendship had begun.

Ryu met him in the entryway of Powerhouse. Outside, the gym appeared to be nothing more than an industrial warehouse. Inside, it was a mecca for any athlete or fitness diehard, with everything from obstacle courses to rock-climbing walls to boxing rings and MMA cages, plus all the other standard exercise equipment.

By way of greeting, Tristan and Ryu exchanged smiles and a fist bump—Ryu wasn't much of a hugger unless it was on the ice.

"How's it going, man?" Tristan asked. "Let's go find Lewis."

They hunted down their joint trainer, who put them through an hour and a half of weight work and interval training before they joined a thirty-minute Pilates class. Afterward, they showered and drove separately to Tristan's favorite Thai restaurant.

"How was Sweden?" Tristan asked once they were seated across from each other with glasses of green jasmine iced tea. The panting and profuse sweating they'd done while working their asses off at the gym hadn't allowed for much in the way of conversation.

"It was fine. We worked on focus and protecting the top of the crease. The drills weren't much different than what I do with Coach Marsh." Ryu shrugged. "But I did make a stopover in Amsterdam for a couple of days. The trip was worth it for the canals alone."

Tristan laughed mid-sip and started coughing when tea went down the wrong pipe. "The canals," he said through a wheeze. "The many and varied canals. Yes. I've heard they're pretty memorable."

Ryu's broad grin defined cheekbones that were already sharp as blades. "How have your classes been?"

"Fine. I wanted to ask you for some advice, actually."

"Oh, yeah? What about?"

Tristan cleared his throat and fiddled with his straw. "Um. It has to do with one of my professors."

"What do you mean?"

"I— There's—" Tristan gnawed on his lower lip as he considered how to word his question without revealing he needed advice about a man. He couldn't ask Morley for help. He knew what Morley's suggestion would be, at least if Morley thought Tristan's professor was a woman. Morley would probably start singing "Hot for Teacher" and then wish Tristan success on his cougar hunt. Ryu was infinitely more levelheaded.

For a second, Tristan contemplated telling Ryu the truth. How much easier would it be if they could discuss the situation openly? Two words and it would be out there: *I'm gay.*

Tristan's brain rejected the idea almost as soon as it popped into his head. He wasn't ready for his friends to know. They were good guys. The best. Hell, they probably wouldn't even care. But what if he was wrong?

He wasn't prepared to risk losing them. Not yet. Not anytime soon.

"I think there might be something between me and one of my professors," he finally went on. "Like…sexual tension."

Ryu's dark eyes widened. "And you want to do something about it?"

"I think so, yeah… I mean, Professor Cruz isn't the only person in the Sociology Department. If I wanted to take another class, I'm sure I could find one being taught by another instructor. So maybe…"

Ryu tilted his head, his forehead wrinkled. "There are rules about that, aren't there?"

Tristan shrugged. "Probably. Conflict of interest, you know? But the term will be over in a few weeks."

"Well…" Ryu tapped the tabletop with his thumb.

"I'd be careful if I were you. Wait until the class is finished and grades are in. That way your actions can't be misinterpreted. It won't seem like a bid for favoritism."

Tristan nodded slowly. He knew waiting was the smartest option, even if the idea of holding off for a few more weeks before making a move felt torturous. Then again, he might be getting ahead of himself. He didn't know if Professor Cruz actually wanted him. Or if he was single. Just because Tristan had caught the guy checking out his ass didn't mean Professor Cruz wanted to tap it, or that he'd cross that line if he did.

There might be a way for Tristan to find out, though. He still needed to put together the prospectus for his final paper before discussing it with Professor Cruz. Maybe he could use the assignment as a subtle way to reveal his sexuality, and the meeting itself to gauge Professor Cruz's interest. Yeah…that might work. Tristan already had a topic in mind.

During his meeting with one of his students about her final paper, Sebastian had to remind himself—more than once—that he was supposed to *encourage* them, not tell them why all their ideas were basically wrong. He did like teaching, for the most part—he just had very little patience when someone sat in front of him and clearly showed how she hadn't been listening while he'd been doing it.

"So, like," the girl said, whose name was something with more vowels than were necessary, "I wanted to, you know, like, show that people who were popular in high school were perceived as being bitchy and cliquey when, like, we totally weren't. And work it into how, like, girls who thought that were usually ones who didn't want to take the time to get to *know* us."

"Ashleighy." Sebastian fixed the young woman with his usual sharp stare. "It's an...interesting rough concept, but I should point out you've written every assignment in this class on a very similar topic." *Someone is having a tough time leaving high school behind*, he thought, which was probably uncharitable.

He tried to talk Ashleighy into rethinking her proposal and expanding it a bit, maybe examining something that had to do with nonprivileged white people, but he wasn't sure how much of it got through. In the end, it was up to Ashleighy and she'd be graded accordingly. He couldn't deny that she tried—she was always in class, always turned in her assignments—and she even seemed *interested* in the material...as long as it somehow related to her and her circumstances.

Remembering the situation with Tristan made Sebastian chide himself about making assumptions, though thinking about Tristan was immediately distracting. He returned his attention to Ashleighy and tried suggesting a few books that were a little more diverse in their focus, but he had no idea how much good it did.

She gave him a bright smile and a cheery wave, with an admonition to "Have a good weekend!" as she bounced out the door. He sighed and rolled his eyes, flipping his pen around in his hand idly as he waited for his next—and last—student appointment of the day.

Tristan.

Thoughts of Tristan's prospectus made Sebastian nearly drop the pen. He'd blinked at his laptop the night before when he'd read it while preparing for the meeting today, because Tristan's proposed final assignment was dealing with homophobia in professional sports, and how it informed perceptions of masculinity and affected power dynamics in a team's locker room.

At first, Sebastian had thought maybe Tristan was angling for a good grade because he knew Sebastian was gay, but he'd dismissed the thought fairly quickly. He'd already made a substantial assumption about Tristan when he'd jumped to conclusions about the plagiarizing, and he was determined to give Tristan the benefit of the doubt this time. Especially when it came to something like this.

Besides, there had been a few times when Sebastian had thought he'd seen Tristan looking at him with more than academic interest—even after his colossal fuckup and the resulting apology. While he'd admitted that was probably wishful thinking, seeing this prospectus made him question if maybe Tristan *was* expressing some sort of interest.

The thought, while gratifying and definitely arousing, was best left for the privacy of his bed at night. Tristan Holt was Sebastian's student and—according to the YouTube videos he'd watched and the online articles he'd read—an up-and-coming athlete with a promising future. There was no way he was interested in some academic asshole who'd been a dick to him, even if Sebastian had apologized.

Tristan was right on time, if not a few minutes early, and Sebastian noticed he was wearing the Pink Floyd shirt again. It made him want to smile, but instead he gestured briefly to the chair across from his desk and said, "Have a seat, Mr. Holt."

Tristan's mouth quirked, but he settled his tall—very,

very tall—frame into the chair. He was fresh-faced and bright-eyed, holding an actual notebook and pen on his lap.

"I read your prospectus," Sebastian said, not one to waste words and also not wanting to leer at his student any longer, no matter how nicely defined his legs were. "As you know, it's a subject near to my own academic interests, but it might be a little off from the scope of the course."

Tristan nodded, leaning forward eagerly. "I thought about that, yeah. I really wanted to do this topic, though, so I was hoping maybe there was a way you could help me figure out how to, uh, apply the idea to the class."

Oh, could I ever. Right over my desk. Sebastian dragged his thoughts out of the gutter and nodded. "Certainly." He grabbed a piece of paper and started jotting down some book names. "Here is a list of sources I think would be a good starting place for the academic portion of your paper. Remember that while personal experience is always valuable, a sociologist is, in part, a passive observer, and their work should include references from other scholars."

Sebastian pushed the list over to him, then paused. "I shouldn't ask this, but I'm going to anyway—are there any issues with your team that are putting you or your personal safety at risk in the locker room?"

Tristan blinked those baby blues a few times, then shook his head. Sebastian couldn't tell if he looked pleased or embarrassed that Sebastian had assumed he was somewhere on the LGBT spectrum. "No, but I'm—I'm not out to my team," he said, his chin raised a little. "But I keep thinking about what happened when you told the class you were gay, and I wonder... I guess I want to see if it's the same in a professional hockey locker room."

"Did you follow the coverage about Michael Sam?" Sebastian asked, referring to the college football player who'd come out before the NFL draft a few years ago.

Tristan winced. "Yeah. I felt bad for him, but mostly because of the media. They were so obsessed with the fact that he was gay, I think they hounded him out of wanting to play football."

Sebastian had thought much the same thing, but he'd also wondered what the situation for Sam had been like on his college team. "I'm sure that didn't help."

"But there's a lot that goes on in the locker room that the media doesn't see," Tristan continued, clearly warming up to his topic. "And the whole idea of the power structures we talked about, how people see each other… that's what I wanted to focus on. The inner circle, or whatever."

Sebastian nodded. "That makes sense." He spent a few more minutes helping Tristan narrow down his focus so that it fit with both his interests and the key ideas of the class, and Tristan really did seem interested and invested in the project. "Are you intending to major in sociology?" he asked, unsure if he'd like to see more of Tristan in his classes or if that might be way too torturous.

"International business." Tristan sat up straighter. "I travel a lot with hockey, which I really like, and if something happens and I get injured, I need to have something else on my résumé besides keeping guys from scoring."

Sebastian noticed Tristan subtly knocked at the wood of his desk, and raised his eyebrows in question.

Tristan flushed. "Sorry. Superstition. Hockey players, man. We're like that." He laughed sheepishly.

It was a nice laugh, which didn't help Sebastian's completely inappropriate attraction in the slightest. "So I hear. I just run marathons. Which is probably not the same."

"I thought you might be a runner," Tristan said, and then his flush got deeper, which told Sebastian that maybe he wasn't wrong about Tristan's attraction to him.

If it was wishful thinking, perhaps Sebastian wasn't entirely off base. "I didn't play any sports growing up, and neither of my parents are into it."

"Do they know you're gay?" Tristan leaned forward a bit. He cleared his throat. "Sorry, that's…probably not appropriate for me to ask. But I guess I wondered how it—how it was for you."

It wasn't appropriate, but it told Sebastian that Tristan probably wasn't out to his family. It was never his intention to be anyone's gay mentor, but it was hard to help himself around Tristan, and besides, it was just a question. "It's all right. Yes, they know, and no, it wasn't easy. There are a lot of expectations for young men in my culture, and subverting those wasn't easy. I'm certainly not the only gay Puerto Rican from the Bronx, but it was more about being out than anything."

Tristan nodded eagerly. "Exactly, that's how I feel about being a gay hockey player. Like, I know I'm not the only one, and honestly, I feel like hockey is a tolerant sport—for the most part. That's why I'm interested in why no one's come out yet, especially since they have in other professional sports."

The enthusiasm was always something Sebastian appreciated, and along with Tristan's bright smile and the subtle signals he was giving off—leaning in closer, meeting Sebastian's eyes, that sort of thing—it was time to end their meeting.

"If you need any more assistance with the project, let

me know," Sebastian said, intending it as a dismissal and hoping it didn't come across in the *would you like to see my etchings* sort of way.

Tristan put his notebook away, stood up, and shouldered his backpack. He was at least five inches taller than Sebastian when they were both standing, so with Sebastian still in his chair, Tristan looked even taller. But Sebastian didn't stand up, though it wasn't necessarily out of any desire to show that Tristan's height didn't intimidate him.

It was more the semi he was sporting in his suit pants.

Tristan's gaze shifted to the Pink Floyd poster on Sebastian's wall. "You into Floyd? Cool. Me too. My favorite's 'Comfortably Numb.' What about you?"

"You seem a little young to be a Pink Floyd fan," Sebastian said, despite himself. "And my favorite's 'Wish You Were Here.'"

Tristan grinned that killer smile of his and shrugged his broad shoulders, which were nicely defined beneath his T-shirt. "I had a friend growing up, and his dad always brought us to games and practices and stuff. He had, like, three tapes in his car. Kansas, Floyd, and Zeppelin. So, you know. Lots of happy memories."

That was a much-needed reminder that Tristan was younger than him and, no matter how attractive Sebastian found him, also his student. It kept him from sharing his own memories of classic rock and how his dad, too, had been the one to introduce a young Sebastian to the genre. "If there's nothing else, I believe I have another appointment," Sebastian said, though he didn't. He needed Tristan Holt to get out of his office before his brain tormented him with images of fucking Tristan over his desk.

Never going to happen. While thinking about it when he was alone in his bed was one thing, it was inexcusable to entertain the thought when the object of his fantasies was standing right in front of him.

Tristan blinked, maybe looking a little hurt, but he gave an easy shrug. "Sure, sorry to take up your time. See you next week, Professor Cruz."

Sebastian nodded and watched him go. He told himself firmly to get a grip, then decided to distract himself by grading a few student papers he knew would be terrible. Nothing took his mind off sex like the badly written academic efforts of students who never showed up.

Chapter Seven

Nothing cleared Tristan's mind quite like the sharp crunch of skate blades biting into ice. For Tristan, the noise held a sensory appeal. Whenever his brain got too loud, too cluttered, he closed his eyes and imagined the sound to center himself. It never failed—until lately. Since the prospectus meeting with Professor Cruz, not even the slicing scrape of skates-on-ice could save Tristan's concentration for long.

During class, Tristan forced himself to recite parts of the NHL rulebook whenever he got distracted by thoughts of how his professor's long, lean body might feel against his. Outside of class, he spent more time than was probably healthy having filthy student/uptight professor daydreams. Tristan wondered about the taste of Professor Cruz's come, about how he smelled up close and personal. He imagined that low, growly voice giving him orders. *Fuck.* The other day he'd even tripped and nearly broken his nose by face-planting on the treadmill when he let his mind wander and it drifted straight to the fantasy of Professor Cruz smirking and asking him things like, *Do you want to choke on my dick?* before forcing his cock deep into Tristan's throat.

As Tristan had groaned in pain from his position on

the floor, Morley had laughed himself stupid and aban-
doned his own run to catch his breath. He'd stood there,
chuckling and wiping tears from his eyes, while Ryu
grabbed Tristan a towel to try to staunch the bleeding
from his nostrils. Afterward, Tristan looked like he'd
taken a vicious right hook to the schnoz, which earned
him a double take from Professor Cruz during the following class.

A few days later, he met Ryu and Morley at a small
local rink to run some practice drills. Despite being in
his element—on the ice with a stick in his hand and a
puck on his tape—it took Tristan an unbelievable amount
of energy to focus.

He didn't understand why he was so preoccupied with
fantasies about Professor Cruz when they'd spent maybe
a grand total of twenty minutes alone together. Possibly,
it was the lure of the unattainable, and Tristan's growing assurance that his attraction was far from one-sided.
He'd felt that gaze lingering on him, and he'd watched
Professor Cruz shake his head, consternation clear on
his features, when Tristan looked up and caught him
staring—three different times.

But Tristan couldn't afford to be so distracted. What if
he seriously injured himself or broke a limb? That would
be fun to explain to the coaching staff when training
camp started. Somehow, he didn't think they'd appreciate hearing, *Sorry, guys, I have a hard-on for my professor and can't stop thinking about his dick. Or mine.*

Tristan almost laughed aloud at the thought. Trying to
center himself, he circled the rink for half an hour, practicing his turns and stops and dribbling the puck around
a few makeshift obstacles. He wasn't as good at stick-
handling as some of the forwards on the team, and he

didn't have any flashy tricks up his sleeve, but he liked to think his skills weren't anything to sneeze at, either.

When Ryu banged his stick against one of the goal posts to call his attention, Tristan took a puck down the ice and aimed for Ryu's weak spot—top shelf left. It sailed cleanly over Ryu's shoulder.

Morley guffawed behind Tristan. "Guess training with that Swedish dude didn't help, eh, Ryu? You might want to get your money back. Is there a refund policy?"

Ryu sent him a steely-eyed look through the cage of his mask and knocked the puck out of the crease. "Why don't *you* try me?"

Morley shrugged one big, padded shoulder. Tristan moved aside as he skated to the blue line and tried a quick slapshot. Ryu easily caught the puck, dropped it to the ice, and kicked it away with enough attitude Tristan broke into a grin.

Morley laughed good-naturedly. "Hey, bro, I'm not here to make goals. I'm here to stop the other team from making them."

Ryu ignored him, jerking his chin at Tristan. "Again."

For the next hour, they took shots at Ryu and ran passing drills while skating the length of the ice. Ryu shut down Morley's every attempt and gave him a tiny, vicious smile when Morley growled in frustration. He could've goaded Morley further, but Ryu wasn't much for trash talk. He let his actions speak for him, standing casually in net with his arms draped along the crossbar, which needled Morley more than any insults Ryu might have slung at him.

Tristan was chuckling at Morley's pissed-off expression when the arrival of about a dozen miniature hockey players signaled the end of their time. Unlike most Atlantans, who'd likely pass Venom players on the street and be none the wiser, these kids and their parents actually recognized the three of them.

"Holtzy!" the smallest boy yelled, nearly mowing down his teammate in his rush to get to Tristan. "I wanna be a D-man like you when I grow up. I'm gonna be on the Venom too, and we're gonna win The Cup for sure."

Tristan grinned. "Is that so?"

"Yeah! On my day, I'll eat Fruit Loops and drink beer out of it. Maybe both at the same time. And I might even let my little sister touch it, if she asks nicely." The kid shot him a gap-toothed smile. "Hey, can you sign my jersey?"

The volume increased as Morley and Ryu were surrounded as well. Tristan signed sticks and helmets while experiencing the same out-of-body surrealism that overtook him whenever he got asked for an autograph. It didn't make sense that people would want *his* signature on anything, let alone seem so thrilled about it. It was humbling too. He remembered being a starry-eyed tyke at his first NHL game. He must've been four or five at the time. Even now, meeting some of the players he'd admired as a teenager left Tristan awestruck. He didn't think he'd ever get over the oddness of being on the receiving end of the admiration.

After showers, they met at a nearby restaurant for lunch. Tristan's carb intake was huge during the regular season, but in the summer, when he wasn't burning through calories almost faster than he could consume them, he focused on eating healthier. His meal was a grilled salmon salad, a slice of multigrain bread, and water with lemon.

Morley eyed Tristan's plate in disdain as he chomped

on his bacon double cheeseburger. "I don't get how you can be satisfied with that, bro. That's bird food."

"I like it." Tristan shrugged. "And it's what you should be eating too."

Morley patted his muscular stomach. "It takes more than romaine to keep this tank running, Holtzy. I'm a growing boy."

"You're twenty-seven," Ryu said flatly. He was eating a wrap of some sort with fruit on the side. "The only growing you're going to be doing is outward."

Morley cupped one huge hand over his ear. "I can't hear you from down there, shrimpy. Do you need me to ask the waiter for a stepladder?"

Ryu leveled Morley with the dead-eyed stare he usually reserved for game time. "Take your taunts back to middle school, Morley. Your juvenile humor is wilting the lettuce in my Caesar wrap."

Tristan choked on a bite of salmon.

"Let's talk about something else," Ryu continued. "Like how distracted you've been lately, Tristan." Aside from the coaches and trainers, Ryu was the only teammate who called Tristan by his first name. "Don't think I didn't notice that you whiffed twice today and missed an easy pass from this one over here." He nodded toward Morley. "It's not only that, though. You've been weird every time I've seen you."

"That's probably why he almost broke his face on the treadmill the other day," Morley said around a mouthful of chewed-up burger. "He's been body-snatched."

Ryu's lip curled with disgust. "Swallowing should happen before speaking."

Morley grinned. "That's what she—"

"Really? Could you not?" Ryu's voice dripped with scorn. "That joke is over a decade old."

Morley's voice boomed as he said something about classics enduring through the ages. Tristan tuned out their bickering while he collected himself. He wasn't surprised his friends had noticed his distraction. Of course they had. It would be obvious to anyone who knew him.

Fucking Sebastian Cruz with his deep, sexy voice and that lean, strong body. Something about him turned Tristan's crank like nothing else in a long time. Tristan wanted a chance to explore their chemistry, but whether or not they would get it, Tristan knew he couldn't take another of Professor Cruz's classes again.

It was too damned distracting. He'd imagined himself in the submissive role with someone domineering like Professor Cruz about a thousand times. When he was alone in bed at night, he craved dominance. Someone to help him just…let go. But he didn't know how to ask for what he needed. Usually, given his size, the guys he hooked up with expected him to lead, to take control and do the fucking. Requesting anything different had led to some embarrassing moments. Why he felt like Professor Cruz would understand, and more than that, give him exactly what he wanted, Tristan couldn't explain.

But daydreams were for children, not grown men. He needed to remember that before other aspects of his life began to suffer.

"Yo, earth to Holtzy." Morley's big paw waved in front of his face.

Tristan snapped to attention "Sorry, guys. I'm good. Acclimating to taking classes again, you know? It's harder than I thought it would be." Pun intended.

Morley grabbed his strawberry milkshake and peered,

frowning, into the mostly empty glass. "I still don't get why you're bothering, bro."

"I already explained. Backup plan, remember?"

"Yeah, yeah." Morley slurped the rest of his shake and signaled their waiter. "Hey, can I get another one of these? No, make it chocolate this time. Or can you do half and half?"

Tristan felt the weight of Ryu's scrutiny and looked up. Ryu was regarding him with narrowed eyes, but thankfully, he didn't press the issue once Morley was distracted.

The conversation turned to the recent NHL draft and the new prospects they might see during training camp. Speculating about who might actually join them on the ice in the near future was enough to divert Tristan's thoughts, and soon he put Sebastian Cruz from his mind entirely.

Of course that only lasted until he got home. He stared at the sociology textbook on his kitchen table and contemplated starting his final paper. It wasn't due until the end of July, which meant he had plenty of time to write it. He wanted it to be perfect, though, not something scraped together at the last minute. He couldn't stand the idea of turning in anything less. Not only that, homophobia in professional sports was obviously a subject near and dear to his heart. He owed it to himself and every other queer athlete to give the topic the respect and consideration it deserved.

Decided, Tristan went to change into some sweats. He had plenty of reading to do before he outlined a rough draft. Might as well be comfortable.

Chapter Eight

Sebastian was still brooding about his attraction to Tristan when he met R.J. for dinner and drinks at a trendy sushi restaurant in Buckhead. He'd arrived before R.J. and was already ensconced at a table with a Scotch, trying to sip it like a civilized person instead of gulping it to make himself stop having fantasies about a student.

R.J. raised an eyebrow at the Scotch as he sat across from Sebastian at the table. "Wow. Scotch already? You usually start with a beer."

"What are you, my boyfriend?" There was a bit more of a bite than Sebastian intended to the words. He sighed into his glass and took another sip, mentally chiding himself to calm the fuck down.

"No, but if I was gay, I'd probably be totally into you," R.J. said, unconcerned, barely even looking at Sebastian as he examined the menu. "Well, maybe if you had an attitude adjustment. What's with you lately anyway?" He set the menu aside. "Your asshole levels have been raised to previously unrecorded numbers these last few days, Seb. What's up?"

Sebastian felt comfortable talking to R.J. about this, if no one else. R.J. was more than a fellow colleague, he was a friend. "I... Ugh, this so stupid I can't believe

I'm about to say it. I have…inappropriate interest in a student."

R.J. just looked at him, so Sebastian stared intently at his glass and ran the tip of his finger around the edge. "The hockey player. Before you ask."

"And that's…stupid?" R.J.'s voice sounded amused. "I thought you were down with appreciating the eye candy?"

Sebastian shrugged. "I am. But I think—I think this might be mutual. And that can't happen."

There was a moment of awkward silence—at least, it was awkward to Sebastian—and then R.J. said, very carefully, "But you haven't done anything, right?"

Sebastian shook his head. "No."

"You haven't, like, sent him a racy email or asked him to stay after for a special tutoring session, right?"

"Of course not."

R.J. studied him. "But you think he'd be into that. If you did, I mean."

This was exactly what Sebastian didn't want to think about, and had, of course, spent all weekend thinking about. "Yes. But I won't."

"The class is only for a few more weeks, though, right?" R.J. asked. "What's stopping you from pursuing something after grades are turned in? Are you thinking he's going to show up in another class of yours in the future?"

"I hope to God not," Sebastian said with a frown. He didn't think he could handle Tristan in those sweatpants for a second longer than he had to. Too tempting. "And just because he wouldn't be my student doesn't take away the part where he is *now*."

R.J. rolled his eyes, clearly not as perturbed by the

idea as Sebastian. "Dude. You went to grad school, right? Half my professors were married to former students."

So that phenomenon wasn't limited to the field of sociology. "Yes, but do you know what those professors have that I don't?"

"Uh." R.J. snorted. "Should I really answer that?"

Before Sebastian could say anything, the waitress came to take their order. He really wanted another Scotch, but made himself stick to water and a light beer. He'd hoped that R.J. would drop the subject once the waitress left, but mathematicians, Sebastian was learning, were relentless.

"I know what you're going to say," R.J. informed him, tucking into the edamame appetizer Sebastian had ordered when he'd first arrived. "That you don't have tenure, and they do. But, Seb, man, do you really think you'd be the first nontenured professor to have a relationship with a former student?"

"Why would that matter? It doesn't mean it's a good idea." Sebastian took a few pieces of edamame. "I appreciate that you're trying to find the bright side here, R.J., but you don't have to try to convince me it would be anything other than a mistake."

"Well." R.J. peered at him thoughtfully. "I understand that you don't want anything to happen while he's still your student. But if you guys are into each other, and he's finished with sociology at the end of the summer... I'm still not seeing what the big deal would be if you two hooked up." R.J. lifted his glass and grinned. "Plus, you'd totally be my hero if you hooked up with a hot professional hockey player and somehow scored me some tickets."

Sebastian glared, but the liquor had done its job and

taken some of the heat out of it. "Can we please not talk about this anymore? And you can't say anything about this to anyone. I'm serious. He's not out. Honestly, I shouldn't even have told you, but I needed to talk to someone I trust."

R.J. set his glass down and raised his hands, palms out. "I would *never* repeat what you tell me to anyone, especially about something like this. I promise. And now that I know you're being a broody asshole because you have a crush on one of your students, we can move on." He laughed, clearly unperturbed by Sebastian's scowl.

Sebastian didn't bother to respond to that. Maybe he did have a bit of a crush on Tristan, and maybe he was being a little too hard on himself. So what if Tristan apparently returned his interest? He knew he wouldn't do a thing about it, and even though there would technically be nothing wrong with him pursuing Tristan after the semester grades were turned in… No. He'd worked too hard to get where he was, and he didn't want to do anything to fuck that up.

The conversation switched to other topics, but before they left, R.J. clapped him on the shoulder and said, "So, hey, even if you decide not to go after hockey boy when the semester ends, that doesn't mean *he* won't try something. If he's into you."

"It doesn't change anything." Sebastian was beginning to wish he'd kept his mouth shut.

"At least think about it," R.J. cajoled, tossing some cash on the table.

That definitely wasn't going to be a problem. Sebastian had a hard time *not* thinking about Tristan, especially when he was at home by himself.

In class he played it cool and looked at Tristan as little

as possible, though it did nothing to lessen his attraction. Every now and then Sebastian would find Tristan staring at him, and he'd feel the heat flare up between them. Still, Sebastian stuck to his guns and limited their eye-fucking as much as he could…until the day of Tristan's final presentation arrived.

The students were supposed to present their papers in front of the class, and Tristan's time slot was the first one for the day. Sebastian had prepared himself by getting off in the shower while having inappropriate fantasies of his student in there with him, sucking his cock to earn a good grade. It wasn't the first time he'd ever had that fantasy, of course, but it was the first time he had someone specific in mind. Sebastian hoped that indulging in the fantasy might make it easier to sit in the lecture hall and listen to Tristan give his talk about LGBT issues in professional sports, especially considering Sebastian's professional interest in the topic at hand.

But, as Sebastian settled in his seat and waited, it looked as if maybe Tristan wasn't going to show up. Frowning, Sebastian crossed his legs and checked his watch, noticing the time inch closer to the start of class. If Tristan was late, he'd miss his spot and that would severely impact his grade. All of the implications of that began to whirl like a maelstrom in Sebastian's mind, and he was momentarily paralyzed with visions of himself in a very uncomfortable meeting with the dean, when the door opened just in time, and Tristan came in.

Or, more appropriately, *rushed* in. He was breathing hard, which meant he'd probably run all the way from the parking lot, and his hair was still damp as if from a shower. He was wearing a Venom shirt (the first time, to Sebastian's knowledge, that he'd done so) and those goddamn gray sweatpants. He gave Sebastian what could only be described as a harried look and said amidst his attempts to catch his breath, "I'm sorry I'm late, Professor."

There'd been something similar in that shower fantasy, and Sebastian was glad he was sitting down. He waved a hand. "Get yourself together and prepare for your presentation, Mr. Holt."

Tristan took a few deep breaths, raked his hand through his hair, and grabbed a folder out of his messenger bag. He gave his classmates a sheepish smile. "I haven't slept through my alarm in about two years. Sorry to make everyone wait."

It was such a sincere, effortlessly conscientious thing to do that Sebastian wondered if the universe was trying to torment him. The problem was, his interest in Tristan wasn't only sexual, and seeing what a decent and kind man he was, well, that wasn't helping his determination to pretend Tristan didn't exist until after the grades were in.

Tristan started talking, and Sebastian wanted nothing more than to focus on the material and the subject matter…until he noticed that in his apparent hurry, Tristan hadn't bothered to put on underwear beneath his sweatpants. No matter how Sebastian tried to keep his eyes from straying lower, it was impossible. He couldn't think beyond the hot rush of blood going straight to his own dick, and his mouth was practically dry as he struggled to keep a neutral expression. It wasn't working—in fact, he probably looked like he was glaring daggers at both Tristan *and* his cock.

When Tristan was finished with his presentation, it took Sebastian until halfway through the next one to calm down. And, for the life of him, he couldn't honestly say if it was a decent presentation or not. All he kept thinking about was how this was the last class meeting, and in under a week, the grades would be in and all the dirty thoughts Sebastian was having could technically become a reality.

Going to Professor Cruz's office was probably a bad idea. The *worst* idea. No one had to tell Tristan that. He knew it as he walked down the stairs, as he surreptitiously checked the hall to ensure none of his classmates had spotted him following their professor, as he rapped a quick knock on the door and pushed it open to duck inside without waiting for an answer.

Professor Cruz paused in the middle of setting his messenger bag on top of his desk and stared at Tristan, surprise marking his features.

After a second, he cleared his throat. "What can I help you with, Mr. Holt? Office hours don't start until two."

Tristan closed the door and leaned back against it, his heavy book bag digging into his spine. "I wanted to ask what you thought of my presentation, seeing as I don't think you actually listened to a word of it."

Professor Cruz arched a dark, imperious brow and stopped fussing with his bag to meet Tristan's gaze directly. "Excuse me?"

"I'm pretty sure you were too busy eye-fucking me and glaring at my cock to hear anything I was saying." Tristan shoved his hands into the pockets of his sweats, and sure enough, Professor Cruz's attention shot straight to his crotch. "I couldn't find a clean jock before I left my apartment. I figured no one would care or even notice...but you did, didn't you?"

A muscle ticked along Professor Cruz's jaw, but he stayed silent.

"Yeah, you noticed," Tristan went on. "That's why you looked so mad the whole time. And maybe it means I'm kind of twisted, but that pissed-off scowl of yours never fails to make my dick hard."

After another beat of silence, Professor Cruz shook his head. "This is extremely inappropriate, Mr. Holt."

"I don't think you really want me to be appropriate." Tristan straightened and took a step forward.

Professor Cruz held up a hand, halting him in his tracks. "No. We're not doing this here."

Tristan allowed himself a smile. "Not here. But we *are* doing it."

Professor Cruz sucked in a deep, slow breath and dropped his hand to his side. "Your final grade should be posted by Friday."

And that was all he said.

Tristan's smile dimmed. He'd swaggered in here like a cocky asshole, so sure of Professor Cruz's attraction after the eye-fucking he'd received during his presentation. Now, his confidence wavered.

"Um." He looked around the room, shifting his weight from one foot to the other as a flush crawled up his neck. His gaze settled on the album print hanging behind Professor Cruz's desk, and he pulled back his shoulders, regaining some of his boldness. "There's a Floyd cover band playing at Terminal West on Saturday," Tristan said, referencing a popular Atlanta music venue. "I was thinking of going to see them. They're supposed to be really good. I'm stoked." Before Professor Cruz could reply, he added, "You should come and check it out."

He forced himself to casually stroll from the room

without waiting for an answer—even though a huge, humiliated part of him wanted to tuck tail and run like his ass was on fire.

He'd expressed his interest, possibly making a fool of himself in the process. Now the ball was in Professor Cruz's court. If he didn't show up at Terminal West, Tristan would call it a wrap and start getting the hell over this stupid crush.

Chapter Nine

Being a homebody with a self-confessed athletic-wear addiction meant Tristan didn't have much by way of fashionable clothing. He had his game-day suits, of course. Those were mandatory and custom-tailored to accommodate his height and the brawny physique he owed to a lifetime of sports and manual labor. But even his suits weren't anything flashy: simply plain, solid colors. At heart he was a farm boy, born and bred in rural Wisconsin, and like his parents, he put more stock in comfort and durability than style. Hell, he practically lived in sweats and band T-shirts when not on the ice. He didn't own any club wear.

On the evening of the concert, Tristan stared into his closet for some twenty minutes and considered a shopping trip before quickly vetoing the idea. As much as he wanted to look good for Professor Cruz, a brand-new outfit reeked of desperation. In the end, he settled on a navy-blue V-neck and a pair of worn jeans that perfectly displayed his ass and thighs, which Tristan knew were impressive even by hockey player standards.

When he got to Terminal West, the venue was nowhere near full. Tristan idly searched the sparse crowd as he walked the main floor and balcony, but he didn't

seriously expect to see Professor Cruz. Not this early. The
opening act—a quartet of bearded men wearing skintight
pants and sporting matching undercuts—had only just
begun their set, belting out Beatles tunes with more enthusiasm than talent. Tristan anticipated Professor Cruz
would time his arrival for when Phloydian Slip, the Pink
Floyd tribute band, took the stage.

Tristan ordered himself an IPA and grabbed one of
the open metal stools on the balcony, which gave him a
bird's-eye view of the concert hall. The place had been
decorated in an industrial style—black beams and air
ducts, reclaimed wood, concrete floors, and lots of exposed brick. He soaked in the atmosphere as the band
launched into their rendition of "Love Me Do." In spite
of himself, their twangy sound had grown on Tristan. Or
maybe it was the adorable way the lead singer bounced
in place while he sang.

Tristan would've contemplated getting closer to the
stage to catch the singer's eye, if not for his entirely inappropriate crush on his professor. Well, former professor.
His final grade, an A-minus, had been posted to the student portal yesterday morning. Which meant Tristan was
free to pursue Professor Cruz…if only the man showed
up and wanted to be pursued.

After a few more songs, the lead singer bowed to the
crowd's applause. "Thanks, everyone. You've been great
tonight. We're Revolution. We'll be over at Stationside
if anyone wants to meet us. We have T-shirts and CDs
available too. Come say hello."

As they left the stage, Tristan went to get himself another beer. His past concert experience told him it would
be at least another half an hour before Phloydian Slip

performed. He toyed with the idea of going over to the restaurant to meet the Revolution singer, maybe score a number. But as cute as the guy was, he didn't make Tristan's blood pump. Didn't make Tristan hot like the mere *thought* of Professor Cruz's broody scowl and lean, sinewy body. Tristan didn't want to settle for someone else, not if there was even the smallest chance Professor Cruz might show up. Tristan hadn't exactly been subtle in his invitation.

He returned to the balcony to find his stool taken. Still hopeful, Tristan wandered down to the main floor to watch the roadies as they set up various instruments and sound equipment. He sipped at his beer until the lights dimmed and Phloydian Slip came onstage. The group had clearly modeled themselves after Pink Floyd in all their seventies, floppy-haired glory, and the lead singer could've easily passed for a young David Gilmour.

The band opened with "Comfortably Numb." Tristan paused near the back of the room to let the song wash over him. At his height, he could easily see above the heads of most of the concertgoers, which meant he had a decent view no matter where he parked himself.

For a time the music distracted him. Tristan swayed in place, caught up in the energy of the now-substantial crowd and enjoying the rare opportunity to hear his favorite songs played live. That wasn't always easy for a classic rock fan whose favorite groups no longer performed, and who, generally speaking, wasn't all that into cover bands.

But soon the novelty wore off. Tristan noticed the time and the distinct lack of one Sebastian Cruz. Like the flame of a candle, his excitement flickered and abruptly sputtered out, leaving nothing but wispy smoke in its wake.

Concerts were a lot more fun when you had someone else to share the experience with. Couples and groups of friends filled the venue. Tristan was one of the few who watched alone, conspicuous in the way he stood apart from the others.

He frowned, deposited his empty bottle on the tray of a passing server, and made his way to the bar for another beer. During the regular season he normally limited himself to two, preferring to get his carbs from food instead of alcohol, but fuck it. Training camp didn't start for nearly another two months. After being stood up, he was due another drink or three.

Tristan snorted. Why was he kidding himself? Professor Cruz never had any intention of meeting him. He'd probably regaled his highbrow academic friends with the story of his student's clumsy attempt to ask him out. No doubt they had a good laugh about it while drinking wine and eating canapés or whatever the hell else snobby professors did in their spare time. Tristan already knew what Sebastian Cruz thought of athletes.

He'd just flagged down a bartender and placed his order when he sensed a presence at his side. Tristan turned and found himself face-to-face with the man himself. Professor Cruz was dressed casually in dark jeans, boots, and a button-down shirt. He'd left the top two buttons undone, and Tristan's gaze automatically went to the prominent collarbones covered in smooth golden-brown skin. All the moisture fled his mouth at the thought of putting his lips to the divot at the base of Professor Cruz's throat. Tristan wanted to bite and lick there, inhale until the scent of sweat and *man* made him drunk with lust.

"Mr. Holt."

Tristan swallowed hard. "Professor," he rasped. *Sebastian*, Tristan really wanted to call him. The name appealed to him as much as its owner. Tristan wished he had the right to use it whenever he pleased.

The bartender delivered Tristan's beer and grabbed the money Tristan had placed on the bar top. He jerked his head at Professor Cruz. "What can I get you?"

"Single malt, neat. Glenlivet, preferably. If not, the best you have."

Of course he would drink Scotch and order it neat, the sexy bastard. Tristan pictured him as the leading man in some classic black-and-white film—crystal tumbler in one hand, a thick cigar between his lips, a plume of smoke curling around his sharp-jawed face. The image sent blood rushing straight to Tristan's cock. *Shit.* There went all his bitter thoughts from a few minutes before, carried away by the rumbling bass of Professor Cruz's voice and the sight of his dark-brown eyes and darker, finger-tousled hair.

Tristan almost sighed. He was weak—he knew it—but how could he be strong with Professor Cruz standing here looking like *that*? Tristan wanted to drop to his knees. Only awareness of his surroundings kept him upright.

After starting a tab, Professor Cruz inclined his head, silently encouraging Tristan to follow. They moved away from the bar to a small gap along the back wall.

"How's the band?" Professor Cruz asked, his eyes fixed on the stage.

Tristan watched, wetting his mouth as Professor Cruz

took a slow sip of the amber liquid in his glass. "They're good, I think," Tristan replied. "I stopped paying attention a little while ago."

Professor Cruz glanced at him. "Why?"

Tristan smiled wryly. "I was waiting for you."

The words made Professor Cruz turn to meet his gaze directly. They stared at each other, the air between them crackling like static. Tristan wanted to kiss him. Damn the consequences. He couldn't remember the last time he'd experienced an attraction so strong. It made him feel reckless.

Professor Cruz's eyes went hot as he read Tristan's expression. He shifted closer, invading Tristan's personal space. Tristan didn't bother checking to see if anyone watched them. The dim lighting made for plenty of cover, and most people were focused on the music and the band, not paying attention to a couple of horny guys standing far too close to each other.

"I tried to talk myself out of coming," Professor Cruz said. "This is a terrible idea."

Tristan blinked slowly. "What?"

"Us meeting like this. Just…this."

Tristan shook his head, trying to clear away the fog of lust clouding his brain. It took him a moment to parse the sentence. When he did, he felt abruptly guilty.

He'd invited Professor Cruz to the concert. Sure, they were both consenting adults, and Professor Cruz was a grown man fully capable of making his own decisions—but Tristan had instigated their meeting. What if Professor Cruz had only come out of some sense of obligation? What if he was trying to make it up to Tristan for accusing him of stealing that paper? Tristan had absolutely no interest in an apology fuck. He never took what wasn't freely offered; he wasn't about to start now.

Tristan stepped back. "Sorry. I… I'll…" He turned to leave, but a strong hand grabbed his wrist, exerting enough pressure to stop him.

Without speaking, Professor Cruz tugged him to his side, but kept a firm hold on Tristan's wrist once he was there. The grip made Tristan squirm—in a good way. It called to the part of him that yearned to be restrained. Tristan wanted to feel that grip in bed, wanted to pull against it just to feel those long fingers tighten again. He refrained. Barely.

Professor Cruz nodded his approval once Tristan relaxed. He resumed watching the band as the familiar intro to "Wish You Were Here" began. Tristan had no choice but to follow suit, although most of his attention remained riveted on the enigmatic man beside him.

The rest of the set passed like a film on fast-forward. Professor Cruz bought him another beer, and as the minutes ticked by, every point of contact between them, every touch of their skin, made Tristan edgier and edgier—until he worried he might actually be vibrating with lust.

Finally, *finally*, Professor Cruz leaned close to ask, "Are you ready to get out of here?"

"God, yes. Fucking beyond ready." Tristan's briefs were sticky, damp with the pre-come he'd been leaking since he felt the tight grasp of fingers on his wrist earlier.

Professor Cruz settled his tab while Tristan waited—or rather, while Tristan shifted impatiently and fidgeted. When they stepped out into the muggy night, he turned to pin Tristan with a dark, hot stare. "I caught a cab here. Did you drive?"

Tristan shook his head.

By unspoken agreement, they started down the block, away from the smokers who were chatting outside the venue. Tristan thought about suggesting food or maybe coffee, anything to distract himself from wondering how soon they could get naked and horizontal. But as they passed a darkened loading area, the thin threads of his willpower snapped. Tristan fisted a handful of Professor Cruz's shirt, hauled him into the shadows, and crushed their lips together.

Professor Cruz seemed startled, but only for a moment. Then his hands came up, holding Tristan's head in place as he took control of the kiss. Tristan allowed himself to be crowded backward until a brick wall stopped his progress. Professor Cruz—*Sebastian*—pressed close and licked into Tristan's mouth. He tasted warm, smoky like Scotch.

Tristan chased the flavor with his tongue, moaning into the kiss and thrusting his hips forward. There was enough of a height difference between them that his cock ground against Sebastian's firm, flat stomach instead of his groin. Tristan didn't care. Friction was friction, and he craved more. He ignored the nearby dumpster, the faint smell of garbage, the fact that they could easily be seen from the sidewalk if anyone cared to look.

The kiss was too good, too hot for Tristan to be distracted by such mundane thoughts.

He made a noise that would've embarrassed him under any other circumstances. He clutched at Sebastian's hips, trying to get even closer, shivering at the hard press of Sebastian's erection along his upper thigh.

He wanted Sebastian so much he felt stupid with need.

"Take me somewhere," he panted into Sebastian's mouth. "Anywhere. I don't care. I want to taste you."

Sebastian pulled back, leaving Tristan's lips pleasantly sore and stinging. In the shadows, his eyes looked fathomless.

"Let's go," he said, taking hold of Tristan's wrist again.

Tristan groaned and fought not to come in his jeans.

Chapter Ten

Sebastian had debated going to the show because he'd known this would happen, even if he hadn't wanted to admit it. The combination of the music and the liquor and Tristan, looking incredible and so clearly wanting it, would make it impossible to resist taking him home. Sebastian had given himself a stern talking-to in the cab on the way to Terminal West, but no amount of mental preparation had girded him against the sight of Tristan's hot, needy expression and the obvious sexual attraction simmering between them.

And the heady reminder that the grades were in, Tristan was no longer his student, and there was nothing stopping them from acting on that attraction. Sebastian could tell himself it was still a bad idea all he wanted, but his body wasn't interested in listening to his brain.

The second he'd heard the noise Tristan made when Sebastian grabbed his wrist, that was it. That kiss in the loading dock only sealed the deal, and Sebastian was fighting the urge to put his hands all over Tristan in the cab on the way back to his apartment. Since he couldn't do that—and did, in fact, enjoy the anticipation—he ran his gaze over Tristan with undisguised intent, from the top of his tousled hair to his kiss-swollen mouth, down to where his chest rose and fell with his rapid breathing, and lower to Tristan's lap and the cock he so viscerally remembered pressing against his stomach.

Sebastian shoved cash at the cab driver, paying just enough attention to ascertain that it was enough to cover the fare and the tip before slamming his door shut and waiting for Tristan to follow him into the building. If there hadn't been people in the elevator with them, Sebastian might have gone ahead and pushed Tristan to his knees right there.

Luckily, it wasn't a long way to his apartment, and the second he had the door closed, he didn't waste any time. He shoved Tristan against it like he'd done in the alley, his mouth hot and demanding on Tristan's as he reached down for the buckle of Tristan's belt.

His rational mental voice was insisting he should say something, but it was fuzzy, muted by how good Tristan tasted and how it felt to finally put his hands all over him.

Tristan was moaning into Sebastian's mouth and trying to help him with the belt buckle. It wasn't working, because their hands were getting caught up and tangled in their haste. Making a sound, Sebastian bit him sharply on the mouth and growled, "Palms against the door."

Tristan's response was immediate and left no doubt that he was into Sebastian being in charge, which had been Sebastian's initial impression when he'd taken control of their kiss in the alley. Tristan might be taller and physically stronger, but Sebastian could feel how much it got Tristan going that Sebastian didn't let that stop him. He put his palms flat against the door like Sebastian wanted, and Sebastian was able to get his belt undone, his jeans unzipped, and a hand down Tristan's pants to grab his cock.

Tristan started talking. "I want to—"

Sebastian put his other hand over Tristan's mouth and leaned in to speak in his ear. "I know. And you will. But you're going to come because I can tell you're nearly there." He took his hand away and started kissing him on the neck, lips on the sensitive skin beneath Tristan's ear. "Aren't you."

It wasn't a question.

"Fuck," Tristan hissed, hips moving, pushing his slick cock into the tightness of Sebastian's fist. Sebastian took that as a yes and smiled against Tristan's neck, licking at the slightly salty, tangy taste of sweat and skin.

"Do you want my mouth on you?" Sebastian asked, angling himself so he could continue to lick and suck Tristan's neck, jack him off, and press his own aching cock against the rock-hard muscles of Tristan's thigh at the same time. If he didn't watch it, he'd be coming in his jeans, and he wasn't as young as Tristan.

"I want whatever you want to put on me," Tristan panted. "Holy *fuck*."

Sebastian bit gently at the bottom of his ear. "Then ask me. Nicely."

Tristan gave what sounded like a half laugh, half moan. "Please suck my cock."

Hearing it made Sebastian shiver, though he hadn't expected Tristan would be too shy to say it. He gave Tristan's earlobe a last little bite, then smoothly went to his knees. It hadn't been too long since he'd been with anyone, but he didn't remember it being like this. As he pulled Tristan's jeans down and out of his way, he noticed his own hands were unsteady with the force of his want.

Tristan still had his palms against the door, and he stared down at Sebastian with a questioning expression.

Sebastian was momentarily distracted by the way Tristan looked—fair skin so flushed he looked sunburned, eyes a heavy-lidded blur, mouth parted and his cock hard and wet from pre-come in Sebastian's hand.

"I'll tell you when you can move them," Sebastian said, his voice rough.

Tristan's head moved in a slight nod, and Sebastian leaned forward and took Tristan's cock in his mouth. He relished the taste as he relaxed his throat and took Tristan deep, setting a fast rhythm because now was not the time to tease. Tristan moaned low in his chest, swearing, and Sebastian could see him hitting his palms against the door—but he didn't lift his hands completely. It was so hot, Sebastian had to reach down and stroke himself through his jeans to take off the edge, undoing the button so he could have a little relief.

Sebastian wasn't inclined to draw this out, but he did want to enjoy himself, so he squeezed the base of Tristan's cock a time or two when it seemed like Tristan was getting close. Finally, after he'd teased Tristan and kept him on the edge for what he was sure felt to Tristan like an eternity, Sebastian pulled off and said gruffly, "All right," sure that his meaning was clear enough.

It was. No sooner had the words left his mouth than Tristan was grabbing at his hair, fingers tight and yanking Sebastian closer. At any other time, Sebastian might tell him that *You can have your hands free* didn't mean *Make me choke on your cock*, but he was looking forward to making Tristan do the same, and he could tell from the pulse of Tristan's cock in his mouth that he was on the edge.

Sebastian rubbed the bottom of Tristan's balls, sliding his fingers back to tease—just tease—at Tristan's hole.

It made Tristan groan and thrust hard enough that Sebastian gagged, Tristan's fingers interlaced at the back of Sebastian's head to hold him close as he came hot down his throat.

Sebastian sucked lightly until Tristan made a strangled sound and pushed gently on his head, wriggling a bit in the hold Sebastian had on his hips. Sebastian wiped his mouth with the back of his hand, rising easily to his feet. Tristan looked deliciously wrecked, chest heaving and his pants somewhere around his knees. Sebastian gave him an appreciative once-over. "Now, I think you can take care of me."

Tristan's laugh was low and rough, but he grinned and tugged his jeans up one-handed. He didn't bother to do up the belt, though, only followed Sebastian to the living room. Sebastian had intended to go to his bedroom, but suddenly he couldn't wait any longer, so he sprawled on his leather couch, legs spread, and motioned at Tristan with two fingers.

Tristan sharply sucked a breath in at the gesture. "I knew you being a bossy motherfucker would do it for me."

Sebastian laughed in surprise, reaching down to finish undoing his jeans. "I had a feeling."

Tristan smiled slowly and lowered himself to his knees between Sebastian's splayed legs. He slid his hands up Sebastian's thighs and hooked his fingers in the edges of Sebastian's jeans, pulling them down. "I've wanted to do this for a long time."

"Then stop talking and suck me," Sebastian said, but he reached out and drew his fingers through Tristan's hair as he did so. He liked being in charge of things, but it was the unavoidable truth that they were playing at something here that could be misconstrued very easily, given Sebastian's job. Though, if Sebastian were honest, that was making this whole thing even hotter, and he wouldn't doubt the same was true for Tristan.

Still. Sebastian reached out and took Tristan's chin in his fingers, bringing Tristan's focus up to his face instead of his cock. "Tell me if it's too much, all right?"

Tristan blinked those bright-blue eyes at him, ducked his head, and sucked on Sebastian's fingers as he nodded in response. The sensation of Tristan's mouth on his fingers went right to Sebastian's cock, and he hissed, hips lifting slightly off the couch. He pulled his fingers free and reached down to slide them, wet from Tristan's mouth, over his own cock. He raised an eyebrow. "Now that we're clear, get that mouth on me and suck me off."

Tristan's smile was sly. "Yes, Professor Cruz."

"It's Sebastian," Sebastian muttered, in a completely futile attempt to disguise how hot it was to hear Tristan say that. He reached out and grabbed Tristan's hair, yanking his head down before he could tell Tristan to call him that again.

Tristan's mouth was hot and wet, and Sebastian let his own head fall back, watching with half-closed eyes as Tristan settled in and started sucking his cock. He was good—very good—and enthusiastic, sucking Sebastian hard and fast, using his tongue on the underside of Sebastian's dick.

Sebastian tugged at his hair. "Slow down. Take your time. Show me how much you like sucking me."

Tristan pulled off his dick and worked him with a nice, firm grip. "You're really fucking hot, you know that, right?"

Sebastian huffed a laugh and tugged on Tristan's

hair again, rubbing his thumb over Tristan's bottom lip briefly. "You're not so bad yourself, Mr. Holt."

Sebastian could tell that Tristan was fine with things being a little rough, so he didn't hesitate to take Tristan's head between his hands and drag him back to his cock. He fucked Tristan's throat with sharp, rough jerks of his hips. Just watching Tristan taking it was enough to almost make him come, and the noises Tristan made weren't only sounds of choking, but whimpers too.

"Is choking on my dick making you hard?" Sebastian asked, aware of how rough his voice sounded.

Tristan's answer was a rough noise and a short nod.

"Good. Get your hand on your dick. Jerk off so you come while you're sucking me." He felt Tristan's moan around his cock, and Sebastian's eyes rolled back for a moment. "Unless you get distracted, then I'll make you stop."

Tristan was a professional athlete, and he had no problem both sucking Sebastian's cock and jerking himself off at the same time. Sebastian liked the way he could see Tristan's elbow moving, faster and faster, and he pulled Tristan's head down in time with the movement. He wasn't an athlete like Tristan, but he was a runner and he knew all about timing and rhythm.

Sebastian briefly thought about orchestrating some way he could come on Tristan's gorgeous fucking ass, but he was too close and didn't think he could wait long enough to arrange the logistics of that. "You don't come until I do," Sebastian told him, and Tristan looked up at him and did something close to a nod before swallowing his cock down again.

Sebastian held him there, tightening his fingers in Tristan's hair, and came long and hard in his mouth. It pulsed through Sebastian with a violent intensity that drew a sharp cry from him, sending him falling bonelessly back on the couch with his heartbeat a loud, insistent pounding in his ears.

He did, however, see Tristan tense and hear a moan amidst his harsh, rapid panting, and that was entirely gratifying. He allowed himself a few moments to catch his own breath, unsurprised to find Tristan was doing the same with his face pressed against Sebastian's thigh. Sebastian lightly stroked Tristan's sweat-dampened hair, and he took a second to enjoy the simple intimacy after the pleasure that had so completely wrung him out.

They both pulled back at the same time, Tristan to say in a tone somewhere between embarrassed and amused, "Uh, so I…your floor…um." He glanced up and smiled. "It's kind of a mess. Not sorry."

Sebastian was, once again, struck by a surprised laugh. "Me neither. It's hardwood. Easy to clean."

They both shared a momentary grin at the *hardwood* comment, and when it looked like Tristan was going to say something, Sebastian shook his head and reached out to lightly tap two fingers over his mouth. "Too easy. I'll go get a towel."

Sebastian maneuvered himself up and off the couch, fixing his pants and running a hand through his hair as he made his way into the kitchen. He grabbed a clean towel, dampened it slightly, and then filled up a glass of water. He drank it thirstily, then filled it up again and carried it into the living room.

Tristan had also fixed his own clothing, and was still sitting on the floor with his back to the couch. He gave Sebastian a sheepish smile as Sebastian handed him the towel but didn't say anything, wiping his hands and the floor before accepting the water.

Sebastian sat on the couch and put a hand on his shoulder, squeezing. "I kept telling myself that we shouldn't do this, even though you aren't my student anymore."

Tristan gave him a sharp look. "Do you still think that?"

Sebastian had to grin. "Not even a little."

"Good," said Tristan. "Because it was fucking great."

Sebastian laughed and shook his head in amusement. "It was, yes. Thank you."

Tristan's face screwed up a little. "Thanking me for sex is kind of creepy."

Sebastian rolled his eyes at that and squeezed Tristan's shoulder again. "There's nothing creepy about having manners, Tristan."

"Oh, my God," Tristan laughed. He gave Sebastian that smile again, but it was a toned-down version of his earlier thousand-watt grin. Maybe just a few hundred. He finished the water and set the empty glass next to the towel. He made no effort to get up off the floor and join Sebastian on the couch. "I guess I can't talk you into doing it again?"

"You know that quote about the spirit being willing, and the flesh being weak?" Sebastian reached out and drew his fingers through Tristan's damp hair. "We're not all in our twenties, here. And it's late."

Tristan sighed and let his head go back, eyes closing. "Yeah, I know. I've got to meet some of my teammates at the gym in the morning anyway. Gonna be distracted enough as it is." A smile curved his full mouth, but he kept his eyes closed.

"Can't say I'm sorry about that," Sebastian murmured, tugging lightly at the blond strands of Tristan's hair. "You've had me distracted all semester."

Tristan opened his eyes at that, looking up at Sebastian. "Not sorry at all." His smile faded a bit. "Is this going to get you in trouble? I mean, I know technically I'm not in your class anymore and grades are in, but…still."

Sebastian didn't think it would get him in trouble, at least not officially. If anyone found out about it, though, it might affect his chances of tenure as far as the faculty and administration were concerned. "It's not against the rules anymore," he said, carefully. "The timing, though… It might not look entirely ethical, if anyone found out."

"I won't tell anyone," Tristan assured him, which made Sebastian feel like an ass. If this wasn't technically against the rules, why should he expect Tristan to keep it a secret because he was worried about what his colleagues would think? "But I'd like to see you again, if you want."

"I do want," said Sebastian. "I think that's fairly obvious. And if you don't leave now, you won't get nearly enough sleep for your workout in the morning, because I'll keep you up way too late showing you just how much I do want that."

Tristan jumped to his feet with pure athletic grace and extended a hand to Sebastian. "Hey, I've worked out on little sleep plenty of times. Some caffeine and a protein shake, and I'll be good to go."

Sebastian put his hand in Tristan's and let Tristan pull him to his feet. "In that case, let me show you the bedroom."

Tristan and Sebastian exchanged numbers before Tristan left the apartment the next morning. Sebastian had been true to his word and not only kept Tristan up late, but woke him a couple of times—once for more blowjobs and another to exchange slow, deep kisses and tug at each other's cocks until they made a mess and had to get up to shower.

Despite the lack of sleep, Tristan felt truly refreshed for the first time in weeks. He took a Lyft home to grab his supplies and made himself a quick protein shake to drink on the way to meet Morley and Ryu at Powerhouse.

When Tristan joined them in the lobby, Morley took one look at him and clapped him on the back hard enough to make Tristan stumble. "Congrats on getting laid, Holtzy!"

Tristan laughed, his face heating when several heads turned in their direction, but he didn't deny it. Why bother when he couldn't wipe the grin from his face and self-satisfaction was practically radiating from his pores?

Ryu scrutinized him for a moment, then led the way to the locker rooms so they could change and stash their stuff.

The trainer put them through a long, grueling workout, which left Tristan panting and sore, but not even that could dampen his mood. He actually had a *spring* in his step as he made his way to his Jeep afterward and waved good-bye to Morley and Ryu.

Morley grinned hugely and gave him a thumbs-up as he hefted his massive frame into his cherry-red Hummer. Ryu shook his head, but he had a tiny smile playing around his lips and he returned Tristan's wave before ducking into his own car.

Tristan rocked out to Lynyrd Skynyrd on the ride home, drumming solos on the steering wheel and singing along off-key.

He didn't expect to hear from Sebastian for a few days, and if he did, Tristan figured it would be a late-night text looking for a quick and dirty hookup. So it surprised him to get a message from Sebastian that evening once he was home and settled on his couch for a few hours of *Battlefield*.

Hey, it's Sebastian. Would you be interested in having lunch tomorrow?

Tristan smiled dopily and typed a reply, accidentally hitting extra keys on the small touchscreen and having to delete letters several times because his big hands were even clumsier than normal.

Tristan: Sure. Where at? Time?

Sebastian: How about Grindhouse? I'll pick you up at two, if that works for you.

Tristan: Yeah, that'd be good.

They exchanged a few more messages, and Tristan sent Sebastian his address.

Sebastian's responding See you tomorrow signaled the end of the conversation. Tristan tossed his phone onto the couch and grabbed one of the PlayStation controllers to turn the system on. He was still smiling like a besotted fool, but who cared? No one was there to see him.

Tristan was waiting outside of his building when Sebastian roared up to the curb in a sexy-as-fuck Pontiac GTO. Tristan gaped at the picture Sebastian made behind the wheel, like some modern-day James Dean: black T-shirt, his raven hair slicked back, and dark shades in place over his eyes.

When Tristan stood there staring, Sebastian leaned across the seat and popped open the door. He smirked at Tristan's undoubtedly stunned expression. "Are you coming?"

Tristan shook himself. "I hope so," he said cheekily as he slid into the passenger seat. The interior was all black leather and gleaming wood accents. Tristan was tempted to run his hand across the immaculately clean dash but resisted the urge.

"This is gorgeous," he said instead. "What year?"

"Sixty-five," Sebastian answered as he pulled out into traffic.

Tristan buckled his seat belt. "Wow. How long have you had it?"

"Almost ten years. It was my gift to myself for my twenty-fifth birthday, after I landed my first job as an assistant professor."

"Did you buy it like this or did you restore it?"

Sebastian didn't answer for a moment as he maneuvered around some slower traffic. Once they were cruising again, he threw a quick glance at Tristan. "I restored it. Actually, my father and I did." Sebastian gave a dry laugh. "He's a mechanic, and he got me into two things—classic rock and classic cars. Things have been awkward ever since I came out, but at least we'll always have that."

Tristan couldn't think of what to say for a moment. "Well, it's beautiful," he said eventually. And it was. Sleek and powerful, like the man who drove it. "I thought you were hot before, but damn, seeing you in this car…

it makes me wish you could pull over somewhere so I could suck your dick."

Sebastian made a startled noise, something between a laugh and a groan. "God, you have a mouth on you, huh? I should've known you'd be like this."

Tristan laid a hand on his thigh and scratched his nails against the material of Sebastian's dark jeans. "Do you mind?"

Sebastian looked at him again. "Oh, no. I know just what to do with a boy like you, Mr. Holt."

"Not a boy," Tristan protested, though it sounded weak even to his own ears. What did it say about him that hearing Sebastian refer to him that way made his blood thrum in his veins and his dick perk up? And the *Mr. Holt* only made it hotter.

Sebastian's responding smile seemed knowing, and he patted Tristan's hand before turning his attention back to the road.

Tristan realized he'd unconsciously tightened his fingers. He was gripping Sebastian's thigh hard, not stroking lightly as he'd intended. He loosened his hold but didn't pull away. The contact with Sebastian felt good, no matter how small.

"You can suck me off after lunch," Sebastian said casually. "Except I want you to do it on my bed, nice and slow. If you think you deserve my come, you need to work for it."

Tristan's hand spasmed, his fingers digging into the meat of Sebastian's thigh again. "*Fuck.* Maybe we should skip lunch."

"No." Sebastian's tone was firm. "You can wait."

Tristan groaned. He'd been waiting for weeks, and the

night of the concert had only whetted his appetite. But he knew Sebastian was right—the anticipation would only make things better in the end.

"Yes, Professor," Tristan said. This time he was the one to smile when Sebastian's grip on the wheel tightened, his knuckles whitening.

Yeah, Sebastian liked that, the same way Tristan liked to hear Sebastian call him *Mr. Holt*. The teacher-student dynamic turned them both on, even though it wasn't technically true anymore. They could pretend. It wasn't anyone else's business.

Grindhouse Killer Burgers fell somewhere between a fast-food joint and a sports bar. The atmosphere was loud but relaxed with a combination of sporting events and B movies playing on the scattered television screens. Nobody paid Sebastian and Tristan any particular attention as they found a table and set their number on the edge to wait for their food.

Tristan looked around, and then met Sebastian's gaze. "Aren't you worried we might run across someone from the school? I have to admit I was surprised you invited me out to lunch. I thought you'd only text me when you wanted to fuck."

"I told you I wanted to see you again. I didn't mean only for sex." Sebastian paused. "Unless that's what you want."

Tristan opened his mouth to answer, but a server appeared to deliver their food.

"Do you need anything else?" he asked as he picked up their table number.

Tristan shot him a grateful smile. "No, thanks."

Once the guy had moved away, Tristan nervously toyed with one of his fries. "I... I don't only want sex. I mean, don't get me wrong—I want that with you. A lot. But...this is good too."

Sebastian nodded. "Good." He picked up his burger, which dripped with gooey Swiss cheese and sautéed mushrooms.

And that was apparently that. No need for further discussion.

Tristan made quick work of his own food and tried to snag a sweet potato fry from Sebastian's tray only to get his hand swatted.

"Ask me nicely," Sebastian said.

Tristan swallowed.

Sebastian waited.

Tristan wet his mouth and watched Sebastian's eyes darken. "Can I have a fry, Professor?"

"May I," Sebastian corrected primly.

Tristan grinned. "May I have a fry, Professor?"

Sebastian smirked back. "No, but you may have me instead."

Tristan stifled a groan and shifted in his seat. "Can we go now?" His voice sounded eager and a little breathless.

"I'm not done yet," Sebastian said, and proceeded to finish his burger with a methodical slowness that drove Tristan crazy.

He waited, poised on the edge of his chair, and every torturous second felt longer than the last. Tristan couldn't say if he loved it or hated it.

Then, before all the sweet potato fries were gone, Sebastian shoved a few in Tristan's direction.

He loved it, Tristan decided, as he bit into a fry. He loved every single moment of the torment.

"I'm glad you came to the concert," he told Sebastian without thinking.

Sebastian's gaze shifted away briefly. When he looked back at Tristan, his smile was wry but genuine. "Me too."

Chapter Eleven

A few days later, Sebastian sat back on the comfortable couch in Tristan's apartment, shaking his head and holding up a hand as Tristan tried to offer him the last pot sticker. They'd ordered Thai, and while Sebastian was a runner and had what he considered a fairly healthy appetite, there was no way he could keep up with Tristan. And this was Tristan *before* the hockey season had started. He must eat like a horse to keep that physique of his when he was playing several games a week.

Thinking about hockey made Sebastian study the apartment as Tristan cheerfully finished off the pot stickers. It was a nice place, definitely new, with an updated kitchen full of modern appliances (the most used of which, Tristan told him with a laugh, was his Vitamix blender) and stylish furniture. Nothing flashy, which fit with what Sebastian knew of Tristan's sensibilities, and while it was tidy, it was obvious someone lived here. Tristan had smiled when they'd first walked in with dinner, and Sebastian had seen the small neat pile of textbooks next to Tristan's bookshelf, his sociology book on top.

"You don't keep this one next to your bed?" Sebastian had teased, lifting the book up.

"I doodled your name in the cover," Tristan had joked, grinning.

"With little hearts around it?"

"Nah." Tristan had winked. "Dicks. Not little, though."

Sebastian had laughed and they'd sat down to eat dinner on the sectional sofa in the living room. Once they'd finished, Sebastian carried the remains of their meal into the kitchen, stacking the leftover boxes in the fridge and throwing away the empty containers.

"You didn't have to do that," Tristan said, appearing in the kitchen behind him. "I invited you over, you know."

"It's not a problem." Sebastian gently pushed Tristan up against the counter and leaned in, kissing him softly on the mouth. More of a tease than a kiss, really. He was enjoying the low burn of arousal, and happy that they didn't have to keep their hands off each other. Now that they didn't, though, Sebastian was going to enjoy making Tristan so hot for it he couldn't control himself.

Revenge for those sweatpants.

Tristan wasn't wearing them at the moment. He was wearing jeans and a nice shirt, as if they were going out instead of picking up takeout. Sebastian would have been fine with going out, but he knew exactly why Tristan wanted to be as close to a bed as possible. He wanted that too. Though the sectional would absolutely work if they didn't have the inclination to make it to the bed. Sebastian had made sure to bring a few necessities in his messenger bag, just in case that happened.

Tristan was kissing him with obvious eagerness, his hands settling on Sebastian's hips so he could curl his fingers into Sebastian's belt and tug him closer. Sebastian allowed it, deepened the kiss, and thought about fucking

Tristan over the table they hadn't used, and then pulled away with a brief nip on Tristan's lower lip.

Tristan looked dazed—which was flattering—and annoyed at Sebastian for stopping, which caused Sebastian to grin evilly at him. "In a hurry, Tristan?"

"Yeah, actually," Tristan said, so honestly that it made Sebastian chuckle.

"We waited this long. We can wait a little longer."

"Yeah, but why—"

Sebastian reached out and put two fingers against Tristan's mouth. "Shh. Let's not pretend you don't like it when I make the rules."

Tristan blinked at him, then smiled a little and maneuvered Sebastian's fingers into his mouth. He sucked on them, and it went straight to Sebastian's dick and threatened his self-control, making the table plan look better and better with each passing second. He pulled his fingers free and dragged them wetly down the side of Tristan's face, then tapped lightly. "Be patient, Mr. Holt."

Tristan sucked in a quick breath at the light tap, and his eyes flared hot—it gave Sebastian ideas, and made him wonder how into dominance play Tristan really was. He looked forward to finding out, but if he didn't stop thinking about it, he was going to lose it and shove Tristan to his knees right then and there. And that was not the plan. Not tonight anyway.

"Mmm. No promises, Professor," Tristan said, and then went around him to get a couple of beers out of the fridge. They were good beers too, with actual hops and an alcohol content. "I gotta enjoy these before training camp starts. After that, it's Miller Lite or Mich Ultra." He made a face. "So, you know. Basically water. Although I did read in Martin Brodeur's book that light beer was a perfect replenishing drink for an athlete. Like, it was the best mix of carbs and water and way better than Gatorade." Tristan laughed. "Maybe I can convince Coach to let us put that in our water bottles."

"I think I'd rather have water," Sebastian said, as they walked back into the living room. He took a moment to study the décor, which was, predictably, all centered on hockey (with one or two concert posters thrown in for variety). Tristan had what appeared to be a hockey puck in a shadow box ("My first NHL game," he explained to Sebastian), a framed jersey from the University of Wisconsin, and a few other pieces of memorabilia.

"You know, I feel ridiculous telling you this, but I've never watched a game of hockey in my whole life," said Sebastian. He sat back on the couch, and Tristan settled right next to him. He liked that Tristan wasn't shy about being close, and in fact, seemed to relish that they could sit so close. "I understand the basic premise, but as for the intricacies of gameplay itself… I'm lost."

"Hey, well, lucky for you, you know a guy who can explain it." Tristan picked up the remote off the coffee table and switched on the television. It was absurdly large, which reminded Sebastian for a moment how young Tristan was. Though, honestly, if he'd come into a lot of money at Tristan's age, he probably would have spent it on something similar. Maybe not a television, but he might have gotten his GTO a lot sooner than he had.

Tristan turned on the NHL Network. "Something tells me you don't have this channel."

"You're stereotyping," Sebastian said, teasing, but he kept his face impassive so it didn't show.

Tristan rolled his eyes. "You just said you didn't know

anything about hockey! I figured if you had it, and you wanted to know about it, you'd watch that."

"Yeah. This is my long con to figure out a sporting event. I learned how to fix up my GTO by dating a mechanic too," he joked. "It's so much easier than using Google."

Tristan snorted. "Your sense of humor reminds me of our goalie. All right, here we— Haha, oh, wow. This is a coincidence." He gestured toward the game. "That's the playoff series that my team ended up losing." He pointed with the beer bottle to the television. "I'm number fifty-seven." He cleared his throat. "In the green and gold."

Sebastian bumped him with his shoulder. "I know that much."

"Okay, so, this is hockey." Tristan winced. "Ugh, I can't believe Morley let that guy through the zone. Anyway, so, my job is a defenseman. That means I try to keep the puck in the offensive zone—that's this end of the ice, where the opposing team's goalie is—so our offense can score. And, I mean, sometimes I score goals."

Tristan's tone reminded Sebastian of TAs from grad school, who were just getting that distinctive "lecture" voice. According to his family and friends, Sebastian had been gifted with that voice soon after he'd learned how to talk. It was endearing to sit and listen to Tristan explain the game to him, because he had as much passion for hockey as Sebastian had for sociology.

Tristan was a good teacher, and he was able to break down the fast-moving game into parts and explain to Sebastian how they functioned as a whole. It reminded him, strangely enough, of his father telling him about engines and how all the separate pieces worked together to make the car run.

"Wait, why did everyone stop playing right there?" Sebastian asked, leaning forward. He liked the fast pace of the game, and the sheer athleticism it must take impressed him. It definitely explained why Tristan worked out so much and could eat so many pot stickers, even before the season started.

"That was icing," Tristan explained. "Basically, you can't whack the puck down the ice like that, where it crosses the center line—" he paused the game and pointed to a red line on the rink "—and the goal line, here, without someone touching it. It's so you don't put a guy down next to the opposing team's goalie and shoot the puck down the ice all day so the guy can score goals uncontested."

"Ah." Sebastian nodded. "So it's like soccer, where you try to not score any goals and thereby excite the audience?"

"The crowd, Sebastian," Tristan said with a sharp grin. "'The audience.'" He shook his head and went back to the game. "Okay, so, see, there's me keeping that guy from getting the puck out of our offensive zone and back into his. And there's Morley fucking up and letting him clear the puck on the power play."

"I thought you said you couldn't do that," Sebastian interrupted.

"Well, you can when it's a power play. That's because your team is down a man, so you're allowed. But that means the face-off comes back to your defensive zone... am I losing you?"

"No, I think it makes sense." Sebastian watched a little more. "I missed whatever the guy did to be...not on the ice. In the penalty box?"

"Right. Uh, I don't know, let's see." Tristan rewound

the game to right after he'd initially paused it to explain icing. "Oh, a trip. Ugh, the fucking Marauders. They're such assholes."

"You spend a lot of time on the ice," Sebastian pointed out as they watched a little more. "More than the... forwards?"

"Yup. And yeah, defensemen usually do. We don't get all the glory of, say, Sidney Crosby but, you know. We do our part." He sounded proud, and he should. Sebastian couldn't imagine the skill it took to get to this level, with so many other guys out there trying for a spot.

They watched an entire period with Tristan patiently explaining the mechanics and Sebastian asking a few questions, and by the time they put the game back on "live" mode, it was getting ready to start the third period.

"So, we win this one." Tristan set the remote on the table. "Which is good. I wouldn't want to show you a game where I sucked."

Sebastian smiled and said nothing.

"So, how about this," Tristan said, voice suddenly heated, a playful glimmer in his blue eyes. "I've given you the lesson, and now it's time for the quiz."

"Oh, is that so?" Sebastian liked where this was going, especially because Tristan's hand was on his knee and moving slowly up his thigh. "Are you a hard grader, Professor Holt?"

Tristan snorted. "Not as hard as you are. A ninety-four? Really?"

"I told you," Sebastian said, "You didn't format those footnotes correctly. And there was a part in the middle of your paper that could definitely have been a tighter argument."

Tristan groaned and fell back on the couch. "Why did I ask?"

Sebastian gave him a wicked grin. "You earned the second-highest grade in my class, Mr. Holt. Don't complain."

"Second highest?" Tristan made a face. He didn't look like he was kidding, either. "Who got the first?"

Sebastian raised an eyebrow at him. "This is really what you want to do right now?" He took Tristan's hand and moved it a little higher on his thigh, and nodded at the game. "I'm getting incredibly turned on watching you defend the puck. And you want to talk about grades?"

"Sorry," Tristan said, without sounding the least bit sorry. "I don't like to lose." He paused. "Then again, I got the second highest grade but I also get your dick in my mouth, so I think I won after all."

"I'm glad you feel better about this," Sebastian said drily. "Back to my quiz?"

Tristan laughed. "Right. Okay, so…what's the guy in front of the net called?"

"A control freak?"

"Oh, like you wouldn't be the goalie," Tristan teased. "Come on, I had that figured out from the first day of class. You like being in charge."

"I do," Sebastian murmured, desire curling low in his stomach as blood pulsed hot and went right to his dick. "That's true." He reached out and put a hand on the back of Tristan's neck. "And you like it. I figured that out the first time I put you on your knees."

Tristan sucked in a sharp breath, focus going from the game to Sebastian, which Sebastian found gratifying. God knew Tristan had distracted *him* from work enough times over the last few months. "Yeah. I—I like that. A lot, actually."

"Mmm. So, maybe you should reward me when I get the answers right."

"Okay," Tristan said, eyes wide and caught by Sebastian's own. The eagerness...fuck, Tristan was really into this, and it was something Sebastian liked a lot. He didn't generally have relationships where he was able to devote a lot of time or energy into exploring it. Something about Tristan brought it out in him more strongly than usual, though, and it appeared they were both into it...so why not?

"How—how many offensive lines are there?" Tristan asked.

Sebastian had to think about that one for a minute. "Three?"

Tristan made a buzzer sound and slid his hand slightly lower and away from Sebastian's dick. "Try again."

"Four," Sebastian guessed, mainly because he knew it couldn't be two.

"Yeah," Tristan agreed, voice heavy. He went to move his hand up, but Sebastian stopped him with a light squeeze on his wrist.

"Put your hand on my cock, Tristan."

Tristan swallowed visibly and obeyed. Sebastian made an appreciative noise, then put his hands behind his head and turned his attention back to the game. "Next question."

"What, uh...what's it called when one team has an extra player on the ice 'cause the other team has a player in the penalty box?"

Sebastian definitely remembered that one. "Power

play." He waited for Tristan's answering nod, then said, "Unbuckle my belt."

Tristan did so with hurried gestures, his fingers a little clumsy in his haste. It made Sebastian want to stop playing games and throw him on the ground and fuck him hard. "Next question."

"What position am I?"

"Power bottom," Sebastian said immediately, then gave a low chuckle at the expression on Tristan's face. "Defenseman." When Tristan's fingers went to the button on his jeans, Sebastian shook his head. "That was too easy. I want a hard one."

"That makes two of us," Tristan quipped, and Sebastian had the odd thought that he couldn't remember the last person who made him laugh quite so easily. "Okay, what's it called if you're the team who is *down* a guy, 'cause the refs are maybe blind and think a good hockey play is a penalty?"

Sebastian raised his eyebrows. "I think it's…" He had to search his memory. "Penalty game?"

"Mmm. Close, but not quite." Tristan peered up at him hopefully. "How about I undo one button since it was mostly right?"

"Not a chance."

"Buzzkill," said Tristan.

That triggered his memory. "Penalty kill. You can unzip my jeans now." He lost his breath for a moment as Tristan did so, doing it with enough pressure on Sebastian's dick to make his eyes roll back in his head.

"What's— Ah, what's the— What's it called when you score three goals in one game?"

"Lucky?" Sebastian asked, then laughed at Tristan's look. He knew this one. "Hat trick."

"That's right." Tristan stared expectantly at him, breathing a little harder, his face flushed.

"Take my cock out," Sebastian said, his voice soft. He made an appreciative sound when Tristan did as instructed, taking his cock in hand. He focused on the game again. "Ask me another question."

"Ah…dude, even *I'm* forgetting about hockey right now," Tristan said, his fingers warm and his grip tight on Sebastian's hard cock. "Okay, what's…uh, what's offside?"

Sebastian had no idea. He squinted at the television. "It's…when the players start too soon?"

"Nope. This one is advanced. Probably more in the blowjob category than a handjob," Tristan informed him. He sounded a little smug too. That wouldn't do.

"Who said we were stopping at a handjob—or a blowjob, for that matter?" Sebastian demanded, fixing Tristan with a sharp stare. He already knew that Tristan liked the professor voice, and lucky for him, it came fairly naturally to Sebastian. "Hmm?"

"No one," Tristan said. "And I— This is hot as fuck, Sebastian, but if we have to watch hockey until you get enough questions right to fuck me, this is gonna take a while. I'm pretty sure the game after this is the one where we lose, and I don't think I'm going to be in the mood for anything hot after that."

"Then you better get me ready to fuck you before this game's over," Sebastian said, as if he were unmoved by Tristan's admission—when in fact, he appreciated the subtle cue that Tristan wouldn't want to keep playing this particular game much longer. Honestly, Sebastian wasn't sure how long he could keep it up, either.

"Offside is when a player not carrying the puck

crosses the blue line first," Tristan said, a little breath-less. "And now they can call back goals for that, which is kind of stupid since it can honestly happen ten seconds before the goal is scored and that's an eternity in hockey."

"It feels like an eternity at the moment too," Sebastian said pointedly, and gave a little push of his hips. "The next question, please."

Tristan watched the game for a moment. "What are the two guys on an offensive line besides the center called?"

"Left wing and right wing," Sebastian recalled. At Tristan's nod, he said, "Start stroking me. Not too fast. You're not trying to get me off."

"Mmm." Tristan started moving his hand slowly, giv-ing a little flick of his wrist when he got to the top of Sebastian's dick that made him suck in a sharp breath. "What's the… Fuck, Sebastian," he muttered, shaking his head. His eyes were glued to Sebastian's cock. "What's a Gordie Howe Hat Trick?"

What the hell? Sebastian had no idea, and had to admit that was annoying because he was starting to become more interested in fucking Tristan than learning about hockey. "Who's Gordie Howe?"

"Former player. Died recently." Tristan's thumb dragged across the tip of Sebastian's dick.

"So…he scores three goals? From the afterlife?"

Tristan grinned at him. "Nice try. It's a fight, an as-sist, and a goal."

"Why?"

"It just is." Tristan shrugged. "Okay, what's an assist?"

"That's when someone helps you score a goal," Se-bastian said, and added, "Context clues, Mr. Holt. Take your shirt off."

That clearly surprised Tristan, and he looked a little

disappointed to let go of Sebastian's cock to remove his shirt. But honestly, if he didn't, this was going to end with Sebastian shoving Tristan's head in his lap and having Tristan blow him. Sebastian slowly fisted his own dick, enjoying the show.

"What's the difference between a major and a minor penalty…how many minutes in the box," Tristan clarified, chest heaving with the rapid pace of his breathing.

Sebastian did remember that one. "Two minutes and five minutes. Rub your cock through your jeans."

Tristan was kneeling on the couch now, and he did what Sebastian wanted with obvious enjoyment, palming his hard cock through his jeans. His head tipped back and his eyes went half-closed, and Sebastian had entirely tuned the game out in favor of watching Tristan touch himself and show off for him. "You want me to fuck you, Tristan?"

"Fuck, yes," Tristan hissed, giving Sebastian a heavy stare. "I'll ask you about Corsi statistics if that gets me fucked hard."

"I'll settle for you asking for it," Sebastian said, ready to stop playing games—at least, this particular game. He had a few more in mind. "Convince me you've earned it."

Tristan bit his lower lip, then started undoing his jeans. He waited for a moment when he got to the zipper, clearly making sure it was all right, and that was so hot Sebastian had to squeeze the base of his dick to keep himself under control.

Tristan shoved his jeans down to mid-thigh, along with his underwear. He was kneeling right next to Sebastian, and he started fisting his own cock, hard and fast. "I really want you to fuck me. I think about it a lot. You have no idea."

He had some idea. Sebastian was transfixed by how sexy Tristan looked, how completely uninhibited he was about his body and showing it off. Sebastian's mouth was dry, but he didn't want to look away or stop touching his cock long enough to reach for his half-finished beer on the table.

"How do you want it?"

"Hard," Tristan said immediately, voice low and rough. "Just bend me over and fuck me."

Sebastian was about at the limit of his patience, so that was fine with him. "Then turn the television off and show me where the bedroom is."

Tristan had the remote in his hand before Sebastian had finished talking, and he turned the power off, tossed the controller negligently to the floor, and then climbed in Sebastian's lap. "You have a problem fucking on the couch, Professor Cruz?"

"Not at all." Sebastian grabbed the back of Tristan's neck and pulled him down to kiss him. He wrapped his free hand around their cocks, jacking them off. They both moaned. "I have supplies in my messenger bag."

"Yeah? Well." Tristan threw his head back with a choked groan, then gave a slow grind of his hips. "I have some right behind that couch cushion. I had a feeling we wouldn't make it to the bedroom."

"Mmm. Good thinking." Sebastian kissed him once more, let himself enjoy another few rough strokes with their cocks pressed together, and then said gruffly, "Take your clothes off."

Tristan slid off his lap. Sebastian stood up on legs that weren't quite steady and eyed the back of the couch. Tristan was taller than Sebastian, but if he leaned over the back, it should work.

Tristan stripped with haste that would have been amusing if Sebastian weren't so goddamned desperate for it, and Sebastian rummaged around in the couch until he found the condoms and the tube of lube. "Come here," he said.

When Tristan was in front of him, Sebastian couldn't resist palming his nape and yanking him down for a hot, thorough kiss. Their height difference would never mean Tristan was in control, and Sebastian wanted him to know it. He pressed the condom into Tristan's hand. "Put this on me."

"Fuck," Tristan muttered, and got the condom open while Sebastian pushed his own jeans and underwear out of the way. Tristan smirked and took way too much time sliding the condom on, which made Sebastian mutter and give him a stern look that did nothing to make Tristan go any faster.

Tristan was apparently waiting for further instructions, so Sebastian opened the lube and gestured to Tristan. "Lean over the back of the couch."

The smile Tristan gave him made Sebastian's gut tighten with something other than lust, but the sight of Tristan bent over the couch, ass up in the air…it was impossible to concentrate on anything but how badly Sebastian wanted to fuck him. He lubed up his cock and shuddered a little at the feel of his hand on himself, and he was glad for the condom or else this might be over way too fast. And he'd promised Tristan a good, hard fuck… so that was what he was going to give him.

Sebastian positioned himself behind Tristan and made a few adjustments, then slicked his fingers one last time before tossing the tube to the couch. He reached down and rubbed between Tristan's cleft, lubing his hole and then lining himself up. He steadied Tristan with his hands on Tristan's hips and eased himself inside, breath catching as Tristan's body took his cock. He paused once he was all the way inside, leaning down and mouthing at the sleek muscles of Tristan's back, giving Tristan time to adjust.

"All right?" he asked, voice gravel-rough, kissing Tristan's spine lightly.

"No, 'cause you're—you're not fucking me," Tristan panted out, which was answer enough for Sebastian.

"Then hold on." Sebastian straightened. He got a firmer grip on Tristan's hips and pulled out slowly, then slammed back inside in one deep thrust. They both groaned, and Sebastian found a rhythm. Tristan moved with him, thrusting back on his cock and panting with harsh, rapid breaths.

Sebastian eventually settled one hand low on Tristan's sweat-slick back and kept the other on his hip, trying to keep up as the couch lurched forward on the hardwood floor. Sebastian briefly thought about stopping and switching locations, but Tristan looked over his shoulder and said, "Fuck, do it harder," and that was the end of thinking about logistics.

"You like it?" Sebastian asked, hips snapping forward. "This what you wanted?"

"Mmm, fuck, yeah," Tristan ground out, head thrown back. "Fuck, yes."

Sebastian wanted to make this last, wanted to make Tristan beg to come, but he couldn't—it felt too good and he was already too close. "Get yourself off," he ordered, and the second Tristan got a hand on his dick, his body tightened around Sebastian's cock and Sebastian groaned loudly. "Yeah, that's it, make me come."

It only took a few seconds before Tristan cried out and came, and Sebastian followed him soon after, half collapsing on Tristan's back as he shuddered hard with his own release. He was gasping for breath and half-aware of the couch sliding again, and he could feel Tristan laugh beneath him.

"Uh, shouldn't have...gotten those...furniture feet things," Tristan said, clearly still out of breath.

He was doing better than Sebastian, though, who couldn't quite speak yet. Sebastian snorted and eased out of him, leaning against the couch for a moment to catch his breath.

Tristan straightened, then turned and flashed him a grin. "Not bad, Professor. I'd say definitely a ninety-four. At least."

Sebastian didn't have enough breath to speak, but he somehow still managed a laugh. *Brat.*

Chapter Twelve

Over the next week, Tristan learned what it meant when someone like Sebastian Cruz said, *Your ass is mine*. He spent almost as much time nude—in bed, or bent over tables, or down on all fours—as he did dressed. Outside of his workouts with Morley and Ryu, every spare second of Tristan's time was dedicated to Sebastian. They couldn't stay away from each other, or keep their hands and mouths off each other. Tristan was so obsessed with how amazing Sebastian made him feel, it might have scared him if Sebastian didn't seem equally enthralled.

Until Tristan realized they were into the second week of August, training camp was only a month away, and he hadn't even thought about making plans to visit his family after the summer term had ended as he'd promised.

Trouble was, Tristan wasn't ready for the honeymoon sexcapade period with Sebastian to be over. Not only that, fall semester began at the end of the month, which meant Sebastian would be back to teaching and Tristan would be starting his online courses. Once hockey season kicked off, Tristan could pretty much kiss his free time good-bye. Between traveling, classes, workouts, and practices, he couldn't imagine being able to see Sebastian very often. He wanted to take advantage of the freedom in their schedules while he could.

A couple of days later, they were sprawled out on Sebastian's couch watching a shoot-'em-up thriller while sharing a six-pack and passing cartons of Chinese food back and forth.

Yet another awesome car went up in flames on screen, and Sebastian muttered something about "senseless waste" under his breath. Tristan still couldn't quite believe Sebastian liked these kinds of movies. He'd accidentally discovered Sebastian's Blu-ray collection the previous week. He'd expected it to be all highbrow and artsy, but the reality made him laugh. The drawers beneath Sebastian's television were filled to the brim with action/adventure gems like *Die Hard*, James Bond, the Bourne films, *Lethal Weapon*, and *The Fast and the Furious*. Sebastian pretended to sneer at them and said he only watched them when he needed "mindless entertainment," but Tristan saw right through his posturing. Really, Sebastian loved the explosions, gunfire, and over-the-top violence. Tristan had caught him grinning gleefully a couple of times, which was rare enough for Sebastian it filled Tristan's chest with fond, warm feelings he didn't want to investigate too closely.

But watching another muscle car get demolished abruptly gave Tristan an idea. He grabbed the remote and lowered the volume on the speakers. Sebastian paused with his beer halfway to his mouth and turned to him expectantly.

"How would you feel about taking a road trip with me?" Tristan asked.

Sebastian stared at him blankly for a moment. He set his bottle on one of the coasters scattered across the coffee table, and his face took on a considering look. "I might be amenable. What are you thinking?"

"Well, I promised my parents I'd come home for a visit this month. If I don't do it before the semester starts, it won't happen until winter break."

"Where is home exactly?"

"Wisconsin. My parents own a farm outside Columbus. It's about forty minutes northeast of Madison. It's a small town. Maybe five thousand people."

Sebastian raised his eyebrows. "Your parents are farmers?"

"Yeah. They have an eight-hundred-acre spread. We grow soybeans and corn." Tristan fiddled with the remote as he watched Sebastian's expression. He wasn't sure if a weekend getaway might be too couple-y for what they were doing. They hadn't exactly quantified their relationship. For now it was simply two guys enjoying each other's company and having lots of great sex. Maybe Sebastian would prefer to keep it that way. "I wouldn't expect you to come to the farm. I thought maybe we could rent a cabin on Lake Wisconsin for a few days, maybe spend a night in Indianapolis or Chicago on the way up. I can go see my family afterward."

"Hmm. Me, you, and a cabin on a lake." Sebastian's dirty smile spoke volumes. "Let's do it." He leaned forward and bit sharply at Tristan's lower lip. "Your car or mine?"

In the end, they decided on Sebastian's GTO instead of Tristan's more fuel-efficient Jeep Grand Cherokee. Sebastian loved to drive his car, and Tristan couldn't blame him. Also, he'd been fantasizing about the various ways Sebastian could debauch him in the car, or over the hood, ever since the time Sebastian had roared up to his apartment building to pick him up for their first lunch date.

He'd be making one of those fantasies a reality when they got to the lake. The owner of the property he'd rented had assured Tristan they'd have complete privacy, and he hoped it was true. He'd insisted on reserving the cabin and paying for their stay, since Sebastian would be putting hundreds of miles on his car and making the return trip alone. Sebastian agreed, with the caveat that he'd buy all the food, and they'd decided to split the cost of gas on the way up to Wisconsin.

They left on a Wednesday morning. For the first half of the drive, Tristan served as both navigator and DJ. The GTO's radio had been upgraded to one that looked original but could stream MP3s through either Bluetooth or an auxiliary cable without sacrificing the aesthetic of the dash. Tristan scrolled through Sebastian's playlists, commenting whenever he found something he liked. Their tastes were almost identical. Sebastian's playlists consisted mainly of songs by The Beatles, The Who, The Rolling Stones, Grateful Dead, The Doors, Kansas, Led Zeppelin, and, of course, Pink Floyd. But a collection of Spanish titles made Tristan pause. He eyed the artist names curiously. Don Omar. Daddy Yankee. Wisin & Yandel. Tego Calderón. He didn't recognize any of them.

"What is reggaeton?" he asked, stumbling over the pronunciation.

Sebastian snorted. "It's *reh-geh-tohn*. And, to put it simply, it's a blend of salsa, dancehall, and hip-hop. It originated in Puerto Rico."

"So, it's like Spanish reggae?"

"Not exactly. Reggae en Español is its own separate genre. It's basically reggae but in Spanish, without blending in the hip-hop or salsa." Sebastian shot him a sideways look. "You've seriously never heard of Daddy Yankee?"

Tristan shrugged. "No. I mostly listen to the bands I already know. I couldn't even tell you what's popular right now. I mean, of course I know about people like Britney Spears and Justin Bieber because they're part of pop culture or whatever, but I'm a classic-rock guy. You know that already." Tristan grinned at Sebastian before returning his attention to the playlist. He couldn't tell what any of the titles meant. Apparently recollecting the Spanish he'd learned in high school wasn't like riding a bicycle. "I'm curious now. Which song should I put on?"

"Try 'Danza Kuduro.' It was fairly popular a few years ago. You might have heard it without knowing what it was."

Tristan started the song and listened for a couple of minutes. He didn't feel an inkling of recognition, which wasn't surprising. What *did* surprise him was how badly it made him want to move his hips. He didn't do much more than sway or mime along with guitar or drum solos when he attended concerts or listened to music on his own. Dancing had never been his strong suit. Sadly, he pretty much defined the rhythmless white boy stereotype. He knew his limitations, and normally he wasn't bothered. Now he wondered if Sebastian could dance and how it might feel to press their bodies together and move along to the beat. The idea made him hot, and he sent Sebastian an appreciative once-over.

Sebastian's attention was focused on the road, as it should be, but the fingers of one hand were tapping on the steering wheel and his lips were moving subtly as he sang along.

When the song ended, Tristan paused the playlist before it skipped to another. "I liked it. Makes me wish I knew what they were saying. Do you speak Spanish?"

Sebastian maneuvered around a slow-moving truck, and Tristan took a moment to admire his corded forearms and the easy, confident way he handled the car. "Yes," Sebastian answered. "Fluently. It's all my parents ever spoke at home."

"You said things got awkward with them after you came out, but are you guys still close?"

Sebastian lifted one shoulder. "We're okay. My sexuality is something we never discuss. Out of sight, out of mind. I try to call my mom a few times a month. I listen to her talk about church and the people she works for and she tells me how my father is doing. She doesn't ask about my love life, and I don't volunteer any information. Everyone stays happy." He looked over at Tristan. "What about you? I'm gathering you're close to your family if you're going to visit them. Do they know you're gay?"

Tristan hesitated, biting his lip. Eventually, he stopped gnawing on his flesh and sighed. "No."

Sebastian didn't ask why, but Tristan knew he was probably wondering. Given that they were dating, or something close to it, Tristan felt he deserved an explanation. "I… I don't know why I haven't told them. They're good people, and they love me. I guess it's the what-ifs, you know? What if it changes how they think about me? What if it messes up our relationship? What if they surprise me in a bad way? I know I'm probably not being very fair to them by keeping it a secret, but…" Tristan sighed again and rubbed the back of his neck.

"I understand," Sebastian said softly. "I didn't tell my parents at first for the same reasons. But as I got older, I realized I wanted to live openly. I wanted them to know who I am. They could accept me or not. Approve of me or not. I refused to allow them to stay blissful in their ignorance or to continue pressuring me about marrying a woman—not if it meant I had to hide and pretend for the rest of my life. Sure, it cost me some friends, and there are a few aunts and uncles I don't speak to anymore. Or rather, they don't speak to me. But to hell with them. This is my truth, and I'm proud. But I know the what-ifs are scary. Everyone has to come out on their own terms."

Tristan nodded, although if he were honest, Sebastian's self-assurance made him feel like a coward. His parents had never given him any reason to suspect they'd reject him for being gay. They were easygoing, salt-of-the-earth type of people. They'd probably be hurt to know how long he'd kept his sexuality from them for fear of their disapproval.

But how often had Tristan heard stories about other gay men whose families didn't seem to have a problem with homosexuality until it was in their own home, their own backyard? Until it was their son or brother or father? Maybe some of those people even *truly* believed themselves to be open-minded—until they had to face the reality of having a gay relative. Then came the worry about appearances and what friends or neighbors or their church might think. In those situations, a person's true colors oozed to the surface, and sometimes those colors were ugly.

Tristan didn't think he'd be able to stand it if that happened with his own family. He didn't think he could face the pain, the crushing disappointment of having everyone he knew turn their backs on him.

He shook his head, as if the motion could banish the

thought from his mind as easily as erasing a picture on an Etch A Sketch.

"So when we leave tomorrow, will you let me drive your baby?" Tristan asked. They were about an hour away from Indianapolis and had reserved a room there for the night. In the morning, they'd continue to Lake Wisconsin.

As an attempt to change the subject, the question was obvious and clumsy, but Sebastian only said, "Sure." After a few seconds, he added, "Why don't you put the music back on? Let's complete your reggaeton education. Try 'Gasolina.' There's actually a bit of a debate about the meaning of that song."

Relief unknotted the ball of tension that had formed in Tristan's stomach. "Oh, yeah?" he asked as he searched for it on the playlist.

"Yes. Some people think he's referring to women who love skeet or jizz, whatever slang term you prefer. But in an interview, Daddy Yankee himself said it was about women who liked to go out and cruise the streets."

Tristan laughed and turned to Sebastian. "What do you think?"

Sebastian shot him a quick smile before refocusing on the road. "I think it's ridiculous, but I can't stop myself from singing along."

They got an early start the next morning. Of course, Sebastian was too much of a control freak to sit quietly while Tristan drove. It wasn't long before the corrections started.

"Ease up on the clutch," he said when Tristan was being a bit heavy-footed. Tristan had told Sebastian he knew how to drive a stick shift, and it was true—but he

left out the part about how he hadn't done it on anything
other than farm equipment in years.

"Switch gears now!" Sebastian snapped when the engine started getting noisier and Tristan didn't respond
quickly enough.

Tristan should've been annoyed by the back seat driving. Instead, perversely, it started to turn him on. He
slowed the car down to hear Sebastian bark out a reminder about the speed limit. He sped up so Sebastian
would tell him to stop being a lead foot and ask if he
hadn't noticed the state trooper.

After another "mistake" he glanced over to find Sebastian staring at him with a dark, knowing expression.

"Pull off at the next rest stop," Sebastian said. "Be-
have until then."

Tristan focused on the road and tried to convince Sebastian he really did know what he was doing. Sebastian put a hand on his thigh, a few inches shy of Tristan's
stiff cock, which strained the material of his sweatpants.

When they got to the rest stop and parked, Sebastian
ordered him out of the car. Tristan's hard-on was doing an
outstanding impersonation of a flagpole as it attempted
to break free of his jock, but thankfully, there was no one
around to notice. He followed Sebastian into the men's
room and trembled when Sebastian grabbed him and
forced him into the nearest stall. Sebastian spun them
so Tristan was pressed face-first to the closed door and
leaned up to grind his cock against Tristan's ass.

"Are you trying to make me lose my temper?" Sebastian asked, a fierce whisper in Tristan's ear. "Or do you
just like having me correct you?"

Tristan pushed his hips back and moaned softly. "You
know which one it is."

Sebastian grabbed his hair, yanking Tristan's head to the side. He bit at Tristan's earlobe, sharply enough that Tristan sucked in a quick breath. "You didn't get enough last night?"

Tristan moaned again. Before they'd gone to bed, Sebastian had fucked him right against the window in their hotel room with the curtains wide open. They'd been on one of the upper levels and most of the lights had been off, save for the one by the door, which had left them as nothing more than silhouettes from the outside. But knowing their actions would be unmistakable to anyone watching had made Tristan leak pre-come all over the glass. Afterward, when Sebastian had instructed him to wipe up his mess, not leave it for the housekeeping staff, it had humiliated and thrilled Tristan in equal measure. Out of sheer Midwestern politeness, he would've never left it to some poor cleaning lady to scrub his dried come from the window—but there was something about having Sebastian command him to do it in his sharp professor voice that made Tristan flush, both from embarrassment and the eagerness to please.

"It'll never be enough," Tristan said, and he already sounded wrecked to his own ears, simply from the memory of the night before. "Want you constantly. I'd stay on my knees all day for you if I could."

Sebastian released his hair and stepped back. "Then get down there. Be a good little cocksucker. Get on that filthy floor and suck my dick."

The words made Tristan's face burn hot, but his cock grew harder than ever as he easily went to his knees and undid Sebastian's fly with shaky fingers. He pulled the briefs out of the way to free Sebastian's thick cock and swiped his tongue across the tip, humming in pleasure at the tang of salt and the warm musk of Sebastian's skin. It was more than enough to distract Tristan from the stench of the restroom or wondering about the contents of the suspicious puddle he'd found himself kneeling in.

Tristan licked again, but before he could take Sebastian into his mouth, Sebastian cupped his chin and tipped Tristan's head up so their gazes could meet. Sebastian studied him for a moment, a question in his dark eyes. They hadn't done anything quite like this yet, and Tristan knew Sebastian was checking on him, ensuring Tristan fully approved of the situation before it went any further.

Tristan nodded slightly and brushed a kiss across Sebastian's palm. "All good, Professor Cruz."

Sebastian moved his hand along Tristan's jaw in a soft caress. Then he buried his fingers in Tristan's hair and gave him a broad, dirty grin that made Tristan wish they were already in Wisconsin so they could find a bed and lock themselves away for days.

He returned the grin, allowing Sebastian to guide his movements, parting his lips wide to accept the insistent push of Sebastian's thick cock. After a couple of slow thrusts, Sebastian withdrew and held Tristan still as he smacked his wet dick against Tristan's cheek. "You look good with my cock in your mouth," he said idly, dragging the tip across Tristan's lips, smearing spit and pre-come. "You'd look better choking on it."

Tristan shivered hard. He turned his head, tearing his hair out of Sebastian's grasp to capture Sebastian's cock again. He grabbed Sebastian's ass and yanked him forward, gripping tight while Sebastian *really* fucked his throat. It was rough, fast, and sloppy, and maybe, just maybe, Tristan played up the gagging while staring up at

Sebastian with wide, pleading eyes because he'd learned Sebastian got off on hearing and seeing his need.

Hunger and approval blended into a perfectly tortured expression on Sebastian's face. Tristan moaned to witness it, aroused to the point where he felt feverish with lust.

By the time Sebastian came, his low grunt a sound Tristan felt deep in his balls, Tristan's jaw ached and he had spit dripping liberally down his chin. Sebastian helped him to his feet and shoved a hand into Tristan's sweatpants. He pushed the jock aside and took Tristan's cock in a firm grip. A few tugs was all Tristan needed to reach his peak, and of course, the men's room door swung open noisily right as he started shaking and spilling over Sebastian's fingers.

Tristan buried his face against Sebastian's shoulder and bit down on a mouthful of his shirt to muffle his groan. They were hidden inside the stall, but their feet would be visible to anyone who looked, and Tristan battled awkwardness and nerves as he fought to stay quiet. Sebastian stroked his hair, murmuring soothingly, his other hand still wrapped around Tristan's softening dick.

Once the guy left and the room was silent, Sebastian stepped back. He used a handful of toilet paper to clean Tristan off. His movements were gentle, and he kept looking up into Tristan's face.

Tristan leaned in to kiss him. "I'm okay."

Sebastian nodded, and they went out to the sinks. Tristan winced when he saw his reflection. Dark splotches stained his sweatpants at the knees, his hair stuck up in messy spikes, and his shirt collar was wet from spit.

"I need to change," he said. No way could he tolerate staying like this until they got to Lake Wisconsin. Part of him even considered tossing the filthy sweatpants. Who the hell knew what was in that mystery puddle?

Sebastian washed his hands, his eyes crinkled in amusement. When he finished, he pulled Tristan close for another short kiss. "Stay here. I'll go get you a change of clothes."

Their time at the cabin was as close to perfect as Tristan could have hoped for. They spent hours swimming in the lake and sunning themselves on the private dock. They took morning runs together, and Tristan learned his muscled hockey thighs were no match for Sebastian's long, sinewy legs. They made out in the hot tub until their skin turned pruney and Tristan's head went dizzy from the heat. They had sex on nearly every flat surface, and late one night, Tristan lived out his fantasy about being fucked over the hood of the GTO to a symphony played out by crickets and cicadas. He didn't even care that he ended up with a mosquito bite on his balls. Afterward, all he could think was, *Worth it*.

Before Sebastian dropped him off at the rental facility where Tristan had reserved a sedan to drive to his parents' place, they shared several deep, lingering kisses. Tristan arrived at the farm still wearing a self-satisfied smile he couldn't seem to rein in. His brother teased him about how he must be getting some. His mother asked if he had anyone special in his life. Tristan played coy and said, "Maybe," which his mother accepted without pressuring him for more information, though she laughed giddily and gave him an exuberant hug that smelled of cinnamon from the pie she was baking.

The two classes he'd registered for were online, which meant he didn't have to rush home for the beginning of the fall semester. He had his MacBook and could do whatever needed to be done while at his parents' house. So for a couple of weeks, he did chores around the farm, caught a few baseball games with his dad, spent time with his siblings, and stuffed himself full of his mother's familiar home cooking.

When he returned to Atlanta a week into September, he texted Sebastian to let him know they'd landed as the plane taxied to the gate.

His phone buzzed while he waited in baggage claim about ten minutes later.

I'll see you soon.

Tristan grinned down at the screen and rubbed his thumb over the words. Sebastian always texted using complete sentences and flawless punctuation, and he hated emojis enough to rant about them. No C U soon or winking smiley faces from him. Tristan found it oddly charming…which was a sign he was probably in over his head, because since when did he give a shit about another guy's texting habits, let alone find them *charming*?

Tristan shook his head and put the phone away so he could grab his suitcase. Morley was waiting for him outside in a cherry-red Hummer about the size of a small garage.

The sheer bulk of Hummers had always struck Tristan as absurdly showy, though he'd never say as much to his friend. If Morley was overcompensating for something, Tristan couldn't comprehend what it would be. He'd seen Morley naked enough times to know the man had a cock well in proportion with the rest of his six-foot-seven frame. It was why most of their teammates called him *Tripod*. Tristan and Ryu refused. But it was hilarious to watch Morley scramble to come up with random, family-appropriate stories whenever reporters asked him about the nickname. He couldn't exactly answer, *I have a wine-bottle dick*, on national television. At least not without suffering the wrath of the league.

"Hey, Holtzy!" Morley greeted him with a smile and a back-slap that nearly pitched Tristan into the dashboard.

"Hey, man. Thanks for the ride." Sebastian had wanted to pick him up, but a faculty meeting conflicted with Tristan's arrival time. He'd offered to bring dinner over to Tristan's apartment after his final class instead. "How've you been?"

"Fine. I saw Bellzie the other night," Morley said, referring to the Venom's captain, Daniel Bellamy. "A few other guys are already in town for training camp too. I can't wait to be back on the ice, bro. Summers are great and all, but, fuck, I'd rather be playing."

"Yeah, I hear you." Tristan looked forward to reconnecting with his teammates, even if it meant he'd have less time for Sebastian. The guys were his second family, and he missed them whenever they scattered to their respective home states or countries for the off-season. And Bellzie, well, he'd always been an inspiration to Tristan, and later, a mentor. The very first jersey Tristan had bought with his allowance said *Bellamy* on the back. He still had it hanging in his closet, though now it sported Bellzie's signature above the logo. A few of his teammates had given him shit for requesting that autograph during his rookie year on the Venom, but Tristan gave zero fucks about that. He hadn't been willing to pretend Bellzie was anything less than one of his personal hockey heroes.

"Want to grab some lunch?" Morley asked when they were past the airport traffic.

It was early enough in the day that Tristan agreed. They stopped for a quick meal at their favorite sub shop before Morley dropped him off in front of his apartment building.

Tristan showered, unpacked, and started laundry to pass the time until Sebastian arrived. When Sebastian stepped into his apartment bearing a bag that smelled of Italian food, Tristan barely let him get across the threshold before he went in for a kiss.

It caught Sebastian off-guard, and Tristan silenced his startled laugh by slipping him the tongue. Somehow they got the takeout and Sebastian's messenger bag on a tabletop as they stumbled to the couch, where Tristan shoved Sebastian down onto the cushions and settled on top of him.

Sebastian slid his hands past the waistband of Tristan's sweatpants and made a soft, pleased sound at finding Tristan completely bare underneath. He pulled back and grinned up at Tristan, his mouth wet from Tristan's kisses. "I think that greeting deserves a solid ninety-five percent, Mr. Holt."

Tristan growled. "I'll show you ninety-five percent." He rubbed his hard cock against the bulge in Sebastian's pants and laughed breathlessly when Sebastian groaned and arched up to meet the pressure, as if he couldn't help himself.

Sebastian squeezed one of Tristan's ass cheeks. "Maybe I can spare another point for the lack of underwear."

"Only one? Who are you giving the rest of my points to, Professor Cruz?" Tristan delivered a sharp bite to Sebastian's chin. "Have you already found another student you want to slip some extra credit?"

Sebastian reared back. When he spotted Tristan's smirk, his incredulous expression darkened into something hot. He yanked Tristan's sweatpants down and swatted at his ass. "Fucking brat." He smacked the same cheek in a different spot, harder this time. "I should spank you, leave my handprints all over this fine ass."

Just like that, Tristan could see it—his body draped across Sebastian's lap, his skin sore and burning, covered in Sebastian's marks. With a helpless groan, he jerked and came abruptly, as he hadn't done since his early teens when it hadn't taken much more than a dirty thought or two to send him over the edge.

"Oh, *shit*. Oh, fuck. God." Mortified and trembling from the shock of how quickly it'd happened, Tristan buried his heated face against Sebastian's neck. "Sorry. I'm sorry."

Sebastian didn't laugh, as Tristan feared he might. Instead, he stroked Tristan's back. "No need to apologize. Do you have any idea how amazing it is to watch you come from only the *thought* of me doing something to you?"

Tristan still couldn't lift his head.

"You're sexy as hell, Tristan," Sebastian said, his voice rough. "I like getting you off, no matter how it happens. This isn't something you should ever feel ashamed about. Not with me."

Tristan gnawed anxiously at his lower lip, but he pulled away so he could meet Sebastian's eyes. "Okay."

Sebastian searched his face. "Is that something you want? For me to spank you?"

Tristan swallowed thickly. "I… I don't know. Maybe. Yeah."

Sebastian raised his brows. "Which is it?"

"Yes." Tristan knew his blush had intensified into a deeper, brighter red, but he forced himself to go on. "And that thing you did at the rest stop? Um, when you smacked my cheek with your dick?"

Sebastian nodded but didn't speak.

"I sometimes think about you doing that with your hand." Tristan stopped and had to clear his throat before he could continue. "Slapping me, I mean. But… I don't want to have to ask for it. I want you to surprise me. I want you to do it when the moment feels right." He stared down into Sebastian's unreadable face as embarrassment twisted in his stomach. "Uh. You know, if you're into that sort of thing. If you want to." Tristan cleared his throat again. Might as well go for broke at this point. "And I *really* liked it when you called me a cocksucker. If you wanted to…call me other things, I'd be okay with it. I mean… I'd like it. I think."

Sebastian stayed silent for so long Tristan had to fight not to squirm.

"I've done that before," Sebastian said finally, right when Tristan was considering taking everything back. "Not seriously, though. Not formally. I can be as controlling as you want, and I'm perfectly willing to humiliate you or spank you if it turns you on. I don't deal with safewords or contracts. You say stop and we stop. Anytime, no matter what the circumstances."

"But will you enjoy it too? I don't want you to do it just for me."

Sebastian rubbed a hand over one of Tristan's bare ass cheeks and tapped it lightly. "Oh, I'll enjoy it," he said

with a wry smile. "Immensely. I may not consider myself a Dom in the technical sense, and I'm not officially
involved in the lifestyle at all, but if you hadn't noticed
by now, I *am* a domineering bastard. I'd love to beat your
ass raw. I'd love to slap you across the face and call you
my little cock slut."

Tristan's shiver shook them both. "Yeah," he whispered as his eyelids slid shut. "Do that. Say that."

"I will." He felt Sebastian touch his cheek. "But it'll
be on my time, as and when I choose."

Tristan smiled. "Good." For him, there wasn't any
need to discuss it further. They both knew he wanted
Sebastian to take charge. He was more than fine with
allowing any kinky play to happen on Sebastian's terms.
He didn't want to have to think about it or ask for it. But
if that ever changed, he wouldn't hesitate to say so.

"Now get cleaned up," Sebastian ordered. "The food's
getting cold."

Tristan opened his eyes in surprise. He reached between their bodies to cup Sebastian's erection, which
hadn't flagged during their talk. "But what about you?"

Sebastian smiled. "You'll be taking care of me later,
don't worry," he said. "We'll see if you can get that grade
up to a hundred."

Chapter Thirteen

Sebastian stood next to the glass in the Philips Arena, arms crossed over his chest and staring out at the ice. R.J. stood next to him, drinking an overpriced beer and grinning.

"This is so cool," he said, for what had to be the sixth time. "And, somehow, that still makes you glare. Are you nervous, Sebastian?"

He wasn't trying to glare—at least, until R.J. said that thing about being nervous. "Why would I be nervous?"

"Your boyfriend is going to play hockey?" R.J. smiled. Luckily, Tristan had been fine with R.J. knowing that he was gay, understanding that R.J. was a trusted friend who would never out him to anyone.

"Yes, but again, why would that make *me* nervous?" Sebastian glanced at R.J., who—of course—was wearing a Venom T-shirt. Sebastian owned no hockey-themed clothing at all, except for a shirt of Tristan's that Tristan had left in his apartment. It was too big on Sebastian and it was from Tristan's college team, not his professional one. At some point, Sebastian thought, he should buy something supportive. Like the shirts he saw with players' names and numbers on them, though the thought of wearing Tristan's name on his back was vaguely ridiculous.

Though it was sort of hot too.

They were at the arena for the Venom's opening night game, and Tristan had given Sebastian a couple of tickets. He'd of course asked R.J. to come with him, and they were waiting for the team to come out on the ice for a warm-up skate (R.J. had been the one to tell him to show up early for that, and Sebastian had to admit he was curious to see Tristan on the ice in all that gear of his), and were joined by a few other fans. All of whom were wearing Venom shirts and jerseys—though there were a few for the Marauders, the hockey team from Memphis that had taken the Venom out of the playoffs last year. Some young women were there with their phones and a few signs too.

The whole thing was decidedly out of his comfort zone, but the sociologist in him was fascinated. Sebastian had never been immersed in sports culture, and if nothing else, this would be an excellent observation opportunity. The buzzer sounded before he could mention that to R.J., who'd struck up a conversation with a couple of children. Sebastian never had any idea what to say to children younger than his college students. Somehow they took one look at him and decided he wasn't the kind of grown-up you talked to. Sebastian couldn't say he was sad about that.

There was a cheer from those assembled along the glass as the skaters came out, and Sebastian's eyebrows went up as he saw how tall and imposing Tristan's team looked on their skates. Fascinated, he leaned closer and watched as they began skating laps around the rink. He couldn't remember if he'd ever been on a pair of ice skates. Probably not. Roller blades a time or two as a kid, maybe, but he'd not been very good at it.

R.J. nudged him. "Hey, there's your… Tristan," he amended quickly, now that they had a bit more of a crowd.

Sebastian frowned. Was Tristan his boyfriend? That title always seemed a bit juvenile to Sebastian, regardless of how old he—or his partner—was. He and Tristan were dating, certainly, and it was admittedly a bit more serious than casual. But *partner* seemed a bit too formal—not to mention, Sebastian would never be comfortable using that for someone who was closeted—and yet there was no other word to use. He put it out of his mind, vaguely chagrined that R.J. had spotted Tristan before he had, and focused on his…fine, his boyfriend skating by.

Sebastian smiled as some of the kids pounded on the glass to get the players' attention. He wouldn't be able to stand that if he were out there.

As if reading his mind, R.J. said, "I'm imagining you stopping and lecturing those kids about ruining your pre-game concentration." He grinned.

Sebastian rolled his eyes, but a smile touched the corners of his mouth. "You're probably right." He watched as Tristan flew by in a green-and-gold rush, moving fast and looking even broader than usual in all that gear.

As he skated by for the third time, Tristan met his eyes through the glass. Sebastian raised his hand from his crossed-armed position to give a bit of a wave, though he had no idea if Tristan saw it or not, given how fast Tristan was going. But on his next pass, Tristan tapped the glass with his hockey stick right where Sebastian was standing.

Something warm flared up in Sebastian's blood and

blossomed in his chest. It wasn't lust, though he couldn't lie and say that Tristan didn't look hot as fuck in that uniform. That little stick tap, the acknowledgment that he'd seen Sebastian...

"Oh, my God, the look on your face, dude," R.J. murmured, a laugh caught in his low voice.

"Shut up or I'll scalp your ticket," said Sebastian, but he was smiling.

"We're already here. You can't scalp the ticket."

"I didn't mention that Tristan said I could have two for every home game?" Sebastian gave R.J. an innocent look. "Mea culpa."

"No, you did not mention that, so yeah, tua culpa." R.J. hit him lightly on the shoulder, and they watched as Tristan—after skating up and shooting pucks at the goalie—came over to the glass again.

This time he flipped a puck up and over the glass, sending the kids scrambling for it. He met Sebastian's eyes and grinned, then nodded hello at R.J. Sebastian was ridiculously pleased Tristan didn't do the stick-tap thing for anyone but him.

Boyfriend, indeed.

Sebastian watched the warm-ups until the buzzer sounded, then he obediently followed R.J. up to their seats. Tristan had already explained that the seats were in the so-called "WAGs" section—which apparently stood for "wives and girlfriends"—and they were seated next to a young woman wearing a Bellamy shirt.

"That's the captain," R.J. whispered.

"Shouldn't she be on the ice?" Sebastian whispered back. He ignored the jab R.J. gave him and focused instead on the pregame ceremony. It involved a lot of loud music, flashing lights and a bombastic announcer. It was a heady atmosphere, and Sebastian found himself enjoying it—especially when they announced the starting players and Tristan's face flashed up on the jumbotron.

He looked like such a jock. Sebastian smiled to himself, remembering how he'd completely misjudged Tristan back at the beginning of the summer. He was hot, but there was a brain to go along with that taut body and those pretty blue eyes.

"Who are you here for?" asked the woman next to him, the one in the Bellamy shirt. She was pretty—all the women in the section were pretty, whether they were younger or closer to Sebastian's age—with auburn hair and warm dark eyes.

His breath caught and a zing of panic raced up his spine. Sebastian had to work to keep the glower off his face. He knew exactly how unapproachable it made him look, but it'd been a long time since he'd felt that moment of fear at being discovered for being gay.

Calm down. People give tickets to their friends. There are other men in this section. "Tristan Holt is a friend of mine."

"This guy," R.J. broke in, smoothly, "has never seen a hockey game, can you believe that? Tristan was kind enough to get us tickets."

Technically true, but it bothered Sebastian to have his relationship cast in such a light. He wasn't sure that was fair of him, though, because he and Tristan...well. It wasn't time to think about that, now. But it was obvious by the woman's shirt and the rock on her finger she was married to one of the players—probably the captain, Bellamy—and Sebastian couldn't help the flare of irritation that his own relationship had to be so carefully hidden.

Then again, he could be misjudging the situation and

making assumptions. It wouldn't be the first time he'd had his perceptions challenged, he thought wryly. "Yes. He was a student of mine this summer, and wrote some really thoughtful papers on life as a pro athlete."

"Oh, he's such a sweetheart," the woman agreed. "My name's Tabby Bellamy—my husband, Daniel, is the captain." There was a little one next to her, peering up at Sebastian with her mother's pretty dark eyes. Next to her was a slightly older boy, who must have taken after his father, with his curly brown hair and blue eyes. "This is my daughter, Gretchen, and my son, Nate."

"Hello," said Sebastian, giving a somewhat awkward wave. "I'm Sebastian, and this is R.J."

"They're friends of Holtzy's," Tabby told her children, who shyly peeked at him and then went back to watching the ice.

"Daddy!" The little girl pointed happily. "Look, Mama."

"I think they could recognize Daniel's number before they knew his first name wasn't 'Daddy,'" Tabby joked.

Sebastian's tension eased at Tabby's friendliness, and he answered a few questions about his job as a professor; agreed that, yes, Tristan was a smart kid; and ignored the grin he could *feel* R.J. aiming in his general direction whenever he talked about Tristan.

The game seemed to be taking forever to start, with more announcements and some sort of ceremony before the puck dropped involving a community leader and both captains from the team. Then they had to stand for the singing of the anthem, the inclusion of which in sporting events Sebastian didn't quite understand, and finally—*finally*—it was game time.

As fast as the sport moved on television, it was nothing compared to watching it live. Sebastian had to orient himself and focus for a moment when he realized there was no announcer to provide a play-by-play (he'd maybe been watching hockey games on the NHL Network), but he saw Tristan immediately. He was on the ice a lot, and watching him play in person was really different from watching him play on the television.

It was also incredibly hot. Sebastian had never thought of himself as a man who particularly went for the athletic type, but he couldn't deny how attractive he found the intensity, focus, and sheer physicality of Tristan's sport. And Tristan playing it.

"Um," R.J. whispered, leaning in at one point and nudging Sebastian in the side. "You're drooling, dude."

"Can you blame me?" Sebastian whispered back.

"No, actually," R.J. said, in a normal voice, and clapped when the Venom's goalie made a fantastic save at the other end of the ice.

R.J. and Tabby hit it off like a house on fire, and between the two of them—literally, as that was where he was sitting—Sebastian found he could easily follow the game and ask questions when he needed. Tabby's hockey knowledge was off the charts, and she also dropped some interesting tidbits about the other players and generally kept them entertained when there were stoppages.

Sebastian had to admit it was fun to see the Venom score a goal, as the whole arena went nuts and jumped up to cheer. It was also Daniel Bellamy who put up the first goal of the Venom's new season, and it was cute to watch Bellamy's kids clapping so enthusiastically for their dad.

"They used to cry when we lost games," Tabby said, in an aside to Sebastian. She giggled. "Daniel always said he didn't mind, because he had to do press interviews about what went wrong, so it's like the kids were doing it for him. They did cry after the Venom lost in the playoffs. Hell, so did Daniel. So did *I*."

Sebastian had grown up in a culture that said men shouldn't cry about anything, but he certainly didn't hold to such an outdated belief of masculinity. He just wasn't sure he could care enough about a sporting event to cry over the outcome, though admittedly that was before he met Tristan. Maybe, if they were to stay together…

Not the time to think about that. Sebastian turned his attention back to the game, though at some point he had to admit he was mainly watching Tristan to the exclusion of everyone else. And Tristan, as a defenseman, spent a lot of minutes on the ice. During the first intermission, Sebastian and R.J. went to get a beer and wander around the stadium a bit.

R.J. went to buy a Venom hat, and tried to talk Sebastian into buying a Holt jersey, of which there were more than a few. "I guess you could get him to give you one."

"I'm not sure I want one he's worn while playing," Sebastian said, as they waited in line. "Besides, it would be too big on me."

"Aw." R.J. grinned at him. "That's cute, Seb."

Sebastian ignored him, and they went back to their seats with fresh beers and a hot pretzel, R.J.'s new hat perched on his head. Sebastian wondered if he should have gotten a shirt like Tabby's with Tristan's name and number, thinking to himself how funny it was to see a bunch of straight men walking around with other men's names on their backs. It made him grin to think about, and he settled into his chair and sipped his beer as the second period started.

The game moved fast, and Sebastian enjoyed the second period the most, since Tristan was active defending the Venom's goal. A few times Tristan checked a player into the glass and got a resounding cheer from the fans, Sebastian among them. There was something sexy about watching Tristan do that—muscle his way in and take the puck, knock other players away from it and use his stick to mess up their plays. Tristan was aggressive in a way that Sebastian wasn't used to, at least when it came to sex, and it made a lot of sense why Tristan liked Sebastian to take control in the bedroom.

By the time the game ended in a Venom win, Sebastian wanted nothing more than to throw Tristan down and fuck him—hell, he wouldn't even have to take off the uniform. Or maybe he would; Sebastian wasn't exactly sure how that worked, but he knew he'd be more than happy to find out. He stood and clapped with the others as the Venom players all skated to center ice and saluted their fans with their sticks. Sebastian and R.J. stuck around long enough to hear the "three stars" of the game, and then they made their way toward the exit.

"That was *great*," R.J. enthused, as they moved along with the crowd. "Feel free to keep bringing me along, okay?"

"Maybe everyone will think *we're* dating," Sebastian pointed out, politely stepping back to let an elderly woman walk ahead of him.

"Dude, I don't care about that and you know it." He grinned. "I bet you could find more than a few guys who wouldn't care, either, if it meant they could score those seats every game."

Sebastian rolled his eyes at his friend, checking his phone as they emerged into the night air. It was October, but that meant the days were still warm in Atlanta, a contrast to the chilly arena. Sebastian got a text message from Tristan as he was walking toward his car, which read, Hope you could follow along :)

Smiling, Sebastian texted back, I had some help but thanks. Good game.

"Dude," R.J. said. "You seriously are smitten, Cruz. I didn't even know you could smile like that."

Sebastian was horrified to feel his face heat and hoped the parking lot lighting was too dark for R.J. to notice his flush. "Maybe that was my mom."

"It totally wasn't your mom. Hey, you know, it's cool that you like him so much." R.J. tugged on the brim of his cap. "And not because it means I get free hockey tickets. It's good to see you have things to do other than scowl and run marathons."

"If you want any more of those free tickets, stop talking," said Sebastian, and he bid R.J. farewell as he found his car. After the cursory inspection to make sure there were no dints or dings on his precious GTO, Sebastian got in and patiently maneuvered his way out of the post-game traffic. As he waited to merge onto the highway, his phone notified him of an incoming message from Tristan: I'm done here in a few. You want some company?

Sebastian texted back, I want you on your back as soon as possible, to which Tristan responded with a winking-face emoticon.

On the way home, Sebastian cranked up the music and did his best not to dwell on the things he didn't want to think about—namely, how he hated pretending Tristan was just his "friend" even though he wasn't sure he had the right to think of Tristan as anything else—and instead replayed all those checks Tristan threw, how fiercely he'd played, and okay, fine, that stick tap before the game started. By the time he got home, he was half-hard and ready to do exactly as he'd said and put Tristan on his back—or against the door.

Tristan showed up about twenty minutes after Sebastian got home, and when Sebastian opened the door, his mouth went dry. Tristan wasn't wearing his uniform—obviously—but he wasn't wearing the sweatpants and T-shirt Sebastian had expected. Instead, he was in a suit tailored to his muscular frame, the tie undone and the shirt unbuttoned at the collar.

"Jesus," Sebastian muttered, pulling him in and shutting the door by pushing Tristan back against it. "I was not prepared for you in a suit."

"Surprise?" Tristan's face was flushed, pupils dilated, and he seemed to have no problem with the way Sebastian was shoving him around and getting up in his space.

"It drives me crazy how you make everything look good." Sebastian kissed him hotly, hands running over Tristan's chest and the firm muscles of his abdomen beneath the dress shirt.

"You—ah—you liked the game, then?" Tristan panted against Sebastian's mouth, trying to shrug out of his suit jacket and kiss Sebastian at the same time.

Sebastian didn't answer, only reached down to get Tristan's belt undone. He'd show Tristan just how much he'd enjoyed the game. They could talk about it later.

Later became the next morning. Sebastian woke up way too early for how late they'd been up, gave up trying to fall back asleep—Tristan took up way too much of the bed, and had the same heat setting as a blast furnace—and decided to go for an early-morning run. He'd already showered and was making breakfast when Tristan ambled out of the bedroom, wearing nothing but his boxer briefs.

That was distracting, but Sebastian had come to the realization while on his run that they were going to need to talk.

"Morning." Tristan yawned, stretching. "Sorry I slept so late."

"You were up late," Sebastian reminded him, pouring some egg whites into a skillet.

"So were you," Tristan pointed out, taking a seat at the island on one of the barstools. "And you're up and making breakfast. And you went running, huh? Don't lie."

"I did. But I also didn't play an exhausting game of hockey for sixty minutes." Sebastian went to get a bottle of water from the fridge. "And I'm older than you."

"Mmm. But you did fuck me like you were playing hockey." Tristan smiled crookedly, taking the bottle of water Sebastian handed him and downing it. "Thanks. What's for breakfast?"

"Egg-white omelet, some wheat toast, and juice. There's coffee if you want some." Sebastian gestured to the Keurig.

"Water's fine," said Tristan. "And that sounds good. I usually have a protein shake."

Sebastian made a face. "There's barely anything with nutrients in that," he chastised gently, sliding the omelet on a plate. He slid it over to Tristan, who was done with it before Sebastian even had the bread in the toaster.

"Sorry, hey, you make a good disgustingly healthy omelet," Tristan said, grinning at him. "I wouldn't say no to another one."

Sebastian made the toast and made another—more

substantial—omelet for Tristan, with whole eggs instead of only the egg whites. Sebastian's own light breakfast was probably nowhere near enough calories for someone who'd engaged in the level of physical activity that Tristan did.

They talked a bit about the game as Sebastian finished up cooking and they both ate breakfast, and Tristan went to clean up but Sebastian stopped him with a wave. "I have to talk to you about something, so let them be for a minute."

Tristan's easy, morning-after smile seemed to dim a little at that. "It'll drive you crazy if they're not done. I'll make it quick, then we can talk."

True. And Tristan knowing that about Sebastian was the reason they were going to have to talk. They finished the dishes in a relatively short time, and then Tristan sat back at the island with a cup of coffee and said, "Okay, what's up?"

"I— Last night at the game," Sebastian started, thinking about how to say what he wanted. He'd thought about it on his morning run, but it was harder with Tristan sitting here across from him, all wide blue eyes and open, honest expression. "Tabby Bellamy asked me who I was there to see, so I said you were a friend of mine."

"Okay," Tristan said, slowly.

"Is that what we are?" Sebastian asked, palms braced on the slick surface of the island.

Tristan's hands were wrapped around the coffee mug, which seemed dwarfed by them. "Y-yeah? I mean, obviously you're my friend."

"Let me rephrase that." Sebastian took a deep breath and waited for Tristan to meet his eyes. "Is that *all* we are? Because of course we're friends, but Tristan, if that's all you want from this, then I think I need to know that sooner rather than later." He raked a hand through his hair. "I like you," he said, simply. "And I don't know what you want, but if you want this to be an exclusive relationship, I have to let you know, now, that I'm not sure how long I'm going to be comfortable saying that all we are is *friends*."

Tristan stared down at his coffee, shoulders slightly hunched. He seemed to be thinking, so Sebastian remained quiet and let him. Eventually he raised his head and met Sebastian's gaze. "In my mind, we've been dating. I don't do casual, not really. I rarely hook up on the road, and I—I want to be with you. I like you too. A lot. And I know how you feel about that, but Sebastian, I'm…not ready to come out. It's not that I don't want to, exactly, it's that…well, there's no out gay player in the NHL, and I'm not sure I want to be the first one."

Sebastian nodded. "I realize it's not the same for you and that there's more to consider. I'm not trying to pressure you, Tristan. But I'm not going to be comfortable being in the closet for anyone, especially if it's a serious committed relationship."

Tristan nodded. "I do get it. I just don't know what to say. I want to see where this thing with us goes, Sebastian, but if you're not…if it's not something you can accept, I'll understand." His mouth twisted wryly. "I won't like it, but I'll understand."

The smart thing to do would probably be to let Tristan finish his coffee, give him a kiss good-bye, and send him on his way with the T-shirt he'd left that was currently in Sebastian's laundry basket. But he hated the idea of ending something before it'd barely gotten started, and besides, it wasn't fair of him to pressure Tristan or ask for him to make such a monumental life decision based on the couple of months they'd been together. "I want to see where it goes too," Sebastian said gruffly. "And I'm willing to accept that you are in a place where you can't be out, but I also need *you* to know that if things get more serious, it means having this conversation again."

Tristan pushed back from the island and stood up. "I hear you. I do. I know how much being out means to you and believe me, I admire you for it. I want to be, it's just…"

"It's not that easy," Sebastian finished for him. "I know. I think we're on the same page, and honestly, that's why I brought this up."

Tristan came around the island so they were standing face-to-face. "Thanks. For bringing it up. It's good to know that you do that. Bring things up." Tristan's fair skin flushed. "Uh, sorry. I'm bad at talking about relationships. I think. I've never really had to do it before."

"Don't worry. I'm good at talking enough for the both of us." Sebastian let his eyes run over Tristan's body, finally focusing on how he was wearing a pair of boxer briefs and nothing else.

"I gotta bring something to this relationship besides the free hockey tickets," Tristan joked, and leaned down to kiss him.

Sebastian drew his fingers along the cock slowly beginning to tent out Tristan's briefs. "Oh, trust me, you bring a lot."

Tristan huffed a laugh against his mouth. "More than you can handle, Professor?"

Sebastian bit his lower lip. "You wish. Let's go work

off those omelets." He gave Tristan's ass a smack, and smiled at Tristan's sudden indrawn breath.

There might be a time when they needed to make some hard decisions, but it wasn't now.

Chapter Fourteen

"Hey, guys! Who's ready to work out with me?"

Tristan grinned at the group of children clustered around him as a bunch of short arms shot up. He was in the gymnasium of a local Atlanta junior high, along with Ryu and Bellzie, as part of the Venom's HeartSmart Program, which promoted fitness and healthy eating. Tristan's contract obligated him to participate in a few of these charity activities every season, but unlike some of his teammates, who grumbled when it was their turn, he actually looked forward to participating. He enjoyed being out in the community, doing something tangible to make a difference, and the kids always seemed so excited. He couldn't help but get caught up in their enthusiasm.

Tristan clapped his hands. "You kids on the left, spread out a bit. We're going to do some basic exercises—jumping jacks, push-ups, sit-ups, stuff like that. The others are going to run through the obstacle course with Ryu and Bellzie. But don't worry, okay? We'll switch in half an hour so everyone gets a turn. After that, we're all going to sit down and talk about the importance of nutrition and staying in shape. Sound good?"

After a chorus of "Yeahs," Tristan nodded at Ryu,

who had a strained expression on his face. Bellzie, on the other hand, smiled broadly, his hair a mess of brown curls and his blue eyes sparkling.

The smile might have surprised people who only knew Daniel Bellamy as the hard-nosed hockey player who always stepped up for his teammates and never backed down from a fight, but outside of the rink, Tristan knew him to be unfailingly kind. He always volunteered for outreach programs involving children, he owned a nonprofit, no-kill animal shelter, and he even rescued homeless cats and dogs in his spare time. *Literally* rescued— driving or flying around the country to help transport them to new homes. He'd also founded an organization, Pucks and Paws, with his equally lovely wife to help with the cause.

Sometimes Tristan could barely believe Bellzie was a real person who actually existed. If it hadn't been for Tabby, Bellzie's beautiful—and ridiculously sweet and genuine—wife, Tristan probably would've fallen in love with him years ago.

As it was, Tristan still nursed a bit of a crush and perhaps a lingering case of hero worship. Not that he'd ever admit it to anyone.

"Come on. I bet you guys can fly through this thing." Bellzie waved the kids over to the obstacle course the three of them had set up earlier with Venom-donated equipment. "Who thinks they can beat my time?" There were a few "Me's," and Bellzie laughed. "Oh, is that so?"

A couple of kids replied, and he grinned, interacting easily with the group as they walked. Ryu trailed awkwardly behind. He looked so stilted and uncomfortable as one of the preteens tried to engage him in conversation that Tristan wanted to laugh.

Instead, he turned back to his own group. A dozen sets of eyes stared at him expectantly.

"Okay, guys. Let's start with twenty-five jumping jacks! Katrina, why don't you count them out for us?"

The little blonde girl smiled and nodded eagerly.

After a few minutes, they moved on to push-ups. Tristan demonstrated some alternatives to make the push-ups easier and more child friendly, then spent the rest of the time offering encouragement and correcting their forms as needed.

By the time they left the school, he'd worked up a surprising amount of sweat. Compared to the stuffiness of the gym and the collective odor of a few dozen perspiring preteens, the fresh breeze and low-sixties weather felt like stepping into paradise—or maybe onto a freshly pressed sheet of ice.

Tristan sighed in appreciation as the wind cooled the drying moisture at the base of his spine. Despite the steadily declining temperatures as late November approached, for a native Wisconsinite like himself, it might as well have been summer. He couldn't say he missed the brisk autumns or brutal winters of home.

"Thank fuck that's over with," Ryu said as they crossed the parking lot to their cars.

Bellzie laughed. "I thought you were going to break into hives when that one boy hugged you."

Ryu shuddered. "There should be a 'don't touch the hockey players' disclaimer before we're forced to engage with them."

"What are you going to do if they ignore that rule?" Tristan asked with a grin. "Cross-check them?"

"I wish," Ryu muttered under his breath.

Bellzie clapped him on the back. "You'll survive the cooties, Ryu. Take a shower when you get home."

"Oh, I intend to."

Bellzie stopped next to his hybrid Lexus SUV. Because of course he'd drive an eco-conscious vehicle. "Sorry to skip out on lunch," he said as he withdrew his keys from his pocket. "Tabby and I are taking the kids to a birthday party. Rain check?"

Tristan nodded. "Sure, Bellzie. See you tomorrow." He turned to Ryu as Bellzie started his car. "Thai?"

"Yep. Meet you there."

It was a week before Thanksgiving when Tristan realized he wouldn't be able to go home for the holiday. The Venom had a game the night before and then a matinee on Black Friday. He'd spend a few hundred on a flight and then have to leave immediately after dinner. If he was lucky, he might be in Wisconsin for a grand total of twenty-four hours. As much as he wanted to spend the time with his family—and he did, after not having seen them in months—it seemed more logical to save the trip for the Christmas break when he'd be able to stay for a few days. But that meant he'd have to make other plans. He didn't want to spend the day alone is his apartment with a frozen dinner instead of homemade turkey and stuffing.

"What are you doing for Thanksgiving?" he asked Sebastian over dinner that night. They were at Sebastian's favorite Puerto Rican restaurant in Marietta, which he'd introduced Tristan to on a date last month.

Sebastian looked up from his plate of rice and bacalao. Thanks to the menu, Tristan knew that meant codfish. Tristan had ordered the roasted pork shoulder and extra tostones—crunchy, salty fried plantains that he wished he could eat by the dozen.

"Nothing special," Sebastian said. "Grading papers."

"You won't be going to visit your family?"

Sebastian shook his head and gestured vaguely with his hand. "I spoke to my mother earlier this month, and she told me they were going to spend a few weeks in Puerto Rico with her cousins. Honestly, I'm not sure I would have gone back anyway. My father never quite manages to hide his disappointment, and my mother continually invites her friends' daughters over to shove them in my face."

Tristan winced. His mom asked about his love life, but she at least never tried to set him up with random women. "But she knows you're gay."

Sebastian sighed. "Yes. Hope springs eternal. She also laments her lack of grandchildren. Loudly and often. Puerto Rican mothers do enjoy a good guilt trip."

Tristan chuckled. "Isn't that all moms, though? Mine does it too."

Sebastian's mouth quirked up at the corner. "I suppose so. Are you going to your parents'?"

"No. That's why I asked, actually. It's not feasible because of the schedule." Tristan scooped some rice onto a plantain and popped it in his mouth. "We should do something together," he added once he swallowed. "Neither of us can cook, but I'm sure we can buy something to throw in the oven. One of those prepared packages that comes with stuffing and cranberry sauce and all that."

"I like that idea," Sebastian said with a slight smile. "As long as you don't plan to make me watch football."

Tristan scoffed. "Of course not. There are hockey games that day too."

* * *

The packaged-dinner idea ended up being a stroke of ge-
nius on Tristan's part. Everything came precooked with
instructions for reheating, and it was pretty much impossible to screw up, even for a pair of guys who weren't
exactly proficient in the kitchen.

Tristan ate way too much turkey and devoured almost half of a surprisingly good pumpkin pie before
slumping onto the couch in Sebastian's living room. He
groaned when he saw the score on the television screen.
The Memphis Marauders were destroying the Miami
Thunder, which pissed Tristan off because the Marauders had taken the Venom out of the playoffs last season.
Plus, he actually liked the Thunder. Unlike the shithead
Marauders, they weren't a group of raging assholes who
dove and threw dirty hits.

Tristan's irritation added to the day's melancholy
tone—or at least it felt that way to him. He'd been slightly
off all afternoon, missing his family, though he tried to
ignore the feeling and focus on his boyfriend and sharing
their first holiday together. Sebastian seemed relaxed and
happy to have Tristan there. It should've been enough.

Annoyed at himself, Tristan left Sebastian to his paper
grading and went to the kitchen to load the dishwasher.
He'd just finished pouring in the detergent and starting the cycle when he noticed his phone buzzing on the
counter.

Tristan snatched it up, and the name on the screen
brought an automatic smile to his face. "Hi, Mom."

"Hi, sweetie. Happy Thanksgiving! How did your
food come out? Did you and your friend enjoy it?"

"Happy Thanksgiving. It was fine. I didn't burn anything, so there's that."

His mother laughed. "We missed you today. Your father and Brian are watching football. Well, Brian is. Your father is snoring in his La-Z-Boy."

Tristan could perfectly envision the picture she'd described, and it set off a pang in his chest. "I miss you guys too. I would've come up if not for the game tomorrow."

"It's okay, honey. We'll see you at Christmas. It's not like you control the schedule, and it doesn't make sense for you to spend all that money to be here for one day. We understand."

"How's everyone? What's Hannah up to?"

"She's right here, waving for me to give her the phone. You have a good night. I'll talk to you soon. Love you."

His mother passed the phone to his sister, and Tristan spent a few minutes listening to her talk about her classes and the guy she'd been seeing since the Homecoming dance. He eventually got handed off to Brian and then his groggy-sounding father.

Tristan ended the call after another half an hour. The ache in his chest had intensified until it felt stifling, and he had to take a few breaths before he could rejoin Sebastian in the living room. He slumped onto the couch next to Sebastian, who glanced up from his laptop and gave Tristan a long, considering look.

"What's wrong?" Sebastian asked.

Tristan shrugged one shoulder, grumbling something indistinct. He didn't want to bitch to Sebastian about missing his family when Sebastian's parents hadn't even bothered calling him and probably would've made him feel like a disappointment if they had.

Sebastian set his laptop on the coffee table and turned to give Tristan his full attention. "Come here."

Tristan wasn't really in the mood for much of anything aside from lazing on the couch, but he couldn't resist the command in Sebastian's tone. He slid a few inches closer, and Sebastian cupped his nape, giving it a light squeeze.

"Here." Sebastian looked pointedly at his own lap.

Tristan stared for a moment, his heartbeat stalling before kicking into overdrive. Sebastian tugged on his nape, and Tristan took in a shuddery breath and allowed himself to be maneuvered until he was draped across Sebastian's wiry thighs.

Sebastian pulled down Tristan's sweatpants until the waistband rested around his knees. The jock left his ass bare, and as the cool air hit his skin, Tristan shivered, his cock stiffening.

"So fucking perfect," Sebastian said, almost idly. "I think it's time I tan these cheeks, don't you? Put my mark all over them."

Tristan moaned quietly, his dick going from half-interested to fully hard in a matter of seconds. "Yes. *Please.*"

"Tell me if you need me to stop."

That was his only warning before Sebastian began to spank him—quick, light taps at first. A warm-up.

Tristan squirmed, torn between embarrassment and arousal. He'd never been in this position before, not even as a child. His parents didn't believe in corporal punishment. His father had never, ever put Tristan over his knee.

Partially it was humiliating. Tristan couldn't imagine what his teammates would say if they could see him right now, in the middle of the living room with his sweatpants around his knees, being spanked by his boyfriend like a naughty little kid. The thought made Tristan flush and wriggle even more.

And yet…it also thrilled him, the idea of them finding out, of them seeing, *knowing*. As long as it was something that only happened in his head, it turned Tristan on to picture how they'd react.

Sebastian delivered a sharper slap, and Tristan jumped and yelped. Heat diffused through his ass cheek afterward, making his cock flex against Sebastian's thigh. He groaned, swiveling his hips.

Sebastian hit him again, harder. He didn't focus on one particular spot but spread the blows evenly across Tristan's ass, on his upper thighs, and even the sensitive crease where they met.

Tristan knew he was making noise, maybe even babbling. The words themselves were meaningless. All that mattered was the sensation—the heat, the pain that somehow morphed to pleasure, the resounding crack of a palm against his skin.

For a while, Tristan lost himself.

When awareness returned, Tristan had tears streaming down his face, though he couldn't remember when he'd started crying. Sebastian was gently stroking his back, murmuring softly, nonsense Tristan couldn't comprehend. His ass fucking *burned*, and even Sebastian's palm felt hot as it coasted along Tristan's spine. In spite of the waterworks, his cock was still rock-hard and slippery from sweat and the pre-come he'd been leaking on Sebastian's denim-covered thigh, but Tristan didn't feel inclined to try to do anything about it right then.

He let Sebastian soothe him, and basked in the attention. Eventually Sebastian led him to the bedroom, where he made Tristan lie facedown on the bed, and rubbed some sort of cream on his ass that instantly eased some of the stinging.

"You should be fine by morning," Sebastian said. "I don't think there'll be anything for your teammates to wonder about. I'll go harder next time, if you want, when you have a few days off."

Tristan could only respond with a hum. He drifted in a dreamy haze as Sebastian went back out to the living room to turn off the TV and prepare for bed. He didn't stir until Sebastian joined him and caressed the side of his face.

"Are you okay?" Sebastian asked, his eyes dark and fond. "Want to tell me what's wrong?"

Tristan turned his head and pressed a kiss to Sebastian's palm. It took a moment to order his thoughts so he could put them into a coherent sentence. "I… I dunno. I was being a baby, I guess. This is the first time I wasn't able to go home for Thanksgiving. Like, ever. It didn't make sense to go when everything would be rushed, you know? I didn't think it would affect me so much, but then I talked to them, and…"

"I understand."

"I'm sorry," Tristan said. "I didn't mean to spoil your night."

"You didn't spoil anything." Sebastian stroked his cheek again. "Did you like what we did? I thought it might be a good distraction."

Tristan fought the urge to bury his face in the pillow. Instead, he met Sebastian's gaze directly. He didn't really want to have a discussion about being spanked—couldn't they just do it and *not* talk about it?—but it was probably necessary. "Yeah. I loved it."

"It wasn't too much?"

"Not at all." Tristan nuzzled Sebastian's palm. "I'll

stop you if it ever gets to be too much, or if I'm not in the mood. I promise."

"Okay. Good." Sebastian kissed him lightly. "Sleep now."

Surrounded by Sebastian's scent, with his arm a strong, comforting presence around Tristan's waist, it was easy to obey.

Chapter Fifteen

"Tonight's game between the Atlanta Venom and the St. Louis Spirit is going to be entertaining," the announcer enthused. "Atlanta's a young defensive team known for their heavy forecheck. The Spirit bring a lot of speed and a potent offense, and this should be a heck of a good matchup."

The Fox Sports South music started playing, and Sebastian took the beer the bartender put in front of him with a faint nod of thanks. He was idly watching the fifteenth car commercial in a row when R.J. slid into the seat beside him at the bar, clapping him enthusiastically on the back. "Hey, man. How's it going?"

Like Sebastian, R.J.'s only concession to the early winter weather in Atlanta was a zip-up hoodie. R.J. was from Chicago, and also like Sebastian, enjoyed—and mocked—the South's version of winter.

Sebastian's response was a slight smile and a raise of his beer. "Can't complain."

R.J. grinned and ordered his own beer, and they chatted about the end of the semester and the flurry of activity that went along with it—grades, faculty meetings, the obligatory parties neither of them wanted to attend. The talk gradually died down as the game started, and Sebastian's attention strayed to the large television mounted above the bar.

"How's being a hockey boyfriend going?" R.J. asked, nudging him.

"It's fine," Sebastian answered, wincing as the Spirit scored two minutes into the game off a bad defensive turnover. His eyes narrowed as he heard a low grumble from the assembled patrons who were also watching the game. He'd heard that this place, the Blue Line, was the only dedicated hockey bar in Atlanta. He tended to watch Tristan's away games at home while grading, but as their relationship progressed, it was quickly becoming apparent that he couldn't do that anymore. His students weren't getting his full attention, for one. For another, he tended to pace.

R.J. was giving him a look, so Sebastian rolled his eyes and said, "Fine, it's… I've never been a sports person, especially team sports. So I'm not used to caring about the outcome of a game."

"I—"

Before R.J. could finish, the crowd in the bar suddenly started cheering as the Venom captain, Daniel Bellamy, flew down the ice on a breakaway and scored. Sebastian wasn't the cheering type, but he did half rise off his barstool in solidarity with the excited crowd.

"You being a hockey fan is my new favorite thing," said R.J., who'd not only stood up and cheered when the Venom scored, he'd given a high five to the bartender.

"It's stressful," Sebastian admitted, as they watched the game. "There's a lot of ways Tristan could get injured on the ice. None of them are pretty."

"Want me to tell you the statistical likelihood of him

sustaining anything more serious than a broken tooth
or a bloody lip?"

"No, I absolutely do not want you to tell me that,"
Sebastian said, firmly. He finished his beer and nodded
when the bartender asked him if he wanted another one.

The game stayed tied at one-one for most of the first
period, but with two seconds left on the clock, one of
the Spirit forwards slipped the puck behind the goalie
and gave the home team a two-one advantage. There
were some good-natured groans from the crowd, but
not too many.

That all changed in the second period, though. For
whatever reason, the Venom weren't able to counter the
Spirit's last-second goal and found themselves giving
up another in the first five minutes. That turned into a
three-goal deficit ninety seconds later, and Sebastian
winced visibly as the Spirit's goal horn sounded and the
hometown crowd cheered on the television.

They were the only ones cheering. The atmosphere
in the Blue Line was a lot different, with groans and a
few muttered curses filling the air.

"So you're learning that being a sports fan will only
bring you heartache and pain." R.J. sipped his second
beer. "I think only chicken wings will solve this pain.
Want to split some?"

Sebastian was too tense to eat anything, which made
him feel ridiculous. It was a regular season game, and it
wasn't like he hadn't seen the Venom lose before. He'd
been to games where they'd lost, both close games and
ones like this, where the opponent's lead seemed insur-
mountable.

"You need practice before the playoffs," R.J. said
wisely. He patted Sebastian on the arm. "It's a good thing

you have me, your hockey guru. All I ask is some sweet tickets for all the playoff games and when the Venom make the finals."

"They're not going to make the first fucking round if they don't fix their fucking defense," the bartender muttered, wiping at the counter in front of Sebastian like it would effectively erase the Spirit's lead.

Sebastian frowned but didn't say anything. He had to remind himself not everyone was dating a member of said defense. To most people, this was just a game, and they didn't have the same level of investment he did.

At least, that was what he thought before the Spirit scored *again*.

"Goddamn it, Holt," one of the patrons behind him yelled. "That was the third goddamn turnover that was your fucking fault."

"Holt's having a three-point game for the other team," grumbled another.

Sebastian jolted as he felt an elbow in his side.

"Your death glare isn't helping," R.J. said with a pointed look. "This is how hockey fans *are*."

"Irrational?" Sebastian asked, annoyed.

R.J. nodded. "Yeah," he said, completely serious. "People live and die with their team, man. It's just how it is."

"Fucking Holt. Send his ass back to the minors," said the guy sitting a few seats down from Sebastian.

"That wasn't his fault," Sebastian snapped, barely aware of what he was saying before the words were out of his mouth.

"Yeah?" the guy asked, turning toward him with an aggressive glare. "Whose was it? The officials? The puck? The other team? We're paying that kid a lot of money for him to fuck up so much."

"Maybe they'll trade him somewhere for some goddamn offense," the bartender groused.

"If the rest of the team did their jobs, it would help." Sebastian couldn't believe he was saying these things out loud. He still barely *understood* the rest of the team's job, but all he knew was that there *was* a team. Tristan was not responsible for the outcome of an entire game and the idea that he would be was ridiculous.

When the Spirit scored yet another goal, R.J. clapped him on the shoulder. "Dude, I think we gotta go. I'll pick up the check and you can repay me in tickets." He cleared his throat. "When they get these defensive issues sorted out."

"Oh, don't *you* start," Sebastian growled, standing up and shrugging into his hoodie. Despite R.J.'s offer, he got some cash out of his wallet and tried to figure out, in his head, the amount of his bill.

"Twelve bucks should cover it, with tip," said R.J., helpfully. Sometimes having a math wizard for a friend was a good idea. "How about next time, you come over to my place with a six-pack and I'll cook. I think that might be safer for everyone."

"I wasn't going to do anything," Sebastian protested. They headed out of the bar, but as they did so, the assembled patrons gave a half-hearted cheer. Sebastian's phone buzzed in his pocket. The NHL app, alerting him to a scoring change. He paused.

"Stats don't lie, friend." R.J. grabbed the door and hustled him outside into the chilly weather. "This one's a lost cause. Need a lift home?"

Sebastian shook his head. "I only had two beers. But

thanks for meeting me." He smiled wryly. "Next time, you're right. I'll take you up on that offer of hanging out at your place."

"Poor Tris. Tell him—"

"R.J.," Sebastian interrupted him. "I'm not telling him anything having to do with hockey."

Undaunted, R.J. grinned and waved, heading off to his car. By the time Sebastian arrived home, his phone had gone off twice—once more for a Venom goal, and then another for the Spirit. The score was now seven-three in favor of the Spirit. The app informed him that there'd been a goalie change for the Venom, but it didn't stop the Spirit from scoring yet another goal in the third.

The final score was eight-three. Sebastian made himself watch the end of the game, standing in front of the television with his arms crossed over his chest and scowling. His brand-new DVR box blinked merrily as he watched his boyfriend's defeated team head down the tunnel when it was finally over. He'd opted in to Direct TV just to catch Tristan's games, which made him feel a little ridiculous. Sometimes if Tristan had an off night, he'd put other teams' games on if he was over. If someone would have told him last year how much hockey he'd be watching, he would have laughed.

His father had always been a baseball fan, but Sebastian found baseball boring as fuck. Some of the guys were hot, but that was about the extent of his interest. Games had never made him nervous, even when the Yankees had been in the World Series when he was a teenager.

About an hour after the game, Sebastian's phone delivered a message from Tristan that only said, *Ugh.*

He'd learned how to deal with Tristan in a bad mood. He wrote back, I'll make you forget it next time I see you.

If Coach doesn't send me to Macon after that game, came Tristan's response. It was somehow morose even over text. Sebastian didn't know what to say after that. He could usually tell when Tristan was in the mood for some sexting and when he wasn't. It was definitely the latter in this situation.

Sexting. Something *else* Sebastian wouldn't have seen himself doing a year ago.

It was a Friday night, and the only thing he had planned was to go to bed at a reasonable hour and get up and go for a run. It was a shame Tristan wasn't in the mood for some phone sex, because Sebastian would have enjoyed the opportunity to cheer him up.

He settled back in his bed, idly stroking his cock through his pajama pants as he thought about Tristan and spanking his bad mood out of him like he'd done at Thanksgiving. That had been intense, and he'd worried it was too much, but it had seemed to do the trick in pulling Tristan out of his funk. He hated seeing Tristan's eyes dim and shadowed.

Scowling, Sebastian made himself think about smacking Tristan's firm ass, not about his sad eyes. But the recriminations of the other hockey fans were hard to get out of his head, and finally Sebastian gave up and checked his phone again. No message from Tristan, but he was probably headed home and would go straight to bed. Sebastian would contact him tomorrow when he'd had a chance to sleep and rest, and then see about making him forget that game.

He was settling in to read a bit when there was a knock

at his door, which was accompanied by a text message that said, Hey if you're up can I come in?

Tristan.

It was a little after midnight, which meant Tristan must have come straight over from the airport. He padded to the door and opened it to reveal Tristan, a Venom duffel slung over his shoulder. He was dressed in his suit, but sans tie, and his shirt was unbuttoned. He looked tired. "Hey."

Sebastian moved aside so he could come in. "Hi."

"I hope you don't mind that I came over." Tristan dropped his bag in the hallway and pushed the door closed with his foot. "Tonight sucked."

"I watched the game," Sebastian said, then wondered if maybe he shouldn't have. It made Tristan's face fall and his broad shoulders tighten and droop at the same time.

"I sucked."

"Seemed like a game when no one was playing their best." Was that the right thing to say? Tristan had been bummed after a loss before, but not quite like this. He'd never come over right after an away game trip, either.

"I— Um—" Tristan gave him a slight smile, but it was a poor shade of his usual grin "—could use a hug."

"Of course." Sebastian stepped forward and pulled him into an embrace, tightening his arms. "I'm sorry it didn't go well."

"Thanks." Tristan's sigh echoed through his entire body, pressed up against Sebastian's. "I know it's stupid to blame everything on myself, but… I'm kind of blaming it all on myself." He drew back and gave Sebastian a searching look.

Sebastian knew that look. It meant Tristan needed something to get him out of his head, and Sebastian might not know what to *say*, exactly, but he had a good idea of what might work.

"I want you to do it when the moment feels right."

"Come with me." Sebastian took his hand and led him toward the bedroom. "Leave your bag there."

"I should—"

"Don't talk unless I ask you a question," Sebastian interrupted, giving Tristan a glare he knew Tristan would respond to. Sure enough, his fair skin flushed and Tristan nodded, glancing down at the floor.

"Look at me," Sebastian ordered softly, and Tristan raised his head and met Sebastian's eyes. The need on his face was so intense it made Sebastian's cock harden in seconds. "I'm going to take care of you. All right?"

Some of the tension seemed to ease in Tristan's stance—not a lot, but some. He nodded again, and Sebastian tugged him in and kissed him gently on the mouth. "Good." With that, he dropped Tristan's hand and headed to the bedroom, expecting that Tristan would follow.

He did. Sebastian's room was lit only by the bedside lamp, and he went over and flipped on the overhead light. Blinking, Tristan glanced at him curiously.

Sebastian wanted the bright light to not only keep Tristan awake and focused, but also to make him feel exposed, on display. Put the attention on him again, but this time, it would be for something good. Sebastian didn't bother to share any of those reasons with Tristan. It was enough that he wanted it that way.

"Strip," said Sebastian. "I don't want a show. I want you naked, fast. But keep everything tidy."

Tristan shrugged out of his jacket and draped it over the chair by the window. He followed it up with his dress shirt and his undershirt, folding them and placing them on the edge of Sebastian's dresser. Then he sat on the chair to take off his shoes and socks, which he pushed neatly out of the way. His fingers went to his belt to undo his pants. While he was undressing methodically and definitely wasn't doing it to be sexy, Sebastian was still enjoying watching as Tristan bared that gorgeous body of his.

Tristan's fingers paused at the waistband of his boxer briefs, and he raised his eyebrows in question.

"I said naked, didn't I?" Sebastian kept his voice cool and even. His erection was probably obvious in his pajama pants, but he couldn't help that. He didn't want to, either. He wanted Tristan to know how much this turned him on. How much *Tristan* turned him on. "You remember to say stop if something gets too intense, all right? You can answer me."

"Yeah. I remember. I will." Tristan stepped out of his boxer briefs and turned to put them on the dresser, giving Sebastian a mouth-watering view of his ass. Remembering how it felt to spank that ass made Sebastian's cock even harder.

"Come over here and kneel on the bed. Put your hands behind your back." Sebastian didn't have a plan, per se, but he had a good idea of what to do to bring Tristan out of his head.

Once Tristan was kneeling, Sebastian stared at him and made him wait. Made him feel exposed under the harsh lights, waiting for whatever Sebastian told him to do next.

He finally moved so he was standing in front of Tristan. Luckily, Sebastian's bed was relatively low to the ground, or this might not work given how tall Tristan was. As it was, he still had to stretch a little to get a good grip in Tristan's hair. "What's the matter? Tell me."

"I—" Tristan swallowed, hard. "I fucked up, and my team was humiliated on the ice."

Sebastian held his head still and slapped him across the face. It wasn't particularly hard, but that wasn't the point of this. Tristan's skin mottled immediately from the contact, though, which was both arousing and concerning. Sebastian drew his fingers over the reddened skin, and he heard Tristan's quick indrawn breath at the contrast.

"Why was that your fault?" He pulled a little harder on Tristan's hair. "Tell me."

"I didn't do what I was supposed to." Tristan's eyes were very wide. "I'm supposed to defend the puck, not give it up to the other team so they can score."

Sebastian smacked him again. Tristan made a sound, and glancing down, Sebastian saw Tristan's cock begin to harden. He smiled inwardly. Good. "You had a bad game. You didn't play as well as you could have. Neither did the rest of your team."

"But I—"

Sebastian smacked him again, a bit harder this time. Tristan's breath escaped in a soft groan, and his cock was fully hard now. "I didn't say you could talk, did I?"

Tristan shook his head. His chest was moving as his breath quickened.

"Mmm. You'll practice and do better next time." Admittedly, Sebastian was a bit out of his depth here when it came to hockey pep talks. "Won't you." He gave Tristan one last slap, his hand tingling from the contact.

"Yeah," Tristan said, half moan, half whisper. "I will."

Sebastian gentled his hold on Tristan's hair, leaned in,

and kissed him. He softly stroked Tristan's abused cheek with the fingers of his other hand. "Then there's nothing else to worry about right now. Is there."

When Tristan didn't answer right away, Sebastian smiled against his mouth and then pulled back, grabbing and pulling Tristan's hair again. "Is there," he repeated, and smacked him one more time. This should do it.

"No." Tristan's big body was trembling, his arms still behind his back and his cock flushed and hard. "There isn't." He blinked a few times.

"Stay there," Sebastian said firmly, stroking Tristan's face. He pulled off his pajama pants and tugged his shirt over his head so he was naked, then climbed on the bed and positioned himself behind Tristan. "You see yourself in the mirror, yeah?"

The mirror was directly across the bed, and Sebastian enjoyed the sight they made with Tristan, face red and cock hard and ready, kneeling there on his bed with Sebastian behind him.

When Tristan didn't say anything, Sebastian bit him lightly on the shoulder. "I asked you a question."

"I can, yeah."

Sebastian ran his hands over Tristan's back, his chest, and pressed his own hard cock against Tristan's firm ass. "Don't look away." He took Tristan's cock in his hand and started to stroke.

"I'm not—I don't—" Tristan's breath was coming faster and faster, his hips involuntarily pushing his cock into Sebastian's hand.

"I know. You don't like this. All the attention. All the focus. But it feels good, doesn't it?" He found that spot on Tristan's neck he knew drove him crazy and sucked on it lightly. "Tell me. Doesn't my hand feel good on you?"

"Yeah," Tristan panted. "It does." His eyes slid closed after a few more strokes.

Sebastian stopped, let go of Tristan's cock and pinched sharply at his inner thigh. "I told you to keep your eyes open and look at yourself. Look at us."

Tristan groaned, and Sebastian could taste the slight tang of sweat on his skin as he went back to stroking him. "You can feel how hard you make me, can't you?" He pushed himself against Tristan's ass. His thumb glanced over the tip of Tristan's cock. "I asked you a question. You still have to answer me."

"I can feel you— Fuck, Sebastian." Tristan panted, mouth open. The rest of his body was turning red too, as if Sebastian had smacked him everywhere.

"Mmm." Sebastian stroked him harder and faster, slipping his other hand down and teasing Tristan's hole with two fingers. "You're going to watch yourself come for me."

It didn't take long. Sebastian slid a finger inside Tristan's hole, fucking him in time with his hand stroking Tristan's cock. He felt Tristan's body tense, his balls draw up, and his muscles clench hard around Sebastian's finger. When he knew Tristan was close, he added another finger and crooked them to find Tristan's prostate as his hand tightened around Tristan's cock.

Tristan's body jerked and shuddered, and he came over Sebastian's hand with a long, drawn-out moan. His eyes eventually closed from the force of his orgasm, but Sebastian knew that was involuntary. He kept up until Tristan's cock went limp in his hand, and gently withdrew his fingers from Tristan's ass. He kissed Tristan's nape and stroked his sweat-dampened back, waiting for him to calm down.

Tristan's hands were still behind his back. It made Sebastian smile, and it also made his cock so hard it hurt.

"One last thing," Sebastian murmured against Tristan's neck. "Suck me off. You can move now."

Sebastian reclined on the bed, and Tristan had turned and was all over him practically before he was settled. Tristan moved in to try to kiss him, but Sebastian grabbed his hair again. "No. Not yet. Suck me off. You got me this hard, you take care of it."

Tristan's eyes were unfocused, and he was still breathing fast from his orgasm, but he grinned—a much more Tristan-like grin too—and moved to lie between Sebastian's legs. Sebastian enjoyed the sight, running his fingers through Tristan's hair as Tristan covered Sebastian's cock with his mouth. It didn't take long—a few slow sucks and Tristan swallowing him deep—before Sebastian's hips thrust up and he came hard in Tristan's mouth.

When he opened his eyes, feeling sleepy and sated, he saw Tristan braced above Sebastian's hips on the bed, still waiting for instructions. Sebastian gave a low chuckle. "Now we're done. Get up here and kiss me."

Tristan crawled up the bed and collapsed next to Sebastian, reaching to draw him close and kiss him, languid and slow.

"Did you like that?" Sebastian asked.

Tristan nodded. "Yeah. It was… I didn't expect you to do it when we weren't fucking, though."

"I told you it would be as and when I chose," Sebastian reminded him, smiling and stroking Tristan's cheek. "I thought maybe it would help."

"It did." Tristan yawned. "Sorry. I'm tired as fuck and my brain doesn't want to come up with words right now." He gave Sebastian a sheepish smile. "We can talk about it in the morning, if you want."

"We can. After I fuck you," Sebastian agreed.

Tristan kissed him again, a little more heatedly. "Thank you. For…knowing that I needed that. And the kneeling thing. It helped a lot."

"I hope the orgasm did too," Sebastian said drily.

Tristan laughed against his mouth, a huff of air. "Yeah, of course. Those always help. Especially from you."

Sebastian kissed him one last time, then got up to turn off the light. He thought about pulling his pajama pants back on, but why bother? He knew they'd both want to fuck in the morning. That was usually how they woke up when they spent the night together.

Sebastian went to wash his hands and get a glass of water. By the time he got back to the bedroom, Tristan was fast asleep on his stomach. On top of the covers. Sebastian tried waking him, but it was no use. He was dead to the world.

Sighing, Sebastian got up one last time and grabbed a blanket from the closet to drape over them both. Tristan was warm enough that he barely even needed it. Sebastian turned the light off, moved close to Tristan's prone form, and closed his eyes. As tired as he was, sleep didn't come as easily for him as it had for Tristan. He couldn't help thinking about how serious this thing between them had gotten, and what that meant for the future.

Chapter Sixteen

Sebastian was finishing the dishes when his cell phone rang, flashing his parents' number on the screen. He dried his hands on the towel and picked up the phone.

"Hello?"

"Mijo." His mother's voice, familiar and warm in his ear.

"Hi, Mami." He put the last dish away, went to the fridge, and got a beer. It was a little too early for Scotch, but sometimes talking to his parents required some liquid support. They loved him, he knew that. But he also knew they were still hoping him being gay was a "phase," and that one day he'd bring home a nice girl to meet them.

His mom asked him the usual questions about work, the weather, if he was eating well and not relying on a diet full of takeout. Sebastian answered in turn, and then she asked him what he was planning to do for Christmas.

Sebastian immediately felt terrible that he'd been so caught up in everything this last month—school, Tristan—that he hadn't thought to convey his holiday plans to his family.

"Actually, Mami, I'm seeing someone, and I'm going home with him to meet his family," Sebastian said, keeping his tone even but firm.

There was the expected pause: the long moment of silence that broadcasted his mother's disappointment louder than any words. "Ah. And where are you going?"

"Wisconsin," he said. "He—he's a professional hockey player."

"Hockey?" She sounded a bit confused. "There's hockey in Atlanta?"

That made him laugh. "Yeah, there is."

"How did you meet this hockey player?" his mom asked. "I didn't think you liked sports."

"He was my student in a class I taught this summer."

"Oh, mijo," his mother *tsk*ed. "This is allowed, dating a student?"

"He's not my student anymore," Sebastian assured her. "That's how we met, but we didn't start dating until the class was over." Talking about dating to his mother made him feel like a teenager again.

"He plays hockey for the college?" She still sounded suspicious.

"For Atlanta. Professional hockey," he explained, telling her about the Venom.

"And this— He is—" His mother faltered. "This is okay, that he is…"

"Gay?" Sebastian finished for her. "Of course it's all right."

"With the team?" She sounded dubious.

As if his mother had ever hung around any gay professional athletes. "He's going to make sure it is." Sebastian wasn't certain he could promise that, but he didn't want to give his mother any other reason to worry.

There was another awkward pause, and then his mother said, "You make sure you are a good guest, mijo. Polite. Pick up your towels. Bring his mother a gift."

That made him smile. It was typical Ana Cruz advice, but he knew how hard it was for her to accept his sexuality, and this was a small, but significant, moment of progress.

"Of course I will." He didn't mention that of the two of them, Tristan was the one who'd need the towel reminder. That was way too much information to share with his mom.

"I will miss you for the holiday," she said, then launched into a long and detailed gossip session about his family members. Sebastian half listened, the sound of her voice chattering at him in Spanish making him feel both comforted and lonely. He knew there'd be no more discussion about Tristan. That was more conversation about a boyfriend than Sebastian had ever had with his mom.

Before they got off the phone, he said, "Do you want to tell Pop why I'm not coming home, or do you want me to?"

"I will tell him," she said, voice firm. "But you will call us on Christmas."

"Of course," he assured her, and that was that. He tried not to be disappointed that she didn't want to know anything else about Tristan, and he wondered if he should have pressed more, offered more information.

Groaning, he finished the beer and went to take a shower. And hoped to God that he didn't make a fool of himself trying to ice skate.

The Avalon Mall had been transformed for the holidays, the façade strewn with lights and festive garland. In addition to the décor, they'd converted the plaza into an ice rink. Both Sebastian and Tristan were eyeing it suspiciously—Tristan because he was a hockey player and knew ice rinks both indoor and out, and Sebastian because he didn't and had never set foot on one in his life.

Tristan bumped into him with a grin. "Ready?"

Sebastian scowled at two teenagers who, tired of waiting for the two guys to get on the ice, scampered past them and dashed off on their skates. "No."

Tristan laughed. "Come on, Seb," he teased, stepping on the ice. He turned with his back away from Sebastian and was, somehow, ice-skating. "Let's go. I'll teach you everything you need to know." He made the *come here* gesture with his hands.

Sebastian climbed on the ice, immediately grasping the side of the rink and fighting for his balance. Tristan skated toward him and closed the gap, then started skating backward again so he could keep an eye on him.

"Show-off," Sebastian muttered, trying to find his footing. He frowned. "I've been on roller blades, why is this hard?"

"Because you don't roller blade on ice?" Tristan's big body looked utterly at home, his muscles relaxed and his backward skating casual and easy.

Sebastian had yet to figure out going forward without holding on to the side.

"Relax a little," Tristan suggested. "You're tense."

Sebastian shot him a glare. "It's *me*, Tristan."

That made Tristan grin, and Sebastian was happier than he wanted to admit in public that he was able to put that look back on Tristan's face. "I know you can relax," Tristan said, a suggestive gleam in his eye. "I've seen it in person." He skated closer.

"Not in public," Sebastian murmured, but he smiled and tried to do as instructed. Tristan was the expert, and if he said relax… Well, it wasn't easy for him to do, but he'd try.

Tristan maneuvered on his skates so he was next to Sebastian instead of in front of him. "You're getting it," he said, encouraging Sebastian in his shaky attempts to gather some sort of speed and not fall over.

A little girl in a tutu and bright-pink skates twirled past them into the center of the rink, where she did a spin and put her arms in the air.

"Can you do that?" Sebastian nodded toward her.

Tristan pushed forward, spun in a circle, and put his hands above his head. It made Sebastian laugh, and of course that sent him to the boards again to regain his balance. "Very nice."

"Figure skating is hard," Tristan told him.

"Regular skating is hard," Sebastian agreed. "So I can't even imagine." He shook his head. "I also can't believe you do this *and* play hockey."

"I'm so used to being on skates I don't even think about it anymore." Tristan held out his elbow. "Come on. You'll never learn if you don't get off the boards."

If a couple and a young boy hadn't skated by right then, Sebastian might have said something about how someone wasn't going to get off and it wasn't him. Instead, he let go and wobbled a bit, lightly taking Tristan's arm to recover.

"There you go," Tristan encouraged. They were going very, very slow.

"This must be boring for you," Sebastian said, as he watched people zoom by on their skates. Luckily, he wasn't the only beginner on the ice. They weren't the only same-sex couple, either, though maybe people only held hands on the ice out of necessity if one of them was as bad at this as Sebastian was.

"Of course not." Tristan was wearing a Venom stocking cap and a bright-blue scarf that matched the color of his eyes. He was taller than the majority of people on the ice, but no one was giving them the slightest bit of attention. If Tristan was bothered by the idea of being recognized, he didn't show it. All of his attention was on Sebastian.

When they were halfway around the rink, Sebastian had found his balance well enough to skate without having to grab onto the board *or* Tristan. He still didn't skate very fast, and his ankles were protesting with every minute they were out there.

"Ice-skating outside in the South feels so wrong." Tristan shook his head. "I grew up skating on ponds."

"Of course you did." Sebastian faltered, arms flailing for a minute before he got his balance under control. "You're not going to want to do that in Wisconsin, are you?"

Tristan's bright eyes widened. "Oh, I forgot to tell you about the family pickup hockey game on the pond before breakfast?"

Sebastian gave him a little shove, but of course Tristan—who was used to a lot more than that on the ice—barely even moved. In fact, it made *Sebastian* wobble instead of Tristan. "I see why you're good at keeping people away from the puck."

"Sometimes," Tristan said. "You want to go faster?"

"You want to call me an ambulance?" Sebastian ignored Tristan's snort of laughter. "You can skate around if you want. I'll just take my time."

"I came here to skate with you. I think you might like

going faster." Tristan smirked at him. "Unless, you know, you're too scared."

"That isn't going to work on me, Tris. Also it *can't*, because seriously, this is the limit to my speed."

Tristan held his hand out. "Come on. Live a little."

Sebastian hesitated for a moment, then realized this was about more than his lethargic skating. He put his own gloved hand in Tristan's. "Don't kill me."

Tristan started skating faster, and Sebastian studied the way he moved and the way he shifted his weight on his skates. Sebastian felt his muscles loosen a bit, but the exertion had him breathing harder in seconds.

Every second he did this, his admiration for Tristan's on-ice skills grew. And the more it made Sebastian want to take Tristan home and fuck him.

Eventually he was able to let go of Tristan's hand and sort of keep up, but his ankles were still protesting, and Sebastian wasn't sure he was cut out for ice-skating. You were supposed to avoid ice, not put blades on your feet and jump right on it.

Everything went fine until they circled back around to the entrance to the rink—God, had they only gone around *once?*—and other people were coming onto the ice. It was a popular location and getting crowded, which was introducing obstacles to Sebastian's skating experience.

He managed to right himself without falling when a kid blew past him, but the second time, he reached out in a full-out flail to grab Tristan's hand to keep from falling over. But his skate hit a groove in the ice, and his feet gave way under him, sending him tumbling down.

Tristan tried to help him, but Sebastian let go so he didn't end up pulling Tristan down with him. Which was probably a ridiculous worry, since he had no doubt Tristan could keep his balance regardless.

Tristan came to a stop and reached his hand down. His eyes were sparkling, but he didn't laugh. "We all fall down, don't worry."

Sebastian put his hand in Tristan's and let Tristan pull him up, none the worse for wear—except the back of his coat was wet, which he didn't much care for. "I don't think I'm made for this activity."

"You're doing great," Tristan soothed, gallantly offering his elbow. "Here. Hang on."

They went around once more, and by the time they'd passed the scene of his earlier fall, Sebastian was beginning to think he had the hang of it. His ankles were still sore, but had begun to get used to the odd activity, and his balance had improved so much that he could sort of keep pace with Tristan without clinging to Tristan's hand.

"Ha," Sebastian said, smiling a bit, concentrating on putting one skate in front of the other and shifting his balance according to Tristan's instructions. "This isn't so bad."

Two seconds later, his skate hit a rut in the ice and down he went. This time, it wasn't quite as contained a fall, and his ankle bent in a wonky angle, sending a shock of pain through him and causing him to curse as his hands hit the ice hard.

"Fuck," Sebastian muttered, trying to get to his feet. It was difficult since they'd made their way toward the inner part of the rink, so he had nothing to hold on to until Tristan went down on his haunches to help him. Which was embarrassing because it made Sebastian feel about a thousand years old.

"You okay?" Tristan asked, a frown between his

brows. He bit his lip. "They need to get the Zamboni out here."

"I think my shift is over," Sebastian said, wincing as he tried to take the weight off his left ankle. "Put in the backup, Coach."

"They don't have— Er." Tristan smiled sheepishly. "Not the time for hockey lessons, huh." He slid an arm around Sebastian's waist. "Here, lean your weight on me and I'll get you across. Keep your weight off your ankle."

Sebastian did so, gritting his teeth at the idea they'd have to skate all the way around with him leaning on Tristan, his ankle lifted from the ice. But Tristan didn't skate them around; he went straight across the ice and through the skaters practicing spins and twirls in the middle.

They got a few looks from the kids—okay, Sebastian got a few looks, mostly pitying—and eventually made their way to the entrance. Tristan helped him to the bench and went to the locker to retrieve their shoes, while Sebastian undid his skate laces and eased his feet out of the skates. His left ankle was all right when he was sitting, though both of them were aching slightly. When he tried to stand up, though, a sharp pain sent him back to the bench. He rolled it experimentally, reaching down to prod at the muscles.

"Okay?" Tristan asked, looming above him. Tristan, who was still on his skates, was holding both of their shoes.

"Probably just rolled it," Sebastian assured him, reaching for his boots.

Tristan collapsed next to him, somehow managing to gracefully arrange his long limbs so he wasn't knocking into anyone. He undid his skates with haste, and was back in his shoes before Sebastian had laced up his other boot. "I'm really sorry."

"Why? You didn't do anything. I think that was gravity and me never having been on skates before." He stood up, but immediately shifted his weight to his right leg.

"I made you go too fast," Tristan said. He was clearly worried, which was touching but probably unnecessary.

"I've sprained this ankle before running on a trail," Sebastian offered with a shrug. "I don't think anything is broken."

"Still, I can get the car if you want to hang out by the entrance."

Sebastian rolled his eyes and patted Tristan on the arm. "I'm really fine, don't worry about it."

It turned out that he wasn't fine, though, as he had to stop every so often thanks to the pain. Tristan's concern was palpable, and he bore most of Sebastian's weight as they continued toward the car. They'd done some shopping earlier, but luckily they'd stored all their purchases before going ice-skating. They were parked way in the back of the lot, partly because it was crowded and partly because Sebastian hated parking his GTO near other cars.

"I should probably drive," Tristan said, as they neared the car. "Don't you think?"

Sebastian almost refused, simply out of contrariness. Eventually he sighed and handed Tristan the keys with a thoroughly displeased expression. The only thing that made him feel marginally better was critiquing Tristan's driving.

They went back to Sebastian's, and Tristan manfully carried all the bags *and* helped Sebastian to the elevator. Sebastian carefully put weight on his ankle once they were in the apartment, waving his hand when Tristan tried to basically carry him to the living room. "It's not broken, Tris. It's not even sprained."

Tristan put both his arms over his chest and scowled. "Sit," he ordered, pointing at the sofa. "I'll bring you some ice."

Sebastian took one look at the mulish cast to Tristan's face, rolled his eyes, and made his way to the couch. He could feel Tristan's eyes boring into his back. It *did* feel better to sit down, but Tristan was acting as if Sebastian's leg were broken.

Tristan disappeared into the bedroom to deposit the bags, then went into the kitchen. Sebastian heard him rustling around, and then he reappeared with a ziplock bag full of ice, wrapped in a kitchen towel.

"I'm pretty sure this is unnecessary," Sebastian said, to no avail. He winced as Tristan pressed the ice pack to his ankle, which he'd propped up on the coffee table.

"Does that hurt?" Tristan glanced at him sharply.

"It's *cold*," Sebastian said. He patted the couch next to him. "I bet I'd feel better if you gave me a blowjob."

"Ankle injuries can be serious," Tristan said. At Sebastian's chuckle, he added, "What? They can be!"

Sebastian laughed. He couldn't help it. Tristan's expression was so earnest. "I'm sure they are, but you're making a big deal out of nothing."

"What would you be doing, Seb, if I hurt my ankle on the ice?" Tristan demanded.

"Letting the trainers take care of you," he answered immediately. "Since they know what they're doing."

"And if I was here? Home, in your apartment, with an injured ankle? Tell me you wouldn't have me elevate it, and that you wouldn't have made me an ice pack."

"I'd definitely give you a blowjob."

Tristan's mouth curled at the corners. "Leave that on there for ten minutes and I'll think about it."

Sebastian harrumphed, but they settled down with Tristan's head in his lap, and that was at least a step closer to the blowjob that really would make his ankle feel better. As they watched a ridiculous holiday movie, Sebastian drew his fingers through Tristan's hair. "I told my parents I was going to your house for Christmas."

Tristan turned his head, focusing those big blue eyes up at him. "Yeah? Were they okay with it?"

"Well." Sebastian tugged lightly at the blond strands. "I told my mother, and I assume she'll tell my father. They're okay with my missing the holidays, as I've done that before."

"But they're not okay about me." Tristan's mouth set.

"They're not okay with the idea of you," Sebastian corrected. "When they meet you, my mother will be awkward for a minute and then try to feed you. My father will be silent and not look at you."

"Sounds fun," Tristan said drily.

Sebastian's mouth quirked. "I know. But I—I told them that you were my boyfriend, and that things were serious. My mom asked how we met, and I told her the truth."

"That you were perving on me in your class?" Tristan fluttered his eyes. "Dirty, dirty Professor Cruz."

Sebastian did the totally mature thing and flicked Tristan on the forehead. "I told her we met because you were my student, yes. I didn't say I was perving on you. She's my mom."

"Right." Tristan smiled. "I'm glad you told her."

"Me too."

"Was it…" Tristan looked like he wasn't sure he

should ask anything else, but Sebastian nodded and he continued. "Was it okay?"

"It was the Cruz version of okay, I suppose. I don't know what surprised my mom more: that you were my student or that you played hockey. Or that I even knew what hockey *was*."

"She must have seen you ice-skate," Tristan teased, and laughed when Sebastian flicked him again. He caught Sebastian's hand and carried it down to press a kiss on it. "Thanks for telling her. I know you're worried about the student thing."

"I shouldn't be. We didn't do anything wrong." Sebastian watched as Tristan took his fingers into his mouth, starting to suck and tease them. "And I wanted her to know."

Tristan stopped the teasing and gave Sebastian a smile that nearly blinded him. "Yeah?"

"Of course."

"Did you only tell me that so I'd blow you?" Tristan went back to sucking on his fingers, a little more suggestively.

"No, but I won't apologize if it gets your mouth on my dick," Sebastian said.

Tristan's eyes flashed, but right then, the Christmas movie they were watching—the one with the Muppets—started playing a song. They paused, looked at each other, and Sebastian grabbed the remote.

"Good call," said Tristan, and grinned before he reached for Sebastian's jeans.

Chapter Seventeen

The Venom's Christmas break wasn't long—only three days—so instead of driving, they flew to Wisconsin and rented a car at the airport. Tristan's parents had offered to pick them up, of course, when he told them he was bringing "a friend" for the holidays. Tristan politely refused, claiming he didn't want to put his parents through the trouble. Truthfully, he figured he could use the drive time between Madison and Columbus to gird his loins.

Tristan didn't think he could cope with his parents' curiosity about Sebastian immediately after disembarking. If it made him a coward to need that extra forty minutes, well, he was a coward. It wasn't every day a guy came out to his family, which he constantly reminded himself whenever that little, insidious mental voice berated him for being anxious. And if things *did* go badly, at least they'd have a vehicle on hand so they could make a quick escape.

Coming out to his family couldn't be put off any longer, though. His relationship with Sebastian had officially crossed into serious territory, and Tristan wanted to share the news with the closest people in his life. He could give this to Sebastian—even if he wasn't ready to open up to his teammates yet.

Sebastian drove while Tristan jittered in the passenger seat. He bounced his leg and chafed his sweaty palms on the tops of his jean-clad thighs until Sebastian reached over to grip one of his knees and snapped, "Sit still!" in that stern professor tone he used in class.

Weirdly enough, that calmed Tristan down. He sucked in a shuddery breath and sheepishly rubbed the back of his neck. "Sorry."

Sebastian squeezed his knee. "Don't be. I know you're nervous, and I understand, believe me, but you're shaking the whole car, and I'm worried you're going to hyperventilate."

Tristan *did* feel kind of light-headed. Jesus. "Why am I so freaked? They're my parents. They love me. I've never heard them say anything bad about gay people. Like, literally never."

"Your feelings are valid, Tristan, whatever they may be. There are no rules for this."

"I know. I just…" Tristan dragged in another deep breath. "Fuck. I'm scared." The last word came out sounding small, vulnerable.

Sebastian grabbed one of his hands and laced their fingers together. He took his attention from the road long enough to shoot Tristan a quick, comforting glance. "You don't have to do this, you know. If you're not ready."

"I want them to know about me. And you. I really do." Tristan stared at the side of Sebastian's face. He looked worried. "I *am* ready, Seb. But I'm…nervous too."

"If you're sure." Sebastian held his hand a little tighter. "And it's okay to be nervous. That's completely understandable."

They spent the next ten minutes in silence, until the GPS on Sebastian's phone went wonky and Tristan jumped in to direct him the rest of the way. He pointed to the long, winding driveway that led to his family home, and felt his stomach muscles tense as Sebastian slotted their rented sedan next to the truck that belonged to Tristan's father.

Sebastian cut the engine.

"We're here," Tristan announced shakily, but he made no move to get out of the car.

Sebastian only gripped his hand even tighter. Tristan returned the pressure somewhat desperately.

It wasn't long before the front door flew open and Tristan's sister raced down the front steps, her long blonde hair streaking behind her. Sebastian released his hand right before she reached the passenger side of the car. She was smiling hugely, her cheeks already flushed pink from the cold.

"Are you coming in or are you going to sit out here all day?" she asked, her voice muffled by the glass of the window. It was cold enough that puffs of condensation accompanied her words, a noticeable contrast to the weather they'd left behind in Atlanta.

Tristan laughed and pushed open his door.

Hannah launched herself into his arms, making him stagger. "I missed you!"

Tristan hugged her, some of his tension easing. "I missed you too, Han." He heard the driver's door close and turned to gesture at Sebastian. "This is Seb. Seb, Hannah."

Hannah waved at Sebastian across the roof of the car. "Nice to meet you."

Sebastian inclined his head. "Same here." He went to the open trunk and started pulling out their luggage.

"Go on in, Han. You're going to freeze out here. I'm going to help Seb bring the stuff in."

Hannah nodded and crossed her sweater-covered arms over her chest, as if she hadn't really felt the cold before he'd mentioned it. "You're right," she said with a laugh. "I'll see you inside." She took off again, leaving Sebastian and Tristan alone.

Sebastian had already set their bags on the ground and stood waiting for Tristan. "All good?"

Tristan sidled closer. For a second, he was tempted to kiss Sebastian right then and there. If someone was watching from the window, then they'd know. He wouldn't have to broach the subject. Tristan resisted the temptation but leaned in to say, "Thanks for coming with me."

Sebastian's sable eyes warmed, and his mouth crooked into a small smile. "Of course. Thanks for inviting me."

Tristan reached down to grab the handle of his suitcase. "Come on."

The introductions went as Tristan had anticipated. His father and brother seemed slightly taken aback that Tristan's "friend" was a guy and not the girl they'd probably expected, but they grinned gamely and shook hands with Sebastian. His mother pulled Sebastian into a boisterous hug, crushing him to her ample bosom. Sebastian endured the embrace with an awkward pat to her back, though his mildly alarmed expression nearly made Tristan laugh. He had to bite hard on his lower lip to stifle the urge.

When she released Sebastian, Tristan's mom shot him a look that practically screamed her curiosity, but she didn't barrage Sebastian with questions. Instead, she ushered them into the kitchen, sat them at the long farm table his father had custom-made for the space, and started plying them with the meal she'd prepared.

They made small talk over pot roast, mashed potatoes, biscuits, and apple pie à la mode. The atmosphere never quite grew comfortable. Tristan's family was unfailingly polite and welcoming, as they'd always been with his friends, but he could tell they weren't entirely sure what to make of Sebastian, who was clearly older than Tristan and holding himself stiffly as he sat there surrounded by strangers.

Afterward, Tristan's mother led the way upstairs. She paused outside Tristan's childhood room. "You'll be right next door," she said to Sebastian. "I figured Tristan's friend would want to be close in a strange house." She smiled and gestured down the hall. "The bathroom's there, and the linen closet is right next to it. Tristan can give you the grand tour tomorrow if you want to rest tonight. We're going to watch our shows in the den. Feel free to join us."

Sebastian's responding smile was strained. "Thank you, Mrs. Holt."

She fluttered her hands. "Oh, please, call me Priscilla. And my husband is Tom. Make yourself at home." She gave Tristan a quick hug and a significant look that told him there'd be questions coming later. "I'll leave you to it."

She disappeared down the stairs, and Tristan turned to Sebastian. "That went...okay."

Sebastian laughed drily. "Yeah." He sighed and moved toward the door Tristan's mother had indicated. "I'm going to shower and change. I smell like airplane."

Tristan caught his arm and waited for Sebastian to meet his gaze. "You don't have to stay in there."

Sebastian arched his brows. "I think I do. For tonight, at least."

Tristan opened his mouth to protest.

"It's okay," Sebastian said. "I'm not upset. You tell them when you're ready. Until then, I'm your friend. And I am, Tristan. I'm here in whatever capacity you need me to be, okay?"

Tristan leaned forward and rested their foreheads together. "In the morning. First thing." He felt Sebastian's answering nod, followed by a soft brush of lips to his temple. Then Sebastian pulled away and went into the room Tristan's mom had prepared, the door shutting gently behind him.

In the morning, Tristan led Sebastian to the workout area in the basement—which was probably better outfitted than the average household, given Tristan spent his summers there and needed the equipment to train.

Sebastian surveyed the space and turned to give Tristan a searching look when Tristan lingered awkwardly in the doorway. He pulled Tristan into the room, backed him against the wall, and kissed him hard. "Good luck," he said softly, his lips brushing Tristan's mouth. Tristan appreciated that he didn't offer any *It'll be okay* platitudes. They both knew Sebastian couldn't guarantee that.

Tristan kissed him again, rather helplessly. They'd hear anyone approaching before they were seen, and Tristan needed the contact. Fuck the whole situation. It made him feel like a child about to confess to some secret misdeed. Why did it even have to be a big deal?

Finally, Tristan drew away. "Okay. Enjoy your run. I'll be back."

Sebastian squeezed the nape of Tristan's neck and nodded.

Tristan left the room to the whir of the treadmill belt and the pounding of footsteps. He made his way upstairs and found his mother in the kitchen, her usual haunt, where she'd already started making breakfast.

Tristan leaned down to kiss her on the cheek. "Morning, Mom."

"Morning, sweetie." She grinned up at him, her plump cheeks flushed from the heat of the stovetop. The scent of frying bacon was thick in the air. "Did you sleep well?"

"Fine," Tristan lied. Because what he'd done was toss and turn and wish Sebastian was beside him instead of separated from him by a wall.

"How about Sebastian?" She turned to test the warmth of the griddle. "He seems nice."

Tristan reined back a snort. *Nice* was not a word he'd apply to Sebastian. "He's using the treadmill. He likes to run."

"Oh, that's nice. Good exercise." His mother used a pair of tongs to flip a piece of bacon.

There was that word again. Tristan sighed. "Do you need any help?"

She looked around the kitchen. "Well, I already have the pancake batter ready. You can start beating those eggs, if you want. You know I always save them for last. I don't like it when they get all cold and rubbery."

Tristan picked up the bowl she'd pointed to. It was filled with what looked like a couple dozen eggs. He grabbed a fork and started whisking.

For a while, they worked in companionable silence.

His mother poured a few circles of pancake batter onto the griddle and then peered over at him. "So, where did you meet Sebastian?"

Tristan kept his focus on the eggs. "At school."

"Huh. He looks kind of old to be a student."

Tristan didn't know whether to laugh or to cringe. "Um. Well, he isn't. He's a professor, actually. Sociology. I met him when I took those courses over the summer."

His mother's silence made Tristan turn. She gaped at him in wide-eyed surprise. "Your professor?"

"Yes."

"Huh," she repeated. "I'll be honest, when you said you were bringing someone home, we thought maybe it would be one of your teammates...or maybe a girl. Not that Sebastian isn't welcome. Of course he is. It's just... Well, you... You've never brought anyone home to meet us. A romantic someone, I mean. I know you're still young, but we thought maybe you'd finally met someone and maybe it was something serious."

Tristan stopped whisking before the eggs turned to froth. He set down the fork and straightened his shoulders. "I did, and it is."

His mother stared up at him. "What?"

"I met someone, and it *is* serious. Sebastian... He's my boyfriend."

His mother blinked once, slowly. "Oh," she said, and in the ensuing quiet, she returned to tending the pancakes and bacon.

Tristan didn't know what to say or do next. Sweat beaded on his forehead and dampened his armpits. He wanted to cry. He wanted to *puke*. All he could do was stand there, a knot of cold dread growing deep in the pit of his stomach.

"Mom?" he croaked after a couple of minutes. He sounded like someone had ripped out his vocal cords and kicked them around in a gravel pit. "Can you say something else?"

She glanced at him again, and whatever she saw on his face made her hastily shut off the burners and rush across the room. "Oh, God, sweetie, I'm sorry. Don't look like that." She'd pulled him into a crushing hug that had him bent over with his face buried against her lavender-scented neck.

"You didn't say anything," Tristan said, speaking into the material of her shirt. "You need to say something."

"I'm sorry! I'm surprised and processing." She stroked his back. "I... I didn't think you were gay. I... Well, you never said. I had no idea." She drew back to peer into his face. "That is, you *are* gay, right? Or are you, um..." She paused as if searching for the word. "Bisexual?"

Tristan gave a watery laugh. "Yeah, I'm gay. I, uh. I didn't know how to tell you. I was scared."

His mother made a distraught sound and tugged him close again. "No, no. Don't be scared. We love you, baby. We love you. It's only a bit of a shock, you know? You came here with Sebastian and then you say he's your sociology professor, and then..." She petted his hair. "How long has this been going on? Since the class?"

Tristan straightened and rubbed at his damp cheeks. He shook his head. "No. After the class. I think I love him, Mom. And I think maybe he loves me too."

His mother reached up to cup his face. She smiled, but her eyes were wet. "Oh, I'm glad, baby. This isn't a problem, okay? I'm sorry if I reacted poorly. I didn't mean to hurt you. I never would. I hope you know that."

Tristan nodded, unable to answer for the tightness in

his throat. His father walked in as they were standing there holding each other, with half-cooked pancakes and bacon on the stove. His eyebrows shot up. "Is everything all right? What's the matter?"

Tristan's mom pulled out of his embrace and lifted her apron to dry her face. "Nothing at all. Tristan just told me Sebastian is his boyfriend, and I was telling him how happy I was to know he had someone special." She stared hard at Tristan's father as if daring him to contradict her.

His father appeared completely stunned. "Uh," he said eventually. "Of course we're, um, happy to hear that. That's... Well, that's great."

Tristan swallowed and looked between them. "Are you disappointed?"

His father shook his head immediately. "No. *No.* Of course not. I can't say I'm not surprised, but..." He moved forward and tugged Tristan into a rough hug. "You couldn't disappoint me, son. Not about this. I'm glad you felt like you could tell us."

Tristan bit his lip. "It wasn't easy."

"I don't imagine it was," his father said.

His mother joined their embrace. "We support you. I'll tell Hannah and Brian, if you want me to."

Tristan shook his head. "I'll tell them myself, but thank you." He inhaled shakily. "And now I'm going to talk to Seb 'cause I... I need a minute with him. Okay?"

His parents nodded. Then his mom smiled crookedly. "Take all the time you need. I'll get back to cooking. Come eat when you're ready."

Tristan left the kitchen, his relief at their response making him feel buoyant. It hadn't been without some awkwardness, sure, and there'd probably be more to come. He wasn't naïve enough to think he could drop a bomb like this on his parents' heads without there being an adjustment period. But it hadn't gone anywhere near as badly as he'd feared, and now that he'd spoken to his parents, he wasn't overly concerned about his siblings' reactions. They were his family too, and he knew his sister at least had a few LGBT kids in her friend circle. They wouldn't disappoint him. He had faith.

Tristan scrubbed the drying tears from his cheeks and went to find his boyfriend.

Chapter Eighteen

Sebastian had never spent the holidays with a boyfriend's parents before, which was something that had occurred to him the very first night he spent in the Holts' home. The guest room was perfectly fine, a nice double bed with far too many pillows and pictures in old frames on the wall of the Holt siblings in various stages of growing up. The ones of Tristan, gap-toothed and holding a hockey stick, had made him smile briefly before he turned out the light.

Knowing Tristan was in the other room and they were sleeping apart had not made him smile, but only because he missed Tristan's warmth—especially since it was freezing—beside him. He'd like to think that would be the only night he'd have to sleep alone, but he knew that wasn't a given. Just because Tristan planned to come out to his parents didn't mean that they'd be comfortable with their son sharing a bed with an unmarried partner.

Tristan appeared after his conversation, face red and eyes wet, but the tension had eased in his tall frame. He smiled, a little wobbly, but it was enough for Sebastian to know that things had gone well. He finished his run and turned off the treadmill, adjusting for the strange sensation of climbing off the moving belt and being on solid, nonmoving ground.

"Everything all right?" He was certain he knew the answer, but he wanted to ask.

Tristan nodded. "I think they were surprised." He gave a laugh, the first honest one Sebastian had heard from him in a while. "Except I'm not sure they don't think we—" He cleared his throat and flashed a grin.

"Hooked up while you were a student?" Sebastian finished. He took a long drink from the water bottle he'd brought, his breathing gradually slowing. He wasn't surprised. While it was way too uncomfortable to even think about telling Tristan's parents straight-up: *Don't worry, I didn't hook up with your son when he was my student*, he was hoping they'd get enough of a sense of him that they wouldn't think that.

"I mean, it's fine," Tristan assured him, a little too fast. "I don't think they're gonna call the GSU Sociology Department and report you or anything."

Mildly irritated, Sebastian frowned. "That has nothing to do with it. They're your parents. I don't want them to think that's the kind of man I am, the kind of man their son is involved with."

Tristan moved into his personal space, apparently not minding that Sebastian was covered in sweat. "Lighten up, Professor," he murmured, leaning down to kiss him. "You want some breakfast? Actual breakfast too. Not a protein shake."

"I'm not the one who thinks protein shakes count as food," Sebastian retorted, kissing him back. He settled his hands on Tristan's hips, pulling him closer—not enough to get him covered in sweat, which seemed like it might make for an embarrassing breakfast. "I'm glad it went all right. Anything I should know before we go up there?"

"Nah. Just be yourself. Maybe with, like, ten percent less scowling, though. They might not find it as hot as I do."

Sebastian raised his eyebrows but didn't say anything. He *did* want Tristan's parents to like him if for no other reason than it would make Tristan's life easier. "All right. I'll take a shower first, though. I stink."

"You think my mom isn't used to sweaty guys at her breakfast table?" Tristan teased, kissing him again. He pulled away with a laugh at the look Sebastian gave him. "Fine, shower. There's clean towels in the linen closet."

Resisting the urge to ask Tristan where else he thought Sebastian would expect to find towels, Sebastian went upstairs and cleaned up. Breakfast was relatively pain-less, with Tristan's parents asking him the usual ques-tions about where he was from, if he had siblings, the usual sort. They didn't ask about Tristan being his stu-dent, and they weren't giving him suspicious death glares, either. Talking about his newfound appreciation for hockey was a safe subject, as was hearing stories about Tristan as a kid.

It was a pleasant day, and Sebastian found himself gradually relaxing around the Holts' warm, genuine presence. Tristan's brother and sister, who'd clearly been briefed about the situation, were completely at ease with the two of them being a couple. After dinner, while they were all in the kitchen cleaning up, they even teased Se-bastian, although good-naturedly, about him having been Tristan's professor.

"Is that how you got an A?" Hannah asked outra-geously, batting her eyes at Tristan.

"A-minus," Sebastian put in, straight-faced, and Hannah laughed.

"So you're an only child?" Brian asked, drying a plate with a dishtowel. He wasn't quite as tall as Tristan, and his stature was a bit stockier, but the family resemblance was clear. Brian was a nice guy, clearly in line to take over the farm when Tom decided to retire.

"Lucky," Hannah said, depositing a few glasses in the sink for Sebastian to wash.

"I do have a lot of cousins," Sebastian offered. "Catholics, and all that."

"And they're okay—" Hannah cleared her throat. "Wow, sorry, that was about to be really rude of me."

"With me being gay?" Sebastian asked. "I don't mind talking about it. And they're…as accepting as I think it's possible for them to be. Some of my other family members refuse to let me in the door, so."

"Are they gonna be nice to my brother?" Hannah demanded. "Like, if you bring *him* to family stuff?"

"Han," Tristan chastised. "You're way too old for bratty-little-sister mode."

"No, it's all right." Sebastian dried his hands and turned toward Hannah. "She has a right to ask, Tris. And to be concerned about you." He noticed with amusement that both Tristan's siblings were looking at him as if he were giving a lecture. "I wouldn't bring him to extended-family functions, but not because it might make *them* uncomfortable. It's not about them at all."

"Aw." Hannah flashed him a grin almost identical to Tristan's. "Good answer." She patted Sebastian on the shoulder. "Then you guys can come here for the holidays. No problem."

"Okay, Mom," Tristan joked, rolling his eyes. The

conversation slipped into other things, namely Hannah asking for some donations from Tristan for her hockey team fund-raiser.

"It would be super awesome if we could have some signed jerseys." She grinned. "Can I have one from Ryu Mori? He is *so* hot. And he's putting up *way* better numbers than Norell."

Tristan smiled. "Sure." Sebastian knew there was a signed Mori jersey in his bag. His sister's crush on the Venom's backup goalie was not news to Tristan, who'd told Sebastian about it with a rueful shake of his head.

Filled with affection for his boyfriend, happy that things had gone well and that his siblings had no problem accepting the two of them as a couple, Sebastian leaned over and pressed a quick kiss to Tristan's mouth. Tristan's smile was bright enough that it might be able to melt the metric fuck-ton of snow falling outside the Holts' house.

Sebastian would not be sad to leave the weather behind and go back to the relatively mild temperatures of an Atlanta winter, that was for sure.

After the dishes were done, they watched a Christmas special in the living room. Sebastian sat next to Tristan on the couch, but Tristan didn't have enough room for his usual sprawl so he wasn't lying with his head in Sebastian's lap. He also might not have been comfortable showing affection in front of his parents, but a few minutes into *A Christmas Carol* (Sebastian refrained from giving his opinion about how the beloved Dickens classic was a satire about the strict class divide in Victorian-era London), he felt Tristan's head rest on his shoulder, his fingers finding Sebastian's and wrapping tight around them.

Tom and Priscilla might have been avoiding looking at them, but Sebastian had the feeling they were simply trying to be accepting and not stare. He was glad. Tristan clearly had come by his good nature and big heart honestly.

God, you are so infatuated.

With the lights sparkling off the Christmas tree, the probably-a-satire-but-vaguely-uplifting movie in the background, and the warmth of an accepting and loving family... Sebastian couldn't find it in himself to mind.

Christmas morning was full of good cheer, coffee, and a lot of wrapping paper. Tristan's parents exclaimed over the elegantly wrapped presents Tristan had brought with him, and he'd sheepishly admitted the artistry was all Sebastian.

"I figured." Priscilla grinned, sipping her coffee. "Tristan would go through six rolls of wrapping paper for three presents."

Sebastian snorted. "I let him wrap one, then told him to go do some sit-ups and let me take over."

Tristan finished passing out the gifts and settled on the floor at Sebastian's feet, his back pressed against Sebastian's legs. Sebastian felt a bit awkward about the whole thing, though pleased that Tom liked the vintage sign Sebastian had gotten him (on Tristan's recommendation), and Priscilla loved the set of butterfly wind chimes. The Holts were a bit abashed at not having gotten him anything, though of course it was understandable. Why would they have? They hadn't even known his name, much less that he was Tristan's boyfriend.

"Well, next year we'll be sure to fix that." Priscilla patted his shoulder. Sebastian was a little overwhelmed by the casual physical affection. He'd barely gotten used to it with Tristan, much less four other people. "What are some of your interests?"

"He likes running and action movies," Tristan said, a bit quickly. Sebastian shot him a sly smile. Did he think Sebastian was going to answer with something embarrassing? "And, uh, Daddy Yankee."

Silence filled the room. Sebastian bit his lip but couldn't help snickering. Tristan looked mortified, his face on fire.

"He's a singer," Sebastian offered as an explanation. "He's Puerto Rican. Like me."

Hannah, dressed in pajama pants and her new, signed Mori jersey, perked up at that. "Oh, does that mean you speak Spanish?"

"Hannah," Priscilla *tsk*ed. She gave Sebastian a worried glance, as if her daughter might have insulted him by asking him that.

"I do," Sebastian answered. "And it's all right. I'm trying to teach your brother." He grinned over at Tristan. "He's better at sociology."

"Sooo," Hannah asked, making a spot for herself next to Sebastian. "If I had some Spanish homework that was due right after break—"

"My boyfriend is not doing your homework," Tristan interrupted, swatting playfully at his sister. "Believe me. He gave me an A-*minus*."

"You *earned* an A-minus," Sebastian retorted, rubbing a hand over Tristan's hair. Tristan stuck his tongue out, and Sebastian was suddenly very glad they were leaving in the morning. Tristan would be heading out on a long road trip shortly after they got back, and he wanted to have some time together before that happened.

Later that night, when they were getting ready for bed, Tristan said, "I like how you didn't tell them the Spanish you're teaching me is all dirty words and sex talk." He was sitting cross-legged on the bed in his pajamas and no shirt, freshly showered since they had to leave at the ass-crack of dawn to get to the airport.

"You're calling my mother tongue 'dirty words and sex talk,' Mr. Holt?" Sebastian crossed his arms and gave Tristan his "professor stare."

"You aren't teaching me anything I can say in public." Tristan's eyes ran over Sebastian. "And stop giving me that look unless you can handle what it does to me."

Sebastian, who had moved on to examining the plethora of trophies in Tristan's room, raised his eyebrows. "When haven't I handled it?" He picked up one of the trophies, frowning at the top and trying to make out what it was a trophy *for*. "This doesn't have a hockey stick on it."

"My boyfriend, the professor," Tristan said. "Mind like a steel trap."

Sebastian gave him a stern look. "My boyfriend, the smart-ass. With an ass that clearly needs to be spanked."

Tristan's eyes gleamed and he shifted on the bed. "Clearly."

There was no way he was spanking Tristan in his childhood bedroom. To give himself a moment to calm down, he waved the trophy again. "What's this for?"

"Um." Tristan laughed sheepishly. "The spelling bee. In third grade."

It was so wonderfully, perfectly Tristan. Sebastian smiled. "Of course it is. Third place, huh? You know you got that A-minus because you misspelled 'sociology' on your final."

"What? I did not!"

Sebastian put the trophy down and crossed the room. He climbed on the bed and Tristan was all over him, playful smile and warm skin, making Sebastian think about things he really, really shouldn't think about. "You didn't. If I took off points for spelling, three people would have passed my class."

"I'd be one of them," Tristan huffed, settling his weight over Sebastian's lap. Tristan's dick was hard in his pajama pants. So was Sebastian's. Maybe it'd been better to sleep alone. Sleeping with Tristan when he couldn't touch him was driving Sebastian crazy.

"Yeah. B-minus, C-plus," Sebastian teased, putting a hand around the back of Tristan's neck. He tugged him down to kiss him. "You have to get off me. No sex in your childhood bed, Tris."

"I love when you call me that." Tristan kissed at his neck. "And we don't have to fuck, but you can still make out with me. Geez, Seb. It's Christmas."

Sebastian gave a low laugh, which turned into a moan as Tristan rubbed his cock lazily against Sebastian's. "Tris."

"Yeah?" Tristan licked at his ear. "You want something, Seb?"

Sebastian wanted a lot of things. His hands slid down and curved over the hard muscles of Tristan's ass, pulling Tristan forward to grind on his cock. "You're the one who wants to defile your childhood bedroom."

Tristan snorted, starting a slow, lazy undulation of his hips that had Sebastian's eyes rolling back in his head. "'Defile'? This poor bed is long overdue. It was just me and my hand for all those years."

This should not be turning him on, and he should *not* be doing this. It wasn't stopping Sebastian from thrusting his hips up, entranced at the idea of Tristan touching himself, biting his lip in the dark and trying to be quiet. "Fuck," he rasped, kissing Tristan roughly to silence his moan.

"Tell me how to say 'suck me' in Spanish," Tristan murmured when they moved apart to breath.

"Chupame," Sebastian said.

"Since you asked so nice." Tristan grinned and moved down his body. "Shhh. This'll be good, I promise."

Sebastian knew that, and he figured they were too far gone by now to stop anyway. So he tilted his hips up and let Tristan pull his pajamas down enough to free his cock. It was a fast, sloppy blowjob, messy but so, so good. Sebastian held Tristan to him with one hand in his hair, letting him control the pace and the depth, not wanting to make Tristan choke—even though it would've been hot—because of the noise.

He bit back his moan when he came, and the effort of trying to be quiet made his orgasm more intense, colors bright behind his eyes and his muscles tensed and shaking. When he finally trusted himself to open his eyes, it was to see Tristan looking very smug and flopping on his back next to him on the bed.

"How was that, Professor Cruz?"

"A-plus, Mr. Holt." Sebastian was still trying to catch his breath. Tristan's cock was tenting his pants, and breathing became even harder for Sebastian when Tristan slipped his hand inside and started stroking himself through the fabric.

"Chupame," Tristan said, grinning at him. "Uh. Please. Por favor."

His Spanish accent was terrible, but they could work on it.

Sebastian moved down the bed, tugging Tristan's pants off and getting in place over him. "Your blowjobs are better than your Spanish."

"Lucky for me," Tristan murmured.

Sebastian gave him a fierce stare as he took Tristan's cock in his hand. "Keep quiet, Tris. I know how loud you get."

Tristan opened his mouth to say something but snapped it shut as Sebastian lowered his head and started to suck Tristan's cock. He knew how to drive Tristan to orgasm fast and hard, and while he would have loved to take his time—and hear all those sounds Tristan was now smothering with a pillow over his face—it wasn't the time or place. He teased Tristan's hole with his finger, lightly pressing in while taking Tristan's dick deep. When he swallowed around Tristan's cock, he slipped his finger inside—not too hard, not too far, but enough that Tristan's hips bucked as he came in Sebastian's mouth.

The pillow wasn't quite enough to muffle *all* the sounds, but hopefully it was good enough to keep their activities private. Sebastian returned to his place next to Tristan, who took a few minutes before he could pull his pants back up.

Tristan reached out and traced his fingers over Sebastian's mouth. "Thanks for coming. For being here, when I did this."

Touched, Sebastian kissed lightly at his fingers. "You're welcome. Thank *you* for doing it."

Tristan nodded. "I think I always knew it would be okay, and that they wouldn't throw me out or anything. They're hurt, probably, that I didn't tell them earlier. But I think they understand why I didn't."

Sebastian nodded but didn't say anything. He was happy for Tristan, and Tristan's relief in having come out to his family was so palpable, Sebastian didn't want to do anything to ruin the moment.

What about your team?

The question remained unspoken between them, though Sebastian knew it couldn't stay that way. Not for long.

Chapter Nineteen

As game time approached, the volume in the dressing room rapidly increased. Tristan tried to stay focused on the words in his microeconomics textbook, but amid laughter and shouts from his teammates, he couldn't keep his concentration.

Sighing, he slammed the cover shut. Clearly, studying was a lost cause. He'd have to save it for later.

Tristan pushed the book from his lap onto the bench and ground the heels of his fists into his gritty eyes. God, he was exhausted. Calculus formulas and banking statistics spun in his brain. Really, all he wanted to do was burrow under a pile of blankets and stay there for a week. Preferably with Sebastian beside him.

"Hey, Holtzy," a voice asked, "want to come kick the ball around with us?"

Tristan dropped his hands to see Carts, one of the Venom's left-wingers, staring at the microeconomics textbook while he tossed a soccer ball back and forth between his palms.

Carts tipped his chin toward the book. "What's up with that? You going nerd on me, Holtzy?"

Tristan picked up the textbook and shoved it into his

stall. "Just putting in some last-minute studying, man. I have an exam on Thursday."

Carts raised his brows. "An exam? You *have* gone nerd on me. No wonder you're always carrying those books around."

"Yeah, I'm taking a couple of courses at GSU. The new semester started a few weeks ago." And Tristan already felt like he needed a vacation. Between classes, practice, games, homework, travel, workouts, and squeezing in time with Sebastian, he felt as brittle as thin ice and ready to crack. The winter break hadn't been nearly long enough.

Carts looked faintly bemused, as most of his teammates did when Tristan talked about his classes. "Okay, well, are you in?"

Bellzie walked up and patted Carts on his gleaming bald head. "Why don't you go ahead, Carts? I need to talk to Holtzy for a sec."

"Sure thing, Bellzie."

Carts left the room to join a few of the others in the corridor, where they were already kicking around a ball and laughing.

Bellzie settled on the bench next to Tristan, so close their shoulders touched. Like Tristan, he was dressed in trainers, loose shorts, and a moisture-wicking shirt that clung to his well-muscled chest in ways Tristan probably shouldn't be noticing. But hell, being in a relationship didn't mean Tristan couldn't look and appreciate. He'd been attracted to Bellzie from the very start. It was hard to ignore him with his curly halo of hair and those bright-blue eyes and the smile that rarely wavered when Bellzie wasn't on the ice.

"I just wanted to tell you not to let them get to you,"

Bellzie said after a moment. "I've heard some of the comments about the way you're always studying. I think we both know nobody means any harm by it, but I wanted to make sure you weren't taking them seriously. I think it's admirable you're going back for your degree—and a few of the other guys do too, even if they haven't said. It takes a huge amount of dedication to split your time between hockey and school. I know it can't be easy lugging those textbooks around on airplanes and busses and losing sleep and taking shit from your teammates. I'm proud of you."

Tristan swallowed around the sudden thickness in his throat. "Thanks," he croaked.

Bellzie flung an arm around him, squeezing briefly. "If there's anything I can do to lighten your load, let me know. You're going to crush that exam, no problem. For now, focus on the game. One thing at a time, okay?"

Tristan nodded. Bellzie clapped him on the back before going over to Stewie, one of the alternate captains, and starting up a quiet conversation.

"One thing at a time."

Tristan nodded again, this time to himself, and went out into the corridor to join his teammates for a bit of hallway soccer before warm-ups started.

The game ended in a four-three win over the Chicago Windhawks. Tristan notched an early assist and the winning goal in the last few minutes of the third period. Once the final buzzer sounded, he head-bumped Ryu, who'd started in net, with an exuberant laugh and a pat to the side of Ryu's mask.

He was running high on endorphins, which kept the exhaustion at bay for a while, but as he showered and the energy faded, he was grateful it'd been a matinee game and he could nap for a bit before meeting Sebastian for dinner. Otherwise, he might fall asleep at the concert Sebastian was taking him to afterward.

Ryu caught Tristan on his way out of the locker room. "Are you coming with us later? A bunch of the guys want to meet for dinner and drinks tonight. Morley's picking me up at seven."

Tristan shook his head and looked around to make sure no one was close enough to overhear them. "Not tonight. I have a date, actually." He lowered his voice, and added, "With the professor I told you about before."

Ryu's eyes widened slightly. "So you made your move, huh?"

"Only after my final presentation, but yeah. We've been seeing each other since the end of August, and it's...it's great."

"Nice." Ryu gave him a small smile. "You kept that pretty quiet, huh? Well, have fun playing naughty school-boy with your professor. I'll tell the other guys you're busy if they ask."

Tristan laughed. "Good lookin' out. And I'm sorry I didn't tell you sooner. It was new, you know?"

Ryu snorted. "No worries."

With a fist bump, they parted ways. Tristan drove home, texted Sebastian, and indulged in a brief nap before forcing himself to study for another hour. When he couldn't take another second of mind-numbing monetary policy, he showered and started preparing for his date.

Sebastian had surprised him with tickets to see Zephyr, a band that described themselves as being "Led Zeppelin inspired." Tristan had been looking forward to the concert all week. More than that, he was anticipating the three days off until the Venom had another game. There'd be practices, of course, but aside from an exam on Thursday, Tristan didn't have much to do for his classes. He'd have time with Sebastian and time for sleep—two things he desperately needed.

Sebastian pulled up to Tristan's apartment building at half past six. Without stopping to think, Tristan leaned over to give him a slow, thorough kiss.

When Sebastian tried to draw back, Tristan chased his mouth, making Sebastian laugh and lightly pat his cheek. "Later, Mr. Holt."

For dinner, they went to a pub not too far from Terminal West. The place had a loud, rowdy atmosphere, cold beer, and fantastic Reuben sandwiches piled high with corned beef and melted Swiss cheese. Tristan was enjoying himself, laughing at a story about one of Sebastian's students, when Sebastian's attention suddenly shifted to something over his shoulder.

Curious, Tristan turned his head—and his stomach dropped so fast and hard he worried what he'd eaten of his sandwich might come spewing right back up.

"So, this is your professor?" Ryu asked.

He was standing in the aisle next to their table…which meant Tristan's teammates probably weren't far behind.

Oh fuck oh fuck.

Tristan tried to summon a response, and then sat there gaping like a largemouth bass when the words failed him.

Sebastian held out a hand to Ryu. "Sebastian Cruz."

Ryu accepted the handshake and introduced himself. If he was surprised to discover Tristan's mystery professor was a guy, he didn't show it.

"I've watched you play." Sebastian's mouth quirked in a small smile. "I like you better than the other goalie."

Ryu gave a startled laugh, and Tristan finally snapped out of his daze.

"Sorry." He gestured across the table belatedly. "Yeah, this is Seb." Tristan cleared his throat and met Ryu's eyes with a beseeching look. *Please don't be pissed. Please don't say anything. I'll explain later.*

Ryu clasped Tristan's shoulder in an uncommon display of physical support. "Well, I'll let you guys finish. We're on the other side of the bar. I saw you as I was heading back from the restroom. Thought I'd say hello." He didn't have to continue for Tristan to hear the rest of his unspoken message: *and warn you we were here.*

"Crazy that we'd all end up at the same place." Tristan chuckled awkwardly.

"Yeah." Ryu nodded at Sebastian, releasing Tristan's shoulder. "I'll see you later."

When he left, Tristan turned back to Sebastian with his lower lip trapped between his teeth.

"Do you want to leave?" Sebastian asked.

Tristan hesitated before shaking his head jerkily. "No. No, it's fine. If they see us, we're just two friends having dinner, right?"

Sebastian's jaw tightened. He glanced away from Tristan, toward the side of the pub where Ryu and the others sat.

"Let's go," he said after a long, tense moment. "I can tell you're uncomfortable. The venue should be open by now. We'll have a drink there."

Deep, almost dizzying relief washed through Tristan, followed immediately by guilt. He knew he'd hurt Sebastian with the friend comment. He'd been aiming for lighthearted to try to cut the tension, but clearly, he'd missed the mark by a mile.

Sebastian paid the bill and they managed to leave the pub without any of Tristan's teammates noticing. Or at least none of them called out to him if they did.

Tristan's heart was racing to the point where he felt shaky, and his palms were coated in sweat as he settled into the passenger seat of the GTO. He rubbed his hands on his jeans, scrambling for something to say as Sebastian fired up the car.

Tristan failed to think of anything—*again*. Excruciating silence descended between them as Sebastian drove to Terminal West.

After Sebastian cut the engine, Tristan reached over to touch his arm. "Seb. Seb, I'm sorry. I—"

Sebastian didn't even look at him. "Later, Tristan. Please...not right now."

He opened the door and got out of the car before Tristan could answer. Tristan's stomach churned as he rushed to follow Sebastian inside the venue.

Sebastian went straight to the bar and ordered a Scotch for himself and a beer for Tristan. He handed Tristan the bottle without meeting his eyes, his jaw still tense.

"Thanks," Tristan said.

Sebastian only tipped his chin and led the way to a free table. A sparse crowd milled around on the main floor, waiting for the opening act to begin.

Only minutes later, the band ambled on stage. The short wait turned out to be a blessing. Sebastian was noticeably gritting his teeth, his hand clenched into a fist on the tabletop. He'd barely spoken before the music started, and outright avoided looking at Tristan directly, even when Tristan asked him a question.

As a result, Tristan couldn't seem to relax, no matter how much he tried. He couldn't shake the vague feeling of paranoia, either. It was extremely rare for him to be recognized outside of Philips Arena—so rare, it only ever happened at the rink where the Venom practiced—but what if there was a diehard fan in the crowd? What if Tristan forgot himself and touched Sebastian in an intimate way, an overly familiar way that couldn't be misconstrued? What if his teammates showed up here? Had Ryu mentioned a concert? Tristan didn't think so. Then again, they hadn't really discussed their plans in-depth.

Tristan knew the chances were slim. Low enough it was probably ridiculous to even worry about it. Regardless, he couldn't shake the fear.

By the time Zephyr came on, Tristan's shirt was clinging damply to his back, and his neck hurt from keeping his shoulders clenched up tight. The music was great, and Tristan liked the band, but he wasn't in the proper mindset to truly appreciate them. Which was a shame. Under different circumstances, he would've been standing and applauding with the rest of the crowd. He would've loved Zephyr as much as Sebastian had suggested he would.

Sadness swept over Tristan at the thought, especially when combined with Sebastian's obvious anger and the effort he was making to ignore Tristan's existence.

"Let's go," Sebastian said, leaning close enough to be heard but not quite touching.

The crowd was still clapping and calling for an encore, but Tristan didn't care about sticking around for another song or three. He'd been ready to leave since they first arrived.

It took them a while to get to the exit. Outside, Tristan inhaled what felt like his first deep breath in hours.

Neither of them spoke as they got into the car.

Tristan considered trying to apologize again, but Sebastian's frosty demeanor didn't exactly encourage conversation.

We'll talk when we get home. Once they were alone in his apartment, they'd work it all out.

It's going to be fine. Totally fine.

Or so Tristan tried to convince himself.

Chapter Twenty

The whole way back to Tristan's apartment, Sebastian tried to figure out what the hell he was going to say.

"We're just two friends having dinner, right?"

No. Not at all. They were more than friends, and that was why it hurt so much to see Tristan so visibly shaken by someone finding them.

His teammates, his inner voice said. *And he's your boyfriend. Who you are stupidly, madly in love with. Which you were going to tell him tonight, because you're pretty sure he feels the same way.*

The problem was, Sebastian was sure that Tristan *did* love him. Tristan's reaction to his teammate finding them on a date didn't necessarily mean that he wasn't at the same place as Sebastian in their relationship. Hell, he'd come out to his family for Sebastian, had brought him home to meet them. But Sebastian absolutely refused to be with someone who introduced him as a "friend." Someone who was so freaked out about being caught on a date with him, he kept checking over his shoulder the remainder of the night.

Here Sebastian thought he'd been so careful to avoid this. Not careful enough, apparently.

Sebastian pulled the GTO into the lot by Tristan's

building. Tristan hadn't said a word the entire drive back from the venue and looked about as miserable as Sebastian felt. Sebastian put the car in park, but he didn't switch the engine off.

"Aren't you coming up?" Tristan turned to look at him. It was too dark to see his eyes, but the unhappy expression on his face came through loud and clear.

"I don't think it's a good idea," he said softly.

Tristan frowned. "Why? Because I got a little freaked out?"

Sebastian stared out of the window, acutely aware of Tristan's gaze on him. He took a second to compose himself, thinking through what he wanted to say. The weight of this moment lay heavily on his shoulders, and he knew the future of their relationship hung in the balance. "Actually, yes. I told you that if things got more serious, we'd have to have this conversation again, and I think it's probably time." Past time, but there was nothing to be done about that now.

"So come upstairs and let's have it." Tristan laid a tentative hand on Sebastian's leg. "Talk to me. Please."

Sebastian gave a slight shake of his head. "It's more than having this conversation. It's taking time to think about what both of us want, and what we need going forward. I can't be in the closet, Tristan. I *won't*. As much as I want to be with you, and I do, I'll end up resenting you. And if I make you do something you're not comfortable with, then you'll end up resenting *me*. That isn't fair to either of us."

"So what is it you want?" Tristan moved his hand away. Sebastian felt an ache at its absence. "For us to go forward, I mean."

"I need you to be honest," Sebastian said. "About me.

About us. And I know that's not something that's easy for you. That's why I think we both need to take some time to really think about this."

"I do want to be with you," Tristan said softly. His head was bowed, and he was no longer looking at Sebastian. "No amount of time will change my mind about that."

Sebastian closed his eyes briefly, a pang echoing in his chest. "I want to be with you too," he said. "I wish it was that simple, but we both know it isn't."

After a few moments of silence, Tristan said, "So either I come out, or we're through?"

Hearing it put so succinctly made Sebastian wince, but he couldn't necessarily deny the truth of Tristan's words. Still, it was hard to reduce this to something so simple when they both knew the situation was anything but. "I'm saying we both have a lot to think about, but essentially? Yes. I know this isn't fair, and it kills me. But I can't... I can't do this. I can't resent you, and I don't want you to resent me."

"But I'm the one who has to make the decision," Tristan pressed, as determined as he was on the ice when he was trying to keep the opposing team from taking the puck. "You're asking me to make a huge decision about my career. There aren't any out players in the NHL. I don't—I don't know how to even do this, Seb. It's not only me, it's my team, and..." He trailed off, sounding miserable.

Sebastian felt like an asshole, but he didn't know what else to do. It wasn't fair for Tristan to have to come out if he wasn't ready, but it wasn't fair for Sebastian to be forced back into the closet, either. "I know."

"No, you really don't." There wasn't any rancor in

Tristan's voice. Just hurt, and confusion, and a weary resignation that Sebastian hated to hear. He couldn't see Tristan's eyes, but he knew how they'd look. Sad, devoid of their usual cheerful light, like the night he'd shown up at Sebastian's house after that humiliating loss in St. Louis.

"This is something you need to think about, Tristan. And I understand that. I know that I'm asking you to make a huge decision in order to be with me. And I—" Sebastian's voice broke a little. "I know this means I'm probably going to lose you. But I'd rather both of us do what we know is right for us, even if it means not being together. That's why I'm not coming up with you." He knew how that would go. They'd talk, they'd go to bed, and nothing would really get solved between them.

"I—" Tristan's voice sounded choked. He was staring straight ahead, his hand clenched into a fist by his side. "I don't want to lose you."

"I don't want to lose you, either." Sebastian reached out and turned Tristan's face toward him with two fingers on his chin. "But the truth is, I'm in love with you. And because I love you, I can't ask you to make this decision without giving it the thought it deserves."

Before Tristan could say anything, Sebastian leaned in and kissed him. He closed his eyes, savoring the press of Tristan's full mouth against his own. The taste of him, which had become as familiar as breathing. "I'm going to give you the space and time you need, and I'll respect whatever decision you make. This is one of the hardest things I've ever done, Tris. But I hope you understand why I'm doing it."

He pulled away, and heard Tristan sigh. He didn't say anything, just turned and got out of the car. His movements were hurried and clumsy. For such a big guy, Tristan usually moved with an athlete's grace, even in the cramped confines of a car. Clearly he was beset by emotion, and Sebastian understood that, but it didn't make it easier to watch him hurry out of the car and away toward the building.

Tristan didn't look back, but Sebastian stayed where he was until he saw Tristan's tall, broad-shouldered form disappear.

For the next few days, Sebastian kept himself busy with classwork and going on a lot of long, grueling runs. He had tickets for the Venom's home game that weekend, but he resolutely refused to go to the arena. He managed to watch a few minutes of the first period before the sight of Tristan in his jersey made him switch over to an old episode of *Forensic Files*.

Murder and mayhem were easier to deal with than the memory of their last conversation, how hurt Tristan had been when he'd gotten out of the car. Not to mention Sebastian's irritating habit of checking his phone more often than usual, then berating himself for feeling disappointed when there was nothing from Tristan.

Finally, when he couldn't stand the silence or his own turbulent emotions anymore, he called R.J. and asked him to come over for dinner.

"Wait, you can't cook," R.J. said. "Why don't you come over here, instead? You bring the booze, and I'll make *you* dinner."

"Thanks," Sebastian said, secretly relieved he didn't have to cook. He was bad at it when he was in a good mood, much less...well.

He showed up at R.J.'s house, a condo in Druid Hills,

with a bottle of Scotch and a six-pack of Dogfish IPA. R.J.'s house smelled delicious, but Sebastian's appetite had been shit for the last few days and he barely registered the garlicky aroma of R.J.'s famous spaghetti. He put the Scotch on the kitchen island and went to find a glass.

"So, what's up?" R.J. took one look at him and crossed his arms over his chest. "Something tells me this is going to be a sad visit."

Sebastian scowled and filled his glass with plenty of ice. He didn't want to be a weepy drunk. Definitely not before dinner. "It's not happy, that's for sure."

"Tristan?"

Sebastian sat back down and took a long drink of the Scotch. He'd gone for a twelve-mile run that day and had barely managed to choke down something for lunch—he couldn't even remember what it had been. The warmth of the liquor hit his stomach and immediately went to his head. He made a note to drink slower and pushed the glass away. "Yeah."

"Since you didn't bother to glare at me or say anything snarky, it must be pretty bad. What happened?" R.J. took one of the Dogfish IPAs and opened it, storing the rest in his fridge.

Sebastian relayed the incident at dinner in as few words as possible, making sure he gave R.J. all the relevant information. R.J. listened with a sympathetic expression, slowly sipping his beer and letting Sebastian talk.

"I'm sorry, man," he said, when Sebastian was finished. "That's rough. I mean, I can see your point. I know you well enough to know you'd never be okay being with someone who wasn't honest. But I can also see Tristan's

point that it's not easy for him to be open about his sexuality." He shook his head. "That's tough."

That was an understatement. "It is. But I can't go back
to being someone's 'friend,'" Sebastian said, giving the
word a sarcastic inflection. "Coming out is never easy. It
wasn't for me, and I know it isn't for him, either."

R.J. was quiet for a moment. "Have you ever been
given any shit for being gay? You said your family accepted you, and the college seems to be… Well, if you've
had any issues, you've never told me about them."

Sebastian scowled down at the granite countertop.
"It's not a matter of being given shit, R.J. Does my family accept me? Yes and no. They accept that I'm gay, but
it doesn't mean they're happy about it. And by 'family,'
I mean my parents. I have relatives who haven't spoken
to me since I came out. Old friends who pretend they
don't know me if I see them when I'm home visiting my
folks. There's a big difference between the way they accept me and, say, the way you do."

R.J. smiled, but it was a little sad. "I'm glad that you
know I don't have any issue with it, but I'm sorry. That
it's a problem for anyone. It shouldn't be."

"No, it shouldn't," Sebastian agreed. "But it is. At
work, there are a few people who aren't friendly, but
that could be because they think I'm an asshole, not because I'm gay."

"You do have that spectacular resting bitch-face," R.J.
said with a nod. "So there's that."

Sebastian was too mopey to laugh, but it at least got
a hint of a smile out of him. "Right."

"If I recall, your hesitation about dating Tristan was
that the other faculty and the administration would think

you'd been dating him when he was your student," R.J. pointed out.

"Obviously I got over it," Sebastian said, with a bit of a bite. He took another sip of his Scotch. Lashing out at R.J. was not going to help anything.

"Did you?"

"What?" Sebastian's head jerked up, and he leveled a glare at his friend. "We've been dating, haven't we?"

"Yeah. Have you brought him anywhere around your colleagues, though? I don't think I've seen Tristan near your office, and you haven't brought him to any functions."

"I don't go to those because they're dreadful," Sebastian pointed out. "Why are you even going to those?"

"Free food? Free booze? That hot astrophysicist that sometimes shows up?" R.J. shrugged. "My point is, aren't you just as worried about being seen with Tristan? Not because you're gay, but because he was your student?"

Sebastian opened his mouth to argue, then realized he couldn't. He snapped it shut and thought about it. Was he still worried about that? Maybe a little. Sure, Tristan had a schedule that barely allowed the two of them time to spend together, and he couldn't imagine that Tristan would want to hang around a bunch of college faculty and administrators. Hell, Sebastian only put in an appearance when necessary, and that was all about getting tenure.

"Are you still worried that someone will see you two together and that will reflect badly on you? Because if so…" R.J. trailed off.

"That's not the same thing," Sebastian protested, but maybe he was wrong. Maybe it was more similar than he wanted to think. He swore under his breath.

"I'm not trying to make you feel like an asshole," R.J. assured him. "I'm really not."

"I know." Sebastian thought about it. "The thing is," he said slowly, "this isn't Tristan's fault. I'd always thought his teammates were like my colleagues. They existed in this separate world that would somehow never intersect with the one he and I lived in."

"I could have told you that doesn't work." R.J. reached out and tentatively patted Sebastian on the shoulder. "I'm not saying it's wrong that you don't want to be in the closet, you know. But you can't get mad at Tristan for keeping you on the down-low if you're doing that to him too. Even if it's for a different reason."

"So I should parade him around at faculty parties?"

"Or," R.J. said, not reacting to Sebastian's waspish tone, "you could bring him as your date, like literally everyone else does. You know. Since he's your boyfriend and all."

Sebastian thought about that as he watched the ice cubes melt into his Scotch. "I see what you mean, and you're probably right."

"'Probably'? Really, dude?"

"Fine, you're right," Sebastian snapped. "But it isn't the same, R.J. It really isn't. This is a much bigger issue for Tristan and you know it. You said it yourself—there are plenty of professors who have married former students. There isn't one single out player in the NHL, and that's what I'm asking Tristan to do for me. He's young, he's got a long, promising career ahead of him, and I can't ask him to risk all of that for me."

"But you did, didn't you?"

Sebastian closed his eyes. "I asked him to think about what he wanted. R.J., I can't go back in the closet, and that's that. It's not fair to me. Asking him to make this choice isn't fair, either. But what am I supposed to do?"

"I don't know," R.J. said, his voice kind. "But I think you made the right choice. I just want to make sure that you're not doing the same thing he is. If he decides to come out for you, Seb, you can't leave him at home for the rest of your life because he was once your student."

"Have you been to these parties, R.J.? Why would Tristan even want to come to one?" He was being a re-calcitrant asshole and he knew it, but at this point, it was a way of life.

"Because he's your boyfriend, he loves you, and he's proud of you. He supports you and your career. Isn't that why you go to his games, even if you still can't figure out what icing is?"

"I just don't get why sometimes it's okay to send the puck down the ice and sometimes it isn't," Sebastian groused.

"I told you, it's fine when it's a power play and—" R.J. cleared his throat. "Not the time. But…can I ask you: are you in love with him?"

"Do you even need to ask? Have you ever seen me act like this?" Sebastian sighed and pushed his mostly empty drink away. He needed to eat before he had any more or he'd fall asleep right here in R.J.'s kitchen.

"Do you think maybe there's a compromise? Between coming out to the entire NHL, and staying in the closet? I know you have a problem with finding the middle ground, Seb— Oh, don't glare at me. You totally do."

R.J. was right, but Sebastian glared at him anyway. "Whatever."

"I don't want you to lose someone you love because of this," R.J. said. "But I know it isn't easy. Still, I think maybe this is something you should talk to Tristan about *with* him, instead of sending him on his way to figure it out on his own."

Sebastian gave an emphatic shake of his head. "No. I can't do that. I need him to make this choice and I need to respect what it is. I know how hard he's worked to get where he is. I know how much he loves hockey, and yeah, I think he loves me. But sometimes love isn't enough. It's a horrible thing to say, but it's true."

R.J. was quiet for a long time. Finally, he sighed. "You're right. Sometimes it isn't. But didn't someone say love was all about compromise?"

"Hallmark? I don't know." Sebastian shook his head. "I don't know, R.J. I love him too much to ask him to give up everything for me, but I also know myself and how denying who we are to each other...that leads to nothing but resentment and *that* will kill any relationship dead."

R.J. got up off the barstool and went to check the garlic bread in the oven. "I wish I had some kind of answer for you."

So did Sebastian. But the only person with the answer to this particular problem was Tristan, and Sebastian knew it.

Fuck it. He was going to have more Scotch. Luckily, R.J. had a comfortable couch.

Chapter Twenty-One

After Sebastian dropped him off, Tristan broke down for a few hours. He let himself have a good cry—because fuck that macho bullshit about how men should be stone-faced and never express their emotions.

There might not be any crying in baseball, at least not according to Tom Hanks, but there was plenty of crying in hockey. It didn't usually pertain to boyfriend troubles, but hell, Tristan could swear his heart was being torn in two. If he wanted to chug some beer and sob into his pillow, he was goddamned allowed.

He woke the next morning with swollen eyes, a splotchy complexion, and a murderous hangover that made him grateful for the optional morning skate—since he was opting not to move from his couch. No way could he show up at the practice facility looking like he'd been on a three-day bender. The coach would have his ass, and his teammates would give him the third degree. Better to stay home, alone, and lick his wounds.

Once he stopped feeling like his head was going to explode, Tristan buried himself in his studies. He filled his brain with business model components, analytics, marketing strategies, and public policy, and tried very

hard not to think about his boyfriend and their last conversation.

Of course, over the next few days, his mind continually went back to it anyway. He replayed Sebastian saying, *"But the truth is, I'm in love with you,"* about a
thousand times and wished he'd heard those words under
different circumstances. Then maybe he could've said
them back instead of pretty much fleeing the car before
he burst into tears. Because *his* truth was, he didn't have
a damn clue what to do. There was no easy answer he
could give Sebastian in that moment, and so he ran rather
than make a complete spectacle of himself.

He'd known Sebastian's position from the beginning.
And Sebastian had known his. Maybe they'd been de-
luding themselves by getting involved anyway. Maybe
they'd willfully set themselves up for failure when they'd
decided to keep things going beyond that first night.
Maybe, in reality, their relationship had been dead before it'd even gotten off the ground.

Lust made people stupid sometimes. It was one thing
when he and Sebastian simply couldn't keep their hands
off each other. It was an entirely different scenario when
lust turned into need and need turned into love.

Tristan had royally screwed himself by letting it go
so far. Now he couldn't decide if the relationship he so
desperately wanted to keep would be worth the potential
consequences of publicly coming out.

Nearly a week went by. Tristan took his exam—and
thankfully passed it. He checked his phone so often it
felt like it was becoming a tic. He practiced and worked
out with his teammates.

During their next home game, Tristan played like a
demon, throwing hits left and right, racking up a bunch

of penalty minutes, and adding another sweet goal to his season's numbers—and hopefully some highlight reels. But off the ice, Tristan was distracted and sad, and he knew it had to be obvious to his team.

After the game that night, when Ryu texted to say he was outside of Tristan's building, Tristan didn't feel a hint of surprise as he buzzed Ryu upstairs. He'd caught the looks Ryu had been casting him at practices, on the bench, in the locker room. He'd known it would only be a matter of time before Ryu confronted him.

Ryu entered the apartment, studied Tristan for a second, and shook his head pityingly. "Tell me what happened."

They settled on the couch with a couple of beers, and Tristan spilled the whole sad story—from his intense attraction to Sebastian to the plagiarism accusation to the Phloydian Slip concert to coming out to his parents, and every little thing in between.

When he finished, Ryu regarded him contemplatively. "First, I think you should know I'm gay too." Tristan's jaw dropped open, but before he could summon a response, Ryu continued, "I suspected about you, especially when you were really careful not to say whether your professor was a man or a woman, but well… I figured if you wanted me to know, you would've told me."

Tristan started to answer, but Ryu held up his hand.

"Don't get me wrong—I'm not upset or anything. I get it. Trust me. I just wanted you to know about me, so when I say I understand how you feel, you'll know it's not some empty platitude. I mean it. Your secret is safe with me. But I hope you knew that already."

Tristan nodded, swallowing thickly. "Thanks. I, um…

Yeah. Yours too, of course. I'm thankful you trust me enough to tell me."

Ryu inclined his head in acknowledgment.

Sighing, Tristan raked his hands through his hair. "I… This is a lot. I'm only twenty-three, man. This is *huge*. I don't want to lose my friends. I don't want to lose my career. My team."

"You won't." Ryu's tone was as calm as his expression. "I mean, I won't lie and say there won't be problems, but look at how far the league has come. Everyone has to go through sensitivity training now. Teams are having Pride Nights. It's not the same league it was ten, hell, even five years ago. Times are changing. Look at how well your family took it. And Tristan?" Ryu waited until Tristan met his gaze. "Anyone who would cut you out of their life because of your sexuality isn't worth knowing. You're an amazing person. The loss would be entirely theirs, not yours. Feel me?"

Tristan ducked his head to hide the rush of moisture in his eyes. He felt a quick, light squeeze to his biceps, but he couldn't risk looking into Ryu's face again. Not yet. He was too close to losing his composure.

"Tristan…please forgive the cliché, but Sebastian's not the only fish in the sea. There are men who'll understand your position, men who won't mind keeping things quiet until you're ready to retire. If you decide to come out to the team, you can't do it for some guy. You should only do it for yourself, when and *if* you're ready."

"He's not 'some guy,'" Tristan rasped, unthinking. He couldn't allow Sebastian to be reduced to those terms. "I'm in love with him. He makes me happy. He makes me feel smart. Everything about him just…does it for me. I don't want to let him go."

"Then there's your answer."

"Is it that simple, though?" Tristan turned to Ryu. His eyes were damp and probably bloodshot, but it wasn't like Ryu couldn't already tell he was crying. "I mean, really?"

Ryu smiled serenely—and it was so unlike his typical smirk or the wry twist of his lips that usually passed for a smile, Tristan couldn't help but stare at him, shocked.

"It's only as complicated as you make it, Tristan. Will it be easy? No. To be totally honest, it'll probably fucking suck." Ryu cringed, shuddering a little. Then his expression grew serious again. "But here's how I see it. If he loves you, and you love him, if you think he's worth the aftermath of coming out, talk to him. Come to a compromise you can both live with. Communication, right? That's what relationships are all about. Or so I hear." One corner of Ryu's mouth curved up sardonically. "And you can tell him about me if you need to. It might make him feel better to know someone has your back in the dressing room. That's why I wanted you to know about me too. You're not alone, Tristan. Never forget that."

Tristan's laugh was thick with tears, more of a sob than anything. But he felt better than he had in days. Ryu had given him something to think about. At the end of the day, maybe it really *was* as simple as how he and Sebastian felt about each other—or rather, how *he* felt about Sebastian. Tristan had been fighting feelings of resentment about how any compromise between them had to come from his side. Sebastian was already out to his coworkers and friends. What did he have to lose? What was *he* giving up?

But maybe it was time to stop thinking about it in those terms. Sebastian had made his stance clear from the very beginning. Tristan wanted to be with him anyway—then and now.

Maybe it was time to let go of the fear.

Chapter Twenty-Two

The morning after his conversation with Ryu, Tristan rapped on the doorjamb of Coach Adams's office and poked his head inside. "Clancy? Can I speak with you for a minute?"

Clancy sat back in his seat, waving a big hand. "Sure, Tristan. Come on in."

Tristan entered the room and shut the door quietly behind him. On the ice and during training, Clancy Adams was simply "Coach." Off the ice, Tristan and the others always addressed him by his first name. He was a large man, easily two or three inches taller than Tristan, and broad across the chest and shoulders. In the nineties, he'd played the role of enforcer, a dying breed in today's NHL, but back then, he'd been the one his teammates relied upon to dole out vengeance whenever the opposition got out of line. He made a better coach than he had a player, though his intimidation factor hadn't lessened with time.

"What's up?" Clancy asked as Tristan folded his frame into the chair in front of the desk.

The question made Tristan's heart jolt. He'd been coping with stomach-churning stress all morning, opting to skip breakfast for fear he wouldn't be able to keep anything down. The strain of the past week had probably sucked a year or two off his life, and he wondered if this vulnerable exhaustion was what Westley felt in *The Princess Bride* after being strapped down on The Machine with a coolly sadistic Count Rugen at the controls.

Already Tristan resented the process of coming out, that it even had to be a *thing*. Straight might be the default, the status quo, but why did it matter that he wasn't? It shouldn't. But, of course, it did, and so here he was. At this point, he just wanted it to be done. If his seasons with the Venom had taught him anything, it was that Clancy Adams appreciated a forthright approach. No sense in beating around the bush with a man who'd rather cut a path directly through.

So Tristan cleared his throat, firmed his spine, and said, "I'm gay, and I'd like to come out to the team."

For a moment, Clancy appeared nonplussed. Then he carefully closed his laptop and laced his hands across the top. "Okay. Only the team? Or do you mean you'd like to inform the team first, before making a wider announcement?"

"Only the team. And my agent, of course. I'm going to speak to her tomorrow. But I'm not ready for the media circus that would come along with telling the entire league." Tristan's stomach cramped. "No. I have no interest in being the NHL's gay ambassador. We both know that's how it'll go for the first player who comes out publicly. I only want to be honest with my family, and that includes the team."

Clancy nodded slowly. He looked contemplative, but there was no judgment in his expression. "Did you want to do this individually, or did you want me to call a meeting?"

Tristan considered the idea, tempted for a second to

lay it all in Clancy's more-than-capable hands, but there were several players who deserved to hear it directly from Tristan. "One of them already knows. I'd prefer to tell Morley, Bellzie, and a few of the others myself. After that, we'll see."

"Your call, of course. Once it's done, though, I think a meeting would be wise. Let me know."

"I will." Tristan stood. "Thanks for...well, for not freaking out." Clancy's casual acceptance had done wonders to ease the tension in Tristan's belly, which was good because he still had a practice to get through.

Clancy shrugged one massive shoulder. "My brother is gay. I know it wasn't easy for you to come in here and open yourself up to me. If anyone gives you grief over this, you tell me." When Tristan didn't answer immediately, Clancy's dark brows drew together, and he flashed the mean mug that had put the fear of God into his opponents for a solid decade. "I mean it, Tristan. I won't tolerate bigots in my locker room."

Tristan grinned. "Got it, Coach."

Clancy extended a hand, and Tristan reached across the desk to shake it. "My door is always open. Use it if you need to."

With a nod, Tristan left the office. One down. Hopefully he could arrange a lunch for the other guys he wanted to tell face-to-face. As comforting as everyone's reactions had been so far—and Tristan knew and appreciated how lucky he'd been in that regard—he couldn't wait for his coming out to be old news.

As it turned out, it wasn't difficult to corral his teammates into an impromptu lunch after practice once Tristan announced he'd be footing the bill. He invited

Bellzie, Morley, both alternate captains, and Ryu for his quiet, steady moral support.

They met at a nearby restaurant that specialized in globally inspired sandwiches. Tristan had been there before and liked the casual atmosphere and the setup that offered several large tables tucked away in the corners for maximum privacy.

Once they'd placed their orders, it took Tristan a few throat-clearings and a "Hey, guys?" to cut through the loud, animated chatter. His teammates turned to him expectantly, and Ryu, who sat beside him, slipped a hand beneath the table to give Tristan's knee a subtle, uncharacteristic squeeze.

"Um." Tristan faltered. For the most part, he'd done all the rest of his coming out one-on-one. Being the central focus of five sets of eyes sent his nerves into chaos. It didn't matter that in the past—in high school, college, and even during Venom special events—he'd delivered speeches without so much as a flicker of stage fright. He hadn't been dropping the g-bomb and talking about his boyfriend then, had he?

"I'm gay." The words burst free in a nearly unintelligible rush. Morley blinked at him, appearing bemused. The alternate captains—Stewie and Tanger—exchanged a confused glance. Only Bellzie seemed to have heard Tristan correctly, and his warm, encouraging gaze bolstered Tristan's courage when Morley asked, "What'd'ya say there, Holtzy?"

"I'm gay," Tristan repeated. He sucked in a slow breath and kept his voice clear as he continued. "I told Coach this morning. I'll be telling the rest of the team too, but I wanted you guys to know first. I have a boyfriend. He's a professor at GSU, and it's serious. I'm not going public, you know, to the league. It would be too much, and I don't want to face that kind of scrutiny. But I *would* like to eventually be able to introduce him to the team."

A few seconds of silence greeted his pronouncement. Then Bellzie grinned and reached over to clasp Tristan's shoulder. "That's great. I'm sure we'd all love to meet him." He peered around the table. "Isn't that right, boys?"

Stewie and Ryu nodded.

Morley shot Tristan a thumbs-up. "Whatever floats your boat, Holtzy. Ladies, gents, both at the same time." He leered, leaning forward. "Live and let live, bro, that's my motto."

If it was, Tristan had never heard Morley use it before, but he laughed, appreciating the sentiment anyway.

Only Tanger looked uncomfortable, his mouth pulled down at the corners, gaze laser-focused on his glass of sweet tea as he muttered, "Yeah, sure. It's cool."

To Tristan's vast relief, Bellzie mentioned something about the Eastern Conference standings, easily diverting the attention away from Tristan's sex life, and the rest of the lunch went smoothly—aside from Tanger never quite managing to look Tristan in the eye as they ate their food. But that was fine. Well, not *fine*, but not entirely unexpected. Tristan hadn't fooled himself into thinking his revelation wouldn't come without repercussions. It was what it was, and as Ryu had told him, if anyone had a problem with his sexuality, it was their issue and their cross to bear, not his.

Afterward, as they parted ways in the parking lot, Bellzie called out for Tristan to wait. "Do you have a sec?" he asked as Tristan stood there with the keys to his Jeep in hand.

Tristan nodded. "Want to sit in the car?" It wasn't very cold, but between the chill and the light drizzle, he'd rather not have a discussion outside.

"Sure."

Bellzie went around to the passenger door, and Tristan got into the Jeep and cranked the heat. Once inside, Bellzie removed his snapback, revealing flattened brown curls. He tossed the hat onto the dashboard and turned to face Tristan.

"Since you shared with us, I wanted to share something with you," he said, his face unusually serious. "Tabby and I are separated. We're getting a divorce."

Tristan stared at him, stunned. He'd witnessed the implosions of many of his teammates' relationships over the years, but he'd always assumed Bellzie and Tabby were rock-solid. They seemed so happy together, the perfect matchup, living in a comfortable, sprawling house with a pair of good-looking, well-behaved kids and a ragtag group of rescued dogs, like some kind of Americana daydream. Tristan had pictured them aging into one of those adorable older couples who wore matching T-shirts and rode tandem bikes together in the park. They weren't supposed to get *divorced*.

"I—I'm sorry," Tristan stuttered when the silence had gone on too long.

"I am too. But it's time." Bellzie sighed deeply, regret in the sound. "I'm bisexual."

Tristan's eyes almost bulged right out of his skull. He made a brief, startled noise, a squawk really, something he imagined might come out of a goose being hit by a car.

Bellzie shook his head. "Sorry. Oh, God. No. I mean, that's *not* the reason we're getting divorced." He laughed sheepishly. "Man, that was the most awkward segue of all time." Bellzie ran a hand over his head, ruffling the curls. "Tabby knows—she's always known—but the two things aren't related. I just… I wanted to let you know you're not alone. I can't claim to understand exactly what you're going through, of course, but if you ever need to talk, I'm here. Remember that, okay?"

Emotion tightened Tristan's throat. He gripped the steering wheel, his knuckles whitening, and nodded when he couldn't find the words to speak.

Bellzie laid a hand on Tristan's tense forearm. "Why don't you let me tell the rest of the team, huh? I'll do whatever I can to make it easier for you."

Tristan considered the offer. Partly it felt like cheating to let Bellzie take over. It was Tristan's truth; he should be the person to tell it. Yet, if he pictured having to repeat his story even *one* more time, the idea alone exhausted him. Bellzie could spare him that turmoil. Tristan wasn't too proud to accept the help from his captain. His friend. "I'd appreciate that. Thank you."

Bellzie patted Tristan's arm before pulling away. "Also, in spite of the separation, Tabby and I are still living together until everything is finalized. We'll be throwing our annual end-of-season bash in a couple of months, like always. You should bring your boyfriend. You could introduce him to some of the team, and with so many people there, you wouldn't stand out. It might be a good way to test the waters."

"You're probably right. I'll ask Seb."

"Good." Bellzie grabbed his hat from the dashboard and thrust it back over his curls. "I'll let you go. See you tonight."

Bellzie left the Jeep and dashed through the drizzle to his SUV. Tristan checked the mirrors and pulled out of the parking space, turning in the direction that would lead toward home. A pregame nap sounded fantastic now that he'd shed some of the weight he'd been carting around on his shoulders. The day had been both harder and easier than he'd anticipated. He wasn't finished having conversations about it. Tristan knew that, of course. But he trusted Bellzie. By nightfall, his secret would be out to the rest of his teammates. He could only hope that most of them cared more about his skill as a defenseman than who he loved or wanted to have sex with.

Chapter Twenty-Three

The following day, when Tristan stepped onto the ice for the Venom's morning skate, the chorus of Van Halen's "Hot For Teacher" suddenly started blaring at full volume over the arena's speakers.

Tristan stopped so abruptly he lost his balance, and would've sprawled onto the ice face-first had a hand not shot out to steady him. He turned to see Ryu gripping his biceps and staring at him in concern. All around them, their teammates were snickering, and Tristan could actually *feel* the blood draining from his head. Everything went fuzzy around the edges—the ads on the boards, the rows of maroon-upholstered seats, the bright lights overhead—and Tristan feared for a second his knees might give out.

This was it: the reason he'd feared coming out from the very beginning.

Then Morley appeared, grinning his broad, unrepentant grin, his blue eyes shining with mirth. "Sorry, Holtzy. I couldn't help myself." He laughed, jovial as always, and clapped Tristan on the shoulder. "Besides, this song has a kick-ass guitar solo. You should see me rock it out on *Guitar Hero.*"

Tristan dug up a chuckle from somewhere, though it

emerged sounding strained. His mounting anxiety began to recede, and as he looked around, noting the complete lack of malice on his teammates' faces, he was able to push it down even further.

These were his friends. They hadn't acted out of spite. Morley was behaving in typical Morley fashion, and Tristan knew with total clarity he would've done the same thing and acted the same way had Tristan's hot professor turned out to be a woman instead of a man. It wasn't about his sexuality at all.

Relief surged in the wake of that realization.

If Tristan's teammates hadn't felt comfortable enough to joke with him anymore, *then* he'd have cause for concern. This was nothing more than the usual teasing harassment that went on among friends—especially with a man-child like Morley around. It made Tristan hopeful any lingering awkwardness might ease back to normalcy in time.

Clancy appeared at the mouth of the tunnel leading to the dressing room. "Turn that shit off!" he yelled. "It's an affront to my fucking eardrums!" The music stopped abruptly. "That's better." He waved his arm. "Come on, boys. Let's run through some of the plays we discussed. I want to see how the changes look on the third and fourth lines."

One of the assistant coaches started chucking pucks onto the ice as the team split into smaller groups.

Tristan moved to his usual position at the point opposite Morley. Within seconds, he fell into his familiar routine, his brain switching over to hockey mode. And when Bellzie skated by to bump his shoulder, shooting Tristan a blinding smile as he passed, Tristan was able to return it without having to pretend.

* * *

After practice and showers, he and Ryu bowed out of the larger team lunch to meet at their favorite Thai restaurant.

Ryu scrutinized him over plates of fragrant appetizers and cups of hot tea. "Are you all right? I thought you were going to pass out when that song started playing. I would've tried to stop him if I'd known what he planned."

Tristan stirred the peanut dipping sauce with a piece of his spring roll. "It's okay. I'm fine. I realized pretty quickly it wasn't meant to be malicious. Morley is Morley, you know?"

"Oh, yes, I do know," Ryu said, dry as dust.

"I think he's trying to be supportive in his own way. I'd rather have him joking with me than ignoring me like some of the other guys." Tristan sighed. "But, I mean, it's all brand-new. No one's been really awful or anything. It could be a lot worse."

"True." Ryu tilted his head, his brows furrowed. "When I was in college, several of the guys on the team knew about me. A few of them gave me grief, but my college was fairly liberal, so for the most part, it wasn't a big deal. It shouldn't be. We go out there, we play our games like everybody else."

"Yeah. I wish it wasn't a big deal. Maybe someday it won't be. I'm still the same guy."

"I've thought about doing it too. Coming out." Ryu smiled wryly. "For moral support, if nothing else."

Tristan shook his head. "You don't have to do that for me. It's like you told me before: do it only if and when you're ready."

"It wouldn't be for you. Not entirely anyway. But maybe I'll wait until I find my own Professor Cruz."

Tristan grinned. "I'm sure we can locate another scowly gay Puerto Rican if we look hard enough."

"Ha." Ryu's lips twisted. "From what you've told me, he and I are way too alike. We'd strangle each other in a week. What I need is someone more like you."

Tristan's face warmed, and he ducked his head. How Ryu had him pegged, he couldn't guess. Maybe it was his weird goalie senses. Sometimes Ryu seemed all-knowing.

"Yeah." Ryu's voice sounded almost wistful. "Like you. But maybe brattier. I do enjoy a good challenge."

Tristan didn't even know what to say to that, so he stuffed another spring roll into his mouth, making Ryu chuckle.

"That's a pretty blush. I've wanted to tell you before."

Tristan looked up, startled, to find Ryu smirking at him, his dark eyes gleaming.

"I love how bashful you are sometimes," Ryu said. "Those sweet reactions are like catnip to a certain type of man, and from what I've heard about your Professor Cruz, I think we have similar tastes."

Ryu nodded sagely, his feathery bangs falling over his forehead. His hair was long enough now he often wore it in a little bun during practice. Tristan thought it made him appear even more rock star-ish. He wondered if Ryu knew he had a following on Twitter for his "water bottle porn" moments—the times he removed his mask during stoppages of play to cool himself off by squirting water over his head and then shaking out his thick, wet hair. The NHL had twice included shots of it in their "Slo-Mo Monday" compilations. Tristan had never admitted it aloud, but with Ryu's perfect cheekbones and strong, angular jaw, he agreed it looked seductive as fuck.

Still. Tristan flicked a chunk of cabbage across the table at him, which Ryu, of course, dodged. "Asshole."

"Guilty as charged." Ryu's expression turned serious. "I'm proud of you, though. Truly. You've had a lot going on with the classes and everything. Now you've come out to your family and the team. You're one of the good guys, Tristan. You deserve good things."

Tristan blushed again, but this time, he held Ryu's gaze. "Thanks. You do too."

"Okay, enough with the sappiness. It's as uncomfortable for me as it is for you. I feel like I have to go be rude to someone to make up for it."

Tristan laughed, a loud burst that drew the attention of the people at the surrounding tables. "Don't worry," he wheezed when he got himself under control. "I won't tell anyone you were nice. Wouldn't want to spoil your rep."

Ryu smiled back at him—a real, rare smile—and Tristan knew right then, deep in his heart, as long as he had the support of his friends, things were going to be fine.

Now all he needed to do was get his man back.

Chapter Twenty-Four

Tristan didn't call before he went to Sebastian's house that night. By now, he'd memorized Sebastian's schedule. He knew Sebastian would be home because he had an early class the next morning. But, most of all, Tristan didn't want to risk calling and being told to stay away.

Sebastian had obviously meant it when he said he'd give Tristan space. Tristan hadn't heard from him for over a week, and out of respect for Sebastian's request that he think things through, he hadn't tried to contact Sebastian, either. Not that it hadn't killed Tristan to go without so much as a text for all that time, but he'd owed it to both Sebastian and himself to give the situation the consideration it deserved.

And he'd done so. He'd made his decision to come out to the team, and he'd waited to see Sebastian until after it was finished. It was nerve-racking to show up, heart in hand, without knowing what Sebastian's response might be. Sebastian could've decided he didn't want to deal with the drama of dating a hockey player after all. Tristan might've come out for absolutely nothing. But it had been *his* decision, done on his terms, and he wouldn't regret it no matter what happened with Sebastian.

Of course, that wasn't to say Tristan wouldn't be

angry. But he'd done this—come out without consulting Sebastian first—so he couldn't blame Sebastian for his own decisions afterward. Maybe there hadn't been very many choices, true, but there *were* some. Tristan could've given up what they had and walked away to keep his secret. It might've broken his heart, but it was a viable option.

Viable but not fucking endurable as far as Tristan was concerned. He loved Sebastian too much to lose him now.

When he arrived at Sebastian's building, Tristan lucked out and caught the door as someone was leaving. The guy looked vaguely familiar and nodded at Tristan as they crossed paths. He had to be a resident who'd seen Tristan around over the past several months, because he didn't appear particularly concerned about allowing a stranger inside.

With his backpack slung over his shoulder, Tristan took the elevator to Sebastian's floor. He didn't want to seem presumptuous, and yet *not* bringing a bag felt like abandoning hope somehow. Besides, he'd brought a gift for Sebastian, and he didn't want to risk it being seen before he knew exactly where they stood. Tristan did have some pride after all.

He knocked on Sebastian's door and spent the next thirty seconds shifting anxiously in place. Tristan had intentionally worn a pair of the gray sweatpants Sebastian loved so much, because he knew they drove Sebastian crazy. As much as everything else, Tristan wanted proof Sebastian had missed him and still wanted him that way too. And he was hopeful, so very hopeful, the sweatpants would lead to what they normally did.

The knob rattled. Tristan's pulse ratcheted up as Sebastian pulled open the door. Then there he was, dressed in nothing but black lounge pants, his dark hair mussed as if he'd been running his fingers through it, and his sharp jaw shadowed by a few days' worth of stubble. Tristan wanted to eat him alive.

Instead, he just stared.

"Can I come in?" he asked after a beat of silence.

Sebastian wordlessly stepped aside. Tristan entered the apartment and shrugged the backpack off to clutch it in front of him. If it looked like he was using the bag as a shield, well, there was some small truth to that. Tristan couldn't deny he was terrified at the thought of what might happen here tonight.

He turned to see Sebastian standing near the door with his arms crossed over his bare chest. Tristan searched his expression, seeking signs of welcome. "I'm sorry for not calling. I wanted to have this conversation in person."

Something flashed across Sebastian's face—fear, maybe—but it was gone before Tristan could decipher it. "All right. But first, I wanted to—"

"No…" Tristan drew in a deep breath. "Please, let me say this, okay? I need to get it out."

Sebastian nodded, but his body tensed like he was preparing for a blow.

"I've been doing a lot of thinking," Tristan said. "I could bore you with the details, but the most important part is this—I don't want to lose you. I don't want to lose *us*." Tristan swallowed hard. "You know I told my parents about us because I didn't want to keep you a secret from them. Yesterday, I came out to my team too. I don't know if I'll ever be ready to come out to the entire league, but… Well, I hope, I really hope, my teammates knowing will be enough for you." Tristan unzipped the backpack with shaky hands and withdrew the jersey he'd brought for Sebastian. "I want you to come to my games. I want you to wear this. I want them all to know you're with me, and that I'm proud of us, and that I... I love you."

He said the last part a bit helplessly. Sebastian's expression hadn't changed, and a knot was forming in Tristan's belly with every passing second. Then Sebastian breathed noisily through his nose and scrubbed both hands over his face.

"*Damn,*" he said, his voice muffled. "I thought you'd come here to end it. I've never been so afraid." Sebastian sighed, dropping his arms to his sides and looking at Tristan with suspiciously damp eyes. "I was ready to beg you to reconsider and suggest we work out some sort of compromise. That's what I started to say before you asked me to let you finish." He raked his fingers through his hair and shook his head as if to clear it. "I know that's easy to say *now*, but fuck, Tris... In spite of everything I said the last time we saw each other, I don't know if I could have ever really let you walk away."

Tristan dropped what he was holding, rushed across the room, and yanked Sebastian into his embrace. The sense of relief when Sebastian's strong, wiry arms wrapped around him only solidified Tristan's certainty that he'd made the right decision.

He buried his face against Sebastian's neck, squeezing him tight. "I don't want it to be over. I want to be with you."

Sebastian laughed breathlessly. "I don't want it to be over, either. I told you that."

Tristan drew back to meet his gaze. "Is it enough? That I came out to my team?"

Sebastian reached up to cradle Tristan's face in his palms. His dark eyes studied Tristan. "It's *more* than

enough. I know—I mean I don't know, but I can imagine—
how difficult it must've been for you. I don't need you to
come out to the world. I just… I didn't know if I could live
with having the most important people in your life thinking I'm only your friend. It hurt too much to contemplate."

Tristan covered Sebastian's hands with his. "They
know who you are to me now. I promise."

Sebastian pulled Tristan down for a gentle kiss.
"Thank you. I wish you would've told me you were doing
it. I could've been there to support you."

Tristan shook his head. "I had to do it on my own."

Sebastian kissed him again, deepening the contact.
Tristan moaned at the feel of Sebastian's tongue against
his own. It seemed as if ages had passed since Sebastian
kissed him in the car that last time. Tristan hadn't even
been able to enjoy it then. It'd felt too much like good-
bye. "I missed you."

Sebastian bit lightly at his lower lip. "I missed you
too. And I'm truly sorry I hurt you."

"I'm sorry I hurt you too. You know, at the restaurant
when Ryu saw us."

Sebastian nodded. "Thank you. Now pick my jersey
up off the floor, Mr. Holt."

Tristan flushed and·went to collect the items he'd
dropped. He tossed the backpack on the couch and tried
to hand Sebastian the jersey.

"Will it fit you?" Sebastian asked.

Tristan paused, puzzled. "Sure. Might be a little snug
on me, but they run large. Why?"

"Because I've had fantasies about fucking you in your
jersey and nothing else. I want you to put it on and get
on your hands and knees for me."

Tristan gulped—legitimately gulped—loud enough that Sebastian grinned.

"I think you like that idea."

Tristan nodded, convulsively clenching his hands on the material of the jersey. He liked the idea so much his dick was already half-hard.

Sebastian chuckled. "Go to my bedroom, strip down, and put it on. I'll be right behind you."

Tristan didn't so much as hesitate. By the time Sebastian entered the room a few minutes later, Tristan was in the center of the bed wearing nothing but the jersey with his own name stitched on the back. His knees were bent, bare ass up and presented, waiting to be filled.

He heard the whisper of fabric and seconds later, he felt the brush of Sebastian's thighs against his own as Sebastian settled on the mattress behind him. Sebastian aligned his hot, hard cock with Tristan's crease and dragged his shaft down until the slick head bumped Tristan's balls.

"You don't know what seeing you like this does to me." Sebastian's voice was quiet, almost reverent.

Tristan groaned, reaching between his thighs to grip his own dick. "I think I do."

Sebastian trailed his hands from Tristan's shoulders to his ass cheeks. He palmed them, squeezed once, and spread them wide to expose Tristan's hole. "I missed touching you."

Tristan shivered and buried his heated face in Sebastian's pillow, inhaling the familiar scent. He wanted to cover himself in that smell, wanted *Sebastian* on every inch of his skin. "I missed having you inside me." Tristan flushed as he said it, but it was worth the embarrassment to hear Sebastian's soft, pleased sound.

Sebastian continued exploring him—tugging gently
on Tristan's balls, kneading Tristan's thighs, running his
fingertips along the backs of Tristan's calves. He even
trailed his nails lightly along the soles of Tristan's feet.

Tristan could only describe Sebastian's touches as
worshipful. He pushed into every caress, craving each
point of contact. He basked in the attention, moaning
incoherently when Sebastian's mouth got involved in
the proceedings.

Sebastian bit one of his ass cheeks, fiercely enough
that Tristan choked on a cry. He sucked on Tristan's sac
and licked a path to his hole. Once there, he lingered,
teasing Tristan with slick lashes of his tongue until
Tristan was covered in sweat, bumping his hips back,
and chanting "Fuck me" under his breath.

He felt Sebastian trembling as he got the condom on,
slicked up, and held Tristan open so he could work his
way inside. Blindly, Tristan reached a hand back. Sebastian's fingers threaded through his and gripped tightly. A
sharp pang of emotion shot through Tristan's chest, and
his moan verged on a sob when Sebastian finally started
to move. "I love you so much."

Sebastian leaned over him to place a kiss on the nape
of his neck, right above the collar of the jersey. "I love
you more."

Any tenderness ended there. Sebastian knew the way
Tristan liked to be fucked, and he gave it to him hard,
an almost constant, grinding pressure against Tristan's
hole that propelled him toward his orgasm with every
deep, aggressive thrust.

The jersey tightened around Tristan's waist, and he
realized Sebastian had fisted a handful of the material
and was using it to hold him in place. The mental visual

was too much for Tristan to handle. He yanked at his cock and came in a shuddering rush, his muscles clamping around Sebastian's dick with enough force to draw groans from them both.

"Fuck, yes. *Baby.* Choke that fucking dick." Sebastian pressed Tristan down so he was flat on the bed. He covered Tristan's body with his and worked his hips in quick, shallow jabs until he stiffened, muttering something unintelligible as he found his own release.

"God, I needed that," Tristan murmured once he regained the ability to speak.

Sebastian laughed and rolled off him. "Me too." He fell onto his back against the pillows, still struggling to catch his breath, and grabbed a tissue from the nightstand so he could deal with the condom.

Tristan turned his head to look at him more fully. For a couple of minutes they lay there, staring at each other with soft, intimate smiles. It was ridiculously sappy, and something Tristan could've never imagined happening when he first saw Sebastian Cruz in that lecture hall all those months ago.

He loved it.

"Come here." Sebastian held out an arm.

Tristan moved closer and snuggled into Sebastian's embrace.

Sebastian stroked his hair, a light, gentle touch, and rested their foreheads together. "I'm so proud of you," he whispered, his breath warm on Tristan's lips. "I'm with you every step of the way, whatever happens from here on out. Whatever you need."

Tristan's eyes stung. He nodded, managing to croak a "Thank you" past the rawness in his throat. So far, coming out to his team had gone a lot more smoothly than he'd ever anticipated. There would still be hurdles. Tristan wasn't naïve enough to think otherwise. They'd deal with those issues when and if they came to pass.

The future was a lot less frightening, knowing he'd have Sebastian at his side.

Epilogue

Sebastian could recall few things as stressful as dating a hockey player during the playoffs. Even his comps for his PhD program hadn't been this intense. Or, okay, maybe they'd been as intense, but there was one main difference— Sebastian had some say in the outcome.

Sitting on the sidelines while the Venom played in the Stanley Cup playoffs? All he could do was watch.

The first round wasn't too bad. The Venom played the Pittsburgh Condors, and won the series in five games. The most stressful moment for Sebastian had been during the last game, which had been in Atlanta and had gone to sudden-death overtime. He'd been so on edge that at one point he'd turned to Tabby Bellamy and said, "How do you *do* this?"

She'd grinned at him. "You just do. But before you ask, no. You never get used to it."

Sebastian had dragged both hands through his hair and ignored R.J.'s smirking next to him. R.J., who was now dating his colleague Maura, was planning to bring her along to the games if the Venom ended up facing Maura's favorite team, the New York Admirals.

When the puck had found the back of the net thirteen minutes into the double-overtime period, Sebastian

wasn't sure he'd ever screamed so loudly in his life. He'd
high-fived everyone around him in the arena, which was
going crazy. He had to admit that sports were maybe
a little more fun than he'd thought. Tristan had been
wound up as hell after the game…right until the second
he'd gotten to Sebastian's apartment after all the interviews. He'd passed out almost immediately, and their
victory celebration had had to wait until the morning.
Sebastian couldn't blame him, given how long Tristan
had spent on the ice.

Sebastian got a bit of ribbing from Maura about the
series against the New York Admirals, and since Tristan
had scored Maura tickets for the game, it was kind of
interesting to have someone there rooting for the other
team. It would have been an interesting sociological
experiment, if Sebastian weren't experiencing sports-
nerves for the first time in his life. It didn't help that he
was in the middle of grading final exams, either. He had
no idea how Tristan managed to deal with the stress of
uncertainty—like taking exams for the rest of your life,
in front of twenty thousand people.

He did figure out how to deal with Tristan's stress in
private, however. The night before the sixth game against
the Admirals, Sebastian was grading papers and trying to ignore Tristan pacing a hole through his floor. It
wasn't only the pacing that was making it hard for Sebastian to concentrate. Tristan was tense in a way that
he usually only was on the ice, shoulders stiff and jaw
clenched so hard it looked like it might crack from the
pressure. Sebastian couldn't blame him, not with the grueling schedule of playing a competitive sport and all
the travel involved, but it was still driving him crazy.
Waves of anxiety poured out of Tristan, making Sebas-

tian finally put his papers down and say in a firm voice, "Come over here."

Tristan made his way over, his eyes wide. He had a bit of a bruise on his left cheekbone from getting a cross-check to the face (which had *not* been called as a penalty, something that still incensed Sebastian), and blond scruff from his playoff beard. "Sorry," he said sheepishly. "I know I'm probably driving you nuts, huh. I can go work out if you want."

Sebastian did want to give him a workout, but he had a much better idea. "No. I'll worry that you'll hurt yourself, and then I'd have to explain to your entire hockey team that their star defenseman can't play because I got annoyed by him pacing and made him go use the elliptical."

"I was thinking I'd lift." A smile curved the edge of Tristan's mouth.

"Oh, okay, great. Then it'd be, 'Sorry, Tristan has a fractured ankle because he dropped a weight on himself.'"

Tristan crossed his arms and scowled. With the beard, he looked like a very cranky hipster Viking. "Hey. I'm not the one who drops weights. Ahem." He coughed into his fist, a very poorly disguised, "Sebastian."

Sebastian gave him his professor look. "Someone overestimated the amount of weight I could lift."

"You run *marathons*, though."

"Tristan, get on your knees," Sebastian ordered, spreading his legs and pointing to the space between. It never failed to give him a thrill when Tristan complied, quickly and eagerly, steadying himself with his hands on Sebastian's thighs. He looked pleased with himself.

Sebastian picked up one of the exams he had left to grade, undoing his pants with his free hand. "Suck me off.

Don't rush it, either. I have six papers left, and you better not make me come before I'm finished grading them."

Tristan slid his warm fingers over Sebastian's dick, starting to stroke it slowly. "Is my giving you a blowjob gonna mean they get better grades, since I'm so good at it?"

Sebastian reached out and casually smacked him across the face, then spoke with calculated dismissiveness. "I want to hear you sucking me, not speaking."

Tristan made a sound, but applied himself to the task at hand admirably. He sucked Sebastian with all his pent-up nerves and enthusiasm, which got Sebastian to the edge before he'd even finished the first paper. He slapped him again, loving the way Tristan's eyes went hot and unfocused, the way Tristan's face still turned red even though it was covered by blond scruff. "Take your time. Remember you're supposed to make this last." He grabbed Tristan's chin with his hand, forcing his gaze up and speaking sharply. "Don't make me tell you again."

Tristan moaned around his dick, and Sebastian went back to grading. He was definitely going to have to redo them, since he was only pretending to pay attention to the answers and was way too distracted by Tristan's mouth. At the end, he gave up entirely and grabbed Tristan's head with two hands, holding him steady and saying, "Get yourself off before I finish or you can go to bed hard."

Sebastian saw Tristan's elbow moving as he jacked himself off, and Sebastian half closed his eyes and let himself fuck Tristan's throat rough and fast. Tristan might have technically come a few seconds after Sebastian, but he was too caught up in his own orgasm to care.

"Thanks for that," Tristan said, later, when they were in bed. He yawned. "That really did help. You know if we win tomorrow, it'll be a thing, right? Like a super-stition blowjob."

"I *guess* I can handle that," Sebastian drawled, then turned his head so he could kiss him. "If you don't win, that better not mean I don't ever get another one, though."

Tristan laughed, and it wasn't long before he fell asleep. Sebastian stroked his hand through Tristan's hair a few times, then sighed, got out of bed, and went to finish grading.

The Venom won the next game, ensuring that Sebastian's cock would not go unsucked during the rest of the playoffs. He knew by now how seriously Tristan took his pregame superstitions, though apparently he should be glad Tristan wasn't a goalie.

Sebastian's grades were all turned in by the time the Venom met the Memphis Marauders in the Eastern Conference final. The fact that the two teams were arch-rivals made the already intense series even more so, and Sebastian wasn't sure he could handle the Stanley Cup Final if it was somehow *worse*. He was hoarse after the second game, had decided he hated the Memphis Marauders, and found himself muttering to R.J. about the refs having a clear anti-Venom bias until R.J. lost the battle to keep a straight face and cracked up laughing.

Whatever. This was stupid. Why did anyone do this to themselves? Why did Sebastian care so much? Maura tried giving him a book about the sociology of sports fans, but he could barely read a take-out menu right now, much less a book. He couldn't comprehend the stress Tristan was under, and he was torn between wanting his boyfriend's team to make the Cup Final and also secretly hoping Tristan would be able to shave at some point.

The beard was nice, but it was getting a bit mountain-man-ish for his tastes.

The series went to seven games, and everyone who wasn't a fan of either team was thrilled about the "excitement of a game seven." Sebastian wanted to find those people and glare at them for an hour or two, because there was nothing exciting about this. Especially since the game was in Memphis, and he'd already decided he hated the city, the stupid one-way streets downtown, and their barbeque. Who put *coleslaw* on barbeque anyway?

Of course the game went to overtime—not once, but *twice.* Sebastian stood with his arms crossed, scarcely blinking, the roar of the crowd deafening as they watched the players race up and down the ice. He couldn't even imagine how exhausted Tristan was by then, given how long he'd been out there.

When one of the Marauders scored on Norell, the Venom's starting goalie (who Sebastian privately thought shouldn't have played this game), Sebastian felt a pang of disappointment as fans around him erupted into wild cheers. Of course the Memphis crowd was elated. He hoped whoever they played in the final destroyed them and their hateful barbeque. Sebastian stood, trembling with the release of all the tension he hadn't realized he'd been carrying, and watched with pride as his boyfriend skated through the handshake line and shook hands with his competitors.

"I don't think I could do that," R.J. said, watching next to him. Sebastian was glad he'd been able to make the trip, even though he'd spent the entire game silent and glaring at the ice as if he could mentally will the Venom to win.

"I know I couldn't," Sebastian muttered, but he and

R.J. gave each other a fist bump and a wry smile as they slipped out of the crowd, leaving the Marauders celebrating on the ice and the fans cheering ecstatically.

Tristan was disappointed but composed when Sebastian found him after the game. Sebastian had brought his car down, intending to convince Tristan either way to come home with him instead of on the team plane. Tristan didn't seem to need much convincing. His eyes were a bit red, and his smile wasn't the thousand-watt version Sebastian had hoped to see, but he still looked... beautiful. Triumphant even in defeat, and why shouldn't he? It had been an incredible, grueling two months, and to get this far was impressive in and of itself.

Still. Sebastian pushed him gently against the GTO and kissed him. "I found us a hotel room for the night. We can fuck, or I'll order you a brownie sundae and we can watch a movie. Whatever you want." He paused. "As long as maybe you shave, first."

Tristan's laugh was low, but it rumbled through him. He wrapped his arms around Sebastian and hugged him tight. "Thanks. I'm bummed, I mean, obviously. We were so fucking close." His voice sounded a little choked. The Memphis breeze—already hot in May—stirred his damp hair. "But I'm glad you were there. Glad you're *here*. It helps a lot." He sniffed again. "Sorry. Ugh. This probably seems really stupid, right?"

"Listen to me," Sebastian said, taking Tristan's face in his hands. "You fought hard and you lost. You're allowed to be upset. Hell, Tris, *I'm* upset and this is the first year I've followed a team in any sport, ever. I can't imagine how you feel, but if you want to cry, then cry."

Tristan hiccupped and put his face against Sebastian's neck. His breath—and yeah, maybe a few tears—was warm on Sebastian's skin. "I know. It's part of it. But, man. You dream about winning games like this as a kid, you know? Not losing."

"I dreamed about fucking a hot blond hockey player over the hood of my GTO," Sebastian murmured, running his hands up and down Tristan's broad, muscled back.

"Mmm. That sounds nice." Tristan sagged against him a bit. "But maybe, first, that brownie sundae. Or, fuck, maybe a beer. I think I've earned it."

"I think you definitely have. Me too." Sebastian pulled back and kissed him.

Tristan kissed him back, then rested his forehead against Sebastian's. "I hate this part, though. The part where I realize hockey is really over, and I won't be on the ice again until next season. October seems a long way away."

It seemed way too *soon* to have to go through all of this again to Sebastian, but he kept that opinion to himself. "You'll have classes this summer," he reminded Tristan. "And since I won't be teaching any of them... you can always help me grade papers."

Tristan smiled, then laughed. "Sounds good to me."

* * * * *

Don't miss Goalie Interference *and*
Trade Deadline, *the next books in the Hat Trick series
by Avon Gale and Piper Vaughn!*

*Reviews are an invaluable tool when it comes
to spreading the word about great reads. Please
consider leaving an honest review for this or any of
Carina Press's other titles that you've read on your
favorite retailer or review site.*

Acknowledgments

First and foremost, we'd like to thank all our alpha and beta readers, especially Annie, who is a rock star and the best cheerleader any author duo could ever ask for.

Thanks also to our agent, Courtney Miller-Callihan, our editor, Stephanie Doig, and the entire Carina team for giving this book and the series a new home. Also, thank you to our sensitivity reader, Marianne Collazo, for her helpful comments and suggestions.

Lastly, thank you to our readers, who showed us so much love for *Permanent Ink*, our first collaboration.

There will be more of the Venom boys to come. We hope you stick around for the next season!

About the Authors

Avon Gale was once the mayor on Foursquare of Jazzercise and Lollicup, which should tell you all you need to know about her as a person. She likes road trips, rock concerts, drinking Kentucky bourbon and yelling at hockey. She's a displaced Southerner living in a liberal Midwestern college town, and she never gets tired of people and their stories—either real or the ones she makes up in her head.

Avon is represented by Courtney Miller-Callihan at Handspun Literary Agency.

Connect with Avon:
Website: *avongalewrites.com*
Twitter: *Twitter.com/avongalewrites*
Facebook: *Facebook.com/avongalewrites*

Piper Vaughn is a queer Latinx author and longtime romance reader. Since writing their first love story at age eleven, they've known writing in some form was exactly what they wanted to do. A reader to the core, Piper loves nothing more than getting lost in a great book.

Piper grew up in a diverse neighborhood in Chicago and loves putting faces and characters of every ethnicity in their stories, making their fictional worlds as colorful as the real one. Above all, Piper believes there's no one way to have an HEA, and every person deserves to see themselves reflected on the page.

Connect with Piper:
Website: *pipervaughn.com*
Twitter: *Twitter.com/pipervaughn*
Facebook: *Facebook.com/pipervaughnauthor*